To my mom, Elaine Card Walsh, a native of Lakewood, who has supported my life as a writer with her encouragement, as well as with the books she bought for me to read and scores of articles she cut from magazines and newspapers.

The Summer Journal of Robert English
by
Robert English

1973

Monday, May 14

I am housesitting for my history professor, Dr. Laighles, and his wife, Emily. He said his name is Irish and is pronounced Lawless, which was the first thing he told my class on day one of World History I.

It's a few minutes after nine a.m. They left an hour ago for Buffalo for a connecting flight to New York City, then they'll be on to Dublin to spend the summer with Emily's sister, Jillian. I'm housesitting the entire summer until a week before the fall semester begins.

"I'm on sabbatical in the fall, so we might not ever return," Dr. Laighles joked before they left.

He told me to be prepared in the event they stayed in Ireland through Christmas. *Be Prepared*. He obviously doesn't know that I'm an Eagle Scout, Troop 370.

He's writing a book about Ireland's neutrality during World War II and Hitler's plans to invade Ireland had the war continued. In class one day, he talked about this for the entire hour.

"If Hitler had invaded Ireland, it would have been a huge mistake," he told the class, "because the Irish are fierce warriors. They've been a pain in the Brits' ass for over a thousand years. Do you think they'd allow Hitler to just roll through like he did in Poland?"

In his kitchen, Dr. Laighles said he still has a ton of research to do and pictures to take with his new camera, a Pentax ES.

"See here, the ES stands for Easy as Shit." He showed me the camera, which was a marvel of technology. He also bought a tripod.

"I'll be taking a lot of photos and I have these prepaid mailers so all I have to do is toss them in the mail. Then, when they're developed, they'll be mailed to the house. When they arrive, just pile them on the shelf. I'll look at them when we get back."

§

Terrace Avenue—this was my childhood home, before Kimberly died. Once Emily and Dr. Laighles left, I walked the halls of my old house to explore, opening every door, but I felt sacrilegious, as if this place is one of the Great Pyramids loaded with treasures and guarded by evil curses. Snooping is breaking a moral contract. I felt as if I was an intruder.

"Are you coming home for the summer?" my mom asked the last time we spoke a few weeks ago.

"I'm not sure."

"Your father and I want to go on vacation to Yellowstone."

"I'll probably be working as an intern for a professor to earn extra credit," I lied.

If I had mentioned the old house, she and my father would've had a conniption fit and been up here before I could have hung up the phone. They didn't want me even applying to Chautauqua University, let alone attending it. Lakewood is the past. When we moved away, my parents buried our lives there to such a depth, no

Lakewood

A Novel

WILLIAM WALSH

5/31/22

To Bob,

Thanks for the teachable golf lesson. You are putting my game back together & I hope you enjoy this adventure.

My best,
Bill Walsh
"Pine Hills"

LAKEWOOD
William Walsh
Published by TouchPoint Press
Brookland, AR 72417
www.touchpointpress.com

ISBN: 978-1-956851-09-0

Editor: Mallory Matthews
Cover Layout: ColbieMyles.com
Cover image and design concept: Wendell Minor

Visit the author's website at
https://williamwalshthepigrider.godaddysites.com

@touchpointpress

First Edition

Printed in the United States of America.

one could ever return. After time has elapsed, you don't know where to dig, and if you do, you'll only find heartbreak.

The Laighles' furniture and decorations are dark and ornate, which is much different from what we had when we lived here. My parents had second-hand furniture that people had given them or things that they had bought at flea markets and garage sales. They cleaned up and restored most of it. In September 1962, my parents had a huge yard sale. I sat on the porch overlooking the lake, with paper and pencil, trying to catalog everything being sold, but the sheer volume was overwhelming. Plus, no one came over to my card table to talk to me. I was upset at first, but my parents assured me that they would buy new furniture in Atlanta. A lot of it was stuff that came with the house when my folks bought it. Of course, to me, it was just our stuff, since it was there when I was born, but they let it all go—sold everything that wasn't tied down.

My parents did not sell my things. Nor my sister's. Kimberly's stuff is still packed away in cardboard boxes in the attic of our Stone Mountain house.

§

I'm sitting on the staircase, balancing Dr. Laighles's typewriter on my knees. It's manual, a Royal Quiet Deluxe. He was quite proud of this typewriter.

"In the event anything happens while we're jet-setting across the world, I typed a new Will and Testament the other day. Both Emily and I signed it and had it notarized. It's in the bottom drawer.

We're giving everything to the university."

I didn't really know how to respond to the idea of dealing with their will or the possibility that they could die while out of the country, so I said, "That's an old typewriter." I walked over to it while Dr. Laighles sat at his desk. The typewriter was next to his phonograph.

"My folks bought this for me when I finished my doctorate back in 1953," he told me. "I was twenty-six. Two months later, I was hired by Chautauqua University. Teaching in my first semester, I met Emily. She was a new M.A. candidate. We were married the next summer, the same time this place became a university."

It is a heavy machine. The metal is thick, but there is something authoritative about hitting the keys.

The house is quiet. Dr. Laighles's Saint Bernards are here. Harry is lying down on the rug near the stairs, while Bess is curled up on the oval rug. A large shard of light is angling across her body. As I type, I'm watching specks of dust float through the light, moving in and out of the sun.

§

Now, I'm sitting in Dr. Laighles's office where books line the deep walnut shelves, which have recently been oiled. There's a lemon scent in the air, but it's overwhelmed by the lingering smell of his cigar smoke. I have a stack of paper, several ribbons, and the entire summer to write a historical novel, like Hemingway, about World War I. But what do I know of history? I like the idea of researching an event, like what happened to the main characters in Lincoln's assassination, but since I know how it ended, I'd like to write a novel about the week leading up to it, but this time, Lincoln survives the assassination. I would need to create a new outcome. To me, that might be interesting.

This is my childhood home. Eleven years ago, a stranger bought it. As it happened, this stranger turned out to be my history professor. I was born several blocks away in front of the Yacht Club. My mother went into labor on the lawn, and out I popped, right into the arms of a woman who was walking her dog. She was a surgical nurse who had been in the Korean War and stopped to help.

The ambulance arrived a few minutes later and rushed me and my mom to the WCA Hospital, where Kimberly was born minutes later. I'm eighteen minutes older, but of course, I don't remember any of this. It's the story my mom always told us and anyone who would listen. I think WCA stands for Woman's Christian Association.

We moved away to Atlanta in September 1962, after Kimberly died.

Tuesday, May 15

Currently playing on the radio is "Crocodile Rock." I feel like jumping around the kitchen or the main living area, but I won't. Dr. Laighles had the radio tuned to a gospel station. The preacher had a nice-sounding voice, very soothing and friendly. At first, I thought I would listen to what the man had to say, but after a few minutes, I couldn't stand it. He was adamant that the Earth is 4,000 years old. There's just no way that's true! Even if a person believes this crap, this guy's essentially saying that when Christ was here a little less than 2,000 years ago, the Earth was only 2,000 years old. What about the Egyptians, Newgrange, and other civilizations? What about Pangaea, when the Earth was a single continent approximately 225 million years ago? I don't understand how people can deny science. I did the math. If Earth's continents shift away from each other approximately half an inch per year (which is what I've read) it takes the shifting tectonic plates ("the land") approximately 125,000 years to move one mile. If Earth's land masses were at one time together, then it would have taken approximately 300,160,000 years to shift to their current position.

Ignorance cannot be excused or tolerated. I am a man of science and history, and there's no way I can believe such bullshit from this charlatan. I have always been suspect of religion.

Looking into the backyard from the kitchen window, I remember the great oak tree with our treehouse and swing. Someone cut it down sometime during the past eleven years. All that remains is a two-foot-high stump that has turned dark with age and rot.

In our old piano room, Dr. Laighles has a really cool Motorola Stereo cabinet with an AM/FM radio and turntable. I'm sure it cost a boatload of money. He left an album on the turntable, Warne Marsh, *Jazz of Two Cities*. He also had Django Reinhardt's *The Quintet of the Hot Club of France* and Dick Dale and His Del-Tones's *Surfers' Choice* sitting on top of the console. Using my skills of deduction and logic, I conclude Dr. Laighles likes the jazz, while Emily likes the surfer music. I have no proof, but based on their personalities, I'm making a hypothesis.

Here's something I know to be factual. I sat around listening to all three albums and flipping through their *National Geographic* magazine collection. I'm listing my two favorite songs from each album:

    Warne Marsh: *Jazz of Two Cities*
       "Quintessence"
       "I Never Knew"
       My notes: Wow, the piano player is awesome

    Django Reinhardt: *The Quintet of the Hot Club of France*
       "Tiger Rag"
       "Blue Drag"
       My notes: Good album but it sounds like it was recorded
       in a tin box

    Dick Dale and the Del-Tones: *Surfer's Choice*
       "Miserlou"
       "Let's Go Trippin'"
       My notes: Kind of reminds me of the music on *Gilligan's*
       Island when Ginger and Mary Ann are dancing

Wednesday, May 16

I wrote the first page of my novel this morning. I woke up at three-thirty in the morning when Harry started howling at a tree branch scraping the side of the house. After that, I couldn't fall back to sleep.

I sleep downstairs on the sofa, mainly because my old room is where Emily has all her arts and crafts—no bed) and I don't want to sleep in her and Dr. Laighles's bedroom. There are five bedrooms, but I haven't yet felt comfortable claiming one. Kimberly's old bedroom is locked. I'm comfortable sleeping downstairs on the sofa in the TV room with a few blankets. This room has an octagon poker table and a 1962 World Series pinball machine. It's not like most pinball machines with bumpers and lights. This pinball machine is a baseball game with a bat instead of flippers. When you get a hit, the men run the bases. I played yesterday for a few hours.

At this moment, I'm sitting in the front of the house, in the glassed-in Florida room, which overlooks Chautauqua Lake. It's dark outside. Across the lake, toward Greenhurst, there are a few lights emanating off the lake, like stars that have fallen from the sky and landed softly.

§

I've decided that my original idea of writing a novel about the French Foreign Legion during World War I is not going to work. I don't know enough to fake it and I don't feel like spending my summer in the library doing research. I want to get laid since that didn't happen this year, although there was a close call at a frat party this past fall when I made out with a girl. Both of us had too much to drink, but then she told me that she wasn't even in college.

"I go to Lakeside Christian Academy. I'm a freshman."

"How old are you?"

"Fifteen."

What the hell! I thought. I had already felt her boobs by this time but when she told me her age, I got scared and told her I'd be right back. I bolted out the back door and ran across campus back to my room. That was Saturday night. I didn't leave my room until Monday morning.

I have another idea—a World War II story about a young couple in Italy, Isabella and Vincenzo, who are both artists. They pretend they are married so he won't be drafted and sent immediately to the front lines to fight. At the outset of the war and before Vincenzo becomes a POW guard, Isabella asks Vincenzo to mail several letters on his way to the University of Milan to see his old professor about funding his graduate degree. He becomes curious and looks to see who she's mailing letters to. He discovers the letters are for friends in Europe. Except for one letter which is addressed to Cynthia Birdwhistle in New York City. When Vincenzo holds that letter up to the sun, he notices another envelope inside.

He opens the letter addressed to Cynthia and finds a note urging Cynthia to forward the smaller letter to her brother, Haywood. Vincenzo does not say anything to Isabella but knows that she's in love with Haywood Birdwhistle. He also knows that after the impending war, she plans to travel to New York City to be with him. The letter explains her intentions to leave Vincenzo. However, a year later, as Vincenzo works as a guard in the POW camp, he hears the name Haywood Birdwhistle called out during the roll call of new prisoners. It takes a few seconds, but the name registers with Vincenzo. Like most prisoners of war, Birdwhistle's fate is set. That is, unless Vincenzo intervenes to save him. If Birdwhistle lives, he and Isabella will be together after the war in New York City. There, she will be happy for the rest of her life. If Birdwhistle dies, she'll be stuck with Vincenzo.

I like the idea of writing that story much better. It's not about the war. It's about love during war and what one person must give up for another. I haven't decided what Vincenzo will do. Carson McCullers was twenty-three when she published *The Heart is a Lonely Hunter*. I understand her title, especially while living in this big house. I also feel like Nick Carraway. All alone. An observer of life.

§

I threw away the page I wrote this morning about the French Foreign Legion. It wasn't that good anyway. The story was supposed to focus on a band of soldiers who steal gold from various abandoned European banks and bury it in Africa with the intent of returning after the war to smuggle it out. There are no opposing forces to stop them from looting the banks. Initially, I liked the idea, but then I found out that Clint Eastwood starred in *Kelly's Heroes*, which has a similar plot. I haven't seen the movie, yet. I don't really care about that idea anymore.

Thursday, May 17

Officially, the United States' role in Vietnam ended in Paris earlier this year on January 27. Dr. Laighles sees the war lasting for at least another decade internally in this country, until we fight again and forget our current losses. He said people are going to protest this war for decades. I hope he's wrong. Even though President Nixon has begun the withdrawal from Vietnam, I'm still nervous about being drafted. I'm 1-A, but I don't trust anyone in government. With the stroke of a pen, my designation can be changed.

The Pentagon announced that 45,997 Americans have died in combat and 10,928 soldiers have died from other causes since 1961. It's on the front page of *The Columbia Union*, which is delivered each morning. Right now, it's sitting next to the typewriter. That's

5,197 per year or 100 per week. Some U.S. government bigwigs are also talking about ending the draft, which I don't believe will happen. It's possible, I suppose. It will make the president a hero for anyone under twenty-eight.

I know of a few draft dodgers who fled to Canada. If my draft number is called up, I'll probably do the same. I would volunteer if our country was invaded. I would fight on this soil. There would be little choice. If my number comes up, I will say I have a heart murmur, which whispers, "I am a scaredy-cat."

My dad said that as an only child, I wouldn't be drafted, but he calculated that if I had a draft number, it would have been 344, which is very high. Now, I'm almost guaranteed to never get drafted even if my 1-A were eliminated. Still, I don't trust the system or anyone in the system, not when you can avoid the draft by being a senator's son.

"We're not rich," my dad said, "but if you got the dough, you don't have to go."

I didn't know this in high school, and it worried me every day back then.

§

Earlier this afternoon, I took the dogs for a long walk to the Rod and Gun Club. On the return trip, I ran them along the lake until the sky turned cobalt blue then black. The air cooled quickly and a stiff breeze across the lake kicked up. I made it home before the rain.

Lakewood is close to many places: Buffalo, Niagara Falls, Pittsburgh, Cleveland, Lake Erie. I can drive to New York City in seven or eight hours.

During one of his lectures, Dr. Laighles informed the class that the Nazis had planned on bombing New York City.

"In 1944, the Nazis drew up plans to drop a nuclear bomb on Manhattan. Hell, they'd already tested a nuke. If you think the U.S. was first, think again. Germany had already tested one, but I believe they did not have the ability to control and deliver the bomb. Think about this, 1944 was only about thirty years ago, and all they had to do was level New York City. Then what would have happened? The same thing when we bombed Japan, that's what. We destroyed their will to fight. Ours would have been destroyed as well."

Friday, May 18

"Is anyone staying in town this summer?" Dr. Laighles asked my history class back in April. No one raised their hand. "There's no one spending the summer in Chautauqua?"

My only job prospect in Atlanta was cutting, delivering, and stacking firewood with Ryan Hanson at his father's business. He and I had our Eagle Scout ceremony together. I helped with his Eagle project, and he helped with mine. At two bucks an hour, the job was acceptable.

"Well, I need someone to housesit. If you change your mind or know someone, stop by my office."

Late in the afternoon, I stopped by his office to see him, but he was not there. In his message box was a note from Mary Cox explaining her experience babysitting and how she housesat for her aunt in Sommerville, Massachusetts, a Boston suburb. I stole her note and left him a note of my own. I tore up her note and flushed it down the toilet in the men's room.

The morning Dr. Laighles and Emily finished packing the car and left for London, I stood next to a portion of concrete my father had poured in our walkway. With Popsicle sticks, Kimberly and I etched our names and the date, "April 13, 1962."

I wonder if they think the etching is mine. I haven't told them I used to live here. Do they know?

When I first met Mrs. Laighles, Emily, a few weeks ago, she was walking down the staircase carrying a box of old clothes that did not look like anything either of them would wear. She is thin, elegant, and graceful, like a figure skater. She could make washing the dogs look like a tea party in a rose garden.

She and Dr. Laighles are from Chicago. When Dr. Laighles asked me, "What'll it be, whiskey, scotch, gin, or vermouth?" Emily said, "Floyd, do you have to ask everyone that?"

I settled for a Coke.

They walked me around the house and backyard as they pointed to certain things, unaware that I probably knew the house better than they did. I have actually been inside the cupboards. Emily showed me things I had seen a thousand times as a kid and never took notice of. They now seemed more interesting:

- Phone Niche on the Wall: This is a concave compartment where the telephone used to sit. Now, as when I was a kid, the phone is on the wall in the kitchen. There is also one downstairs in the hall. There isn't a phone upstairs so you have to hurry down the stairs to answer it. When I was a kid, my mom had a plant sitting in the phone niche.

- Laundry Chutes: Emily said she still uses the laundry chutes because the washer and dryer are on the first floor. They've thought about installing a laundry room upstairs, but it seems unnecessary since it's only the two of them.

- Milk Door: This is a tiny compartment in one cabinet. I remember this because Kimberly and I would use it to hand each other our lunch—one of us stood outside, while the other stood in the house. I didn't know what it was actually for until Emily told me. The milkman would walk around to the back side of the house and place the milk and butter on one side and the residents would retrieve it later from inside the house. Emily and Dr. Laighles have it wired shut from inside the cabinet.

- The Cold Closet: When I was a kid, it was a broom closet that housed all our junk. One day, my mother opened up the door and a ton of junk fell out. Emily said they use it as cold storage for fruits and vegetables, as well as canned goods. She must have a hundred Mason jars of food stored in there.

§

This past winter, during a two-week period when the temperature rose into the high forties, there was a huge rainstorm and a few violent thunderstorms. The lightning from one thunderstorm sparked a fire in the town of Ripley when it hit a barn. A tree was knocked over on campus near the science building, pinning a girl to the ground. Dr. Laighles ran over to her and when he couldn't pull her free, he lifted the tree enough so another man could pull her out. The history department held a party in his honor and the *Chautauqua University Eagle,* (nicknamed *The CUE*) as well as the *Jamestown Post-Journal*, plastered his picture on the front page.

Dr. Laighles is tall, has a thick mustache like Grover Cleveland. He has a thick beard, like he's a 19th Century politician. He's a big guy, burly.

He shocked everyone at the party when he said, "Anyone associated with the jubilation of this event is a coward. You would have done the same. And, if not, then I'm not interested in your company."

I stood there next to Marcy Summers, a grad assistant, eating a sugar cookie and drinking punch. When Dr. Laighles stormed out, he left everyone wondering if they could have saved the girl. I doubt I could have. I don't have much upper body strength. I wish it wasn't true, but I'm weak. I was just not built for strength. I'm quick and agile instead.

§

A little while ago, I ran the dogs over to campus and bumped into Mitch Lancaster. He's the editor of the *Chautauqua Historian*, the university's historical journal. He may be good in history, but he's failed math twice and is just now taking freshman biology. He's the favorite student in the history department because, as a freshman, he published two articles in a highly respected magazine, *The Civil War Now*. He had just loaded up his Beetle and was about to head home to Memphis for the summer when I ran into him.

Mitch said the following:

Your girlfriend, Caroline, (she's not my girlfriend—
the Ice Queen) she went on a date with Wally
Olmstead to The Tiger Buddha and he kept putting
his chopsticks in his mouth and acting like he was a
walrus, which really pissed her off. When he told
Caroline that he had two pet pigs named Macon and
Bacon and wanted to know if she was into Making
Bacon, she got all huffy. She then excused herself and
went to the restroom. While she was there, he left and
stuck her at the restaurant with the check. In
Stephenson's biology review, Wally wouldn't leave
her alone. He apologized for being a jerk and kept
trying to get a second date. He offered to pay her back
for the dinner. Finally, Stephenson stopped his
lecture and told her to leave if she couldn't be quiet.

"I'm not the one talking. It's Wally and he won't
leave me alone."

"I don't care what the problem is, you work it out
after class."

"There's nothing to work out. This guy's a weird
fucking pervert."

Stephenson, who is a lay-minister and doesn't
tolerate cussing and drinking, kicked her out of

class. She never showed up for her final exam.

"What happened?" I asked.

"I guess she failed."

If I ever have the opportunity to go on a date with Caroline DeBauché, I will not take the Ice Queen out for Chinese food.

Beautiful, though Caroline may be, from my conversations with her, she's a bitter pill.

Saturday, May 19

The New York Times reported that "Richard Nixon won a victory in the House today as it sustained his veto of a bill requiring Senate confirmation of the two top officials for the Office of Management and Budget." He was the first president I was able to vote for, and so I ended up helping defeat McGovern. Although, I felt odd when I did because I've always considered myself a Democrat. I just did not have any confidence in McGovern, not after the 1968 debacle when it looked like the world was exploding. This time last year, I would never have imagined voting for someone like Nixon.

§

I made a huge mistake today. Two mistakes really. I walked the dogs from the house to Allen Park, which I estimate is eight miles away. It rained considerably last night, so it was a beautifully cool morning, just right for a long walk. Of course, it was still wet for the most part. I left at nine, and two and a half hours later, we were in the park. I walked them but also jogged a little bit. It was too far for the dogs. At the baseball field, they both plopped down in the cool grass by the bleachers and would not move. Harry and Bess were already gritty from the walk but got even more dirty in the grass. They are big dogs and when they don't want to move, they don't. There were only two other people around, a man chipping golf balls on the field, and a man practicing with his fly rod. I watched the fly rod-guy until he finished, then asked if he could give me and the dogs a ride home in his truck, which made him laugh when the dogs did nothing but stretch in the grass.

"Those are two lazy dogs," the man laughed.

Around the time the fly rod-guy was leaving, a bunch of boys arrived to play a little league game and they all wanted to pet Harry and Bess. Those lazy mutts rolled over to have their bellies scratched. I had to pick them up, one at a time, all 130 to 150 pounds. I had to drag Harry a few feet in the grass. Holy-hell, I about broke my back. I lifted both dogs, one after the other, into the back of Mr. Card's pickup truck where they plopped down.

I rode with Mr. Card in the front cab.

"I'm installing linoleum in a house over on West Virginia Boulevard, but the woman changed her mind on the style, so her husband's driving over to Erie to buy all new material. I don't know what they're going to do with this other stuff."

"Is it hard to lay down a new floor?" I asked.

"It takes time and patience, and you need to concentrate on doing a good job. Same with wallpaper. But like anything, the more you practice, the better you get. That's what I was doing in the park. I bought a handful of lures from Linwood's, so instead of going on to the next job just to stop a few hours from now, I got some lunch and came to the park to test them out before getting back to work. I'm going fishing next week on Findley Lake."

When we arrived at Dr. Laighles's place, he said, "I know the folks who live here. Emily and the doctor. I knew the folks who lived here years ago, too. I built a treehouse for them, a long time ago. That's what I do. I'm a carpenter. You know'em?"

"I know Emily and Dr. Laighles. I'm not sure about the other people before them. I go to college at Chautauqua. I'm just housesitting for the summer."

"I used to work down the street when I was a kid, at the Green Farm. That's where I met my wife."

The second mistake I made was how dirty the dogs got. I gave them a bath, one at a time. No matter what, you cannot dry a Saint Bernard. Once washed, I tied them up on the back porch until they dried.

Currently, Harry and Bess are zonked out on the carpet lying between me (on the sofa) and the television. There was nothing worth watching until *Kung Fu* at 9:00. Before that, just *Toma*, *The Waltons*, or *The Flip Wilson Show*. Until *Kung Fu* came on, I filtered through Dr. Laighles's books to see if there was anything I wanted to read. Two books looked promising: *1984* and *A Good Man is Hard to Find*. I've heard of one of them.

Sunday, May 20

Early morning: Harry woke me up to go outside. He and I sat on the front porch. I wrapped up in a wool sweater and several blankets up to my neck. Harry plopped down on the Adirondack, his body curled across my feet while his legs hung over the sides. I sipped a hot cup of coffee. The vapors feathered up around my face like ghosts disappearing past my ears. No boats were on the lake, and no cars in town. Across the lake, before closing my eyes, I watched a few headlights travel west toward Dewittville.

When daylight broke, I drove to The Big Tree for breakfast, a restaurant in Sherman's Bay. The ceiling fan wobbled like elephant ears flapping, while men and women read their newspapers, pulling down the corner edge whenever someone walked in. The food was good. I will eat there often.

Afterwards, I visited the Lakewood Drug Store for a journal-book or some direction on how to keep a journal, but all I found were pink, flowery diaries that some young girl's grandmother would buy her. I was too lazy this morning to walk all the way to the university bookstore to look for one.

Mr. Barone, the pharmacist, was behind the counter whistling and when I asked if he had any other kinds of journals, he said no, but he could order one.

"It'll take a few weeks to arrive."

"No thanks. I wanted to buy it today."

"I don't have much demand for journals, but I have some fine pens up by the counter."

I think William Faulkner wrote in a journal. Hemingway, too. I'll just keep typing on single sheets of paper in the meantime. I have no direction. I will make up my own rules. Life has no plot.

Mr. Barone did not recognize or remember me, but my mother grew up with him. I once helped his daughter fix the chain on her bicycle. I think it was his daughter. Maybe. Maybe not. Now that I think about it, it was Mr. Card's daughter. When I was a kid, he installed a new ceiling in our kitchen. Lisa had a small pink Schwinn with streamers hanging from the white grips. She said she had a cat named Blossom. Down by the park, she had gotten her shoestrings caught in the chain and could not hop off her bike without falling over because the strings had wound so tightly that her sneaker was pressed against the chainguard.

"I have an idea," I told her. "Let me pull your foot out and then you can sit on the sidewalk while I unhook your shoe."

And that is what we did. It took about thirty seconds to free her shoe, but the laces were covered in black, dirty oil and had a few puncture marks.

I tied her shoes for her so she did not get her fingers oily.

"Do you know how to double tie your laces?" I asked her.

"No."

"Watch this. It'll keep your laces from coming undone."

§

Since starting this housesitting gig, I've walked through the house, sat on each chair and sofa, some with lion-clawed legs, and studied the paintings and pictures hanging on the walls. I tried as hard as I could to conclude something—what, I don't know. Moments ago, I typed that life has no plot. That's not true. Sometimes the plot is slow. But plot is getting into trouble then getting out.

The same men who drove nails into the beams of this house over one hundred years ago continue to live in this house. The energy it took to pound the nails continues to reside in the wood. It's Einstein's dynamism at work. The man who cut the timber, his energy is in the beams.

In the kitchen, there is a dumbwaiter from when the house was a hotel in the 1920s and '30s. The dumbwaiter didn't work when I lived here, and my father never fixed it, though he tried once. He found a rat's nest with baby rat skeletons in it.

The basement, when I lived here, was my hideout. Me and my friends were outlaws and bandits on a cattle drive, playing down there in the winter when it was too cold to go outside. It's still dark and has a musty smell to it. There's a sign: BE CAREFUL LOW ENTRANCE, written in marker on a small board. The basement looks older than before, unsafe. The steps creak and may be rotted. Thick layers of dust hang like a collection of fog. The walls are lined with graffiti: stick people, stick cats and dogs, tic-tac-toe games, and rudimentary trees, which my parents allowed Kimberly and me to paint. My mom and dad painted the picket fence along her side of the wall. It's watercolor, and although it's faded, some imprints of the pickets remain. They painted fort posts on my side of the basement.

Fort Apache (me) always conquered the Queen of England (Kimberly) when push came to shove in a battle of clay balls. There are a few grease marks on the walls from where the clay hit and stuck. One time when I stood up, Kimberly hit me in the mouth with a clay ball.

My favorite room in the house has always been where we had

our piano, which Emily and Dr. Laighles use for entertaining. It's been years since I studied piano. Mrs. Grattan-Smith came to our house every Wednesday afternoon to give me and Kimberly piano lessons. My parents sold the piano when we moved to Atlanta, along with everything else. It was my great-great-grandfather's piano (on my mother's side), Antom Siguler.

"Your great-great-grandfather was a Civil War hero," my mom said throughout my childhood. "I never met him, but he saved a lot of soldiers during the war."

The piano worked but was in need of repair, as it sounded like a snapping cable each time a key was struck. My parents convinced me that we would get another piano in Atlanta, but we never did. Maybe I will mention that to them the next time I call home.

Harry and Bess follow along after me when I walk around. They sniff the air as if searching for Emily and Dr. Laighles. My favorite game is throwing their ball down the stairs, and when they chase after it, I run through the house, and down the spiral staircase in the back. As soon as they realize I'm nowhere to be found, they start barking and try to find me. There are two staircases in the house, one in the front and one in back. The one in back is a spiral staircase, which has always been spooky. I like to run up and down it because it connects the upstairs hall to the kitchen.

§

I have not spoken to my former girlfriend, Ashley Brown, or my former best friend, Will Croon, since last year. A year as of yesterday. Maybe I should have made note of it yesterday, but I'd forgotten the date. I have not read the six letters Ashley has mailed. I have not heard from Will, and if I don't in another twenty years, that will suit me right fine.

I am still in love with Ashley, but I cannot forgive her or Will for what they did. When I call home, my mother weaves her into the conversation. I've known Ashley since fourth grade. My mother always asks if I've heard from her, and though I say no, I'm sure she knows I'm lying. She told me that Ashley has stopped by the house to talk to her, to ask me to call, to get my mailing address. I hope she hasn't told my mother why we broke up.

Ashley was a year behind me in school, and I was scheduled to start classes at the University of Georgia in the fall. A huge graduation party was thrown at Kyle Onderdonk's house by his parents—there must have been one hundred kids in their backyard—and at around midnight, Ashley and I snuck into their pool shed. There, we started making out on a broken lounger with a foam cushion with a seashell and starfish print. We had our bathing suits off.

"What's the problem with you?" she asked as she put her clothes on. It took less than a minute for Ashley to get fully dressed.

"We don't have any protection. I don't want to get you pregnant."

There was no yelling.

"I want to go home."

I sort of thought we'd hang out the next morning and talk about what happened. Well, what didn't happen.

Around nine o'clock the next morning, Will Croon showed up in my driveway in his Plymouth Road Runner.

"Let's go play Putt-Putt."

On the third hole, Will said, "Last night, after everyone took off from the graduation party, I popped Ashley's cherry."

"What?"

"Yeah, man. She called me up and said, 'let's go for a ride.' We drove around and ended up in Stone Mountain, deep in the Kentucky picnic area. She jumped in the back seat, so I did, too. We kissed for about five seconds, then she undid my belt. I yanked off her shorts and broke that shit wide open."

"What the fuck, Will? That's my girlfriend."

"She said you wouldn't do it with her, so I did. What the hell's wrong with you? Are you a homo?"

"No."

"Well, damn, boy, she loved it."

I didn't even think about it, I just cracked him in the jaw with a wild uppercut. I laid him out in the bushes and walked away. I handed the putter to the man at the golf booth who saw the whole thing.

"Was he cheating?" the man asked.

I walked away and hitchhiked home. That is how my friendship with Will Croon ended.

My mother wouldn't understand, nor my father. When I got home, I told them I was not going to college at U.G.A.

When my dad asked me why, I said, "I've changed my mind. I am going to Chautauqua or Clemson."

I gave them no details beyond the fact that Georgia did not have the program I wanted. That was it. No argument. I told them I was leaving in three days, and if anyone called or knocked on the door for me, I was not home. By the end of the afternoon, I had decided on Chautauqua University over Clemson, but it was a close call.

I wanted to have sex with Ashley, but I knew it would be a mistake. Maybe if we'd prepared for it, things would have been different. I took responsibility for her safety and her future. Maybe I should have slept with her just so I could stop thinking about it all the time.

I guess Will and I are enemies now. We had a lot of fun growing up together, especially at his grandfather's farm down in Cochran.

When Will and I walked home from baseball practice after sunset, we were scared to walk down the dark streets, and every time we came upon a house or a car parked in the street where someone could jump out at us, we raised our voices about how much we had learned in karate class that night. It must have worked as no one ever bothered us.

Will's father was almost never around, and since his mother worked nights, Will slept over at my house on many school nights. He would ride the bus to school with me the next day. Sometimes, he did not want to stay over, so my mother drove him back home about one o'clock after his mother finished her shift.

I was thirteen the first time I visited Will's grandfather. He was retired and did nothing but sit on the front porch of his shack listening to WSB, chewing tobacco, strumming his dulcimer, drinking corn whiskey, and rocking in his chair.

Will's grandfather was always handing out advice, as if for years he'd been storing up nuggets of wisdom for hillbillies, one-legged men, and women with six kids and a broken heart.

"You boys remember this—you need to find you a way of making cash money. Don't never let the government tax your money. Lie like hell if you got to 'cause those bastards are lying to you about every goddamned thing. Don't never let the IRS know where all your money is or how much you're making."

He rarely left the porch, save to use the outhouse, which consisted of an old refrigerator on bricks with a hole cut in the bottom that you stood over or bent down to use. Individual preference, I suppose. When the four-foot hole in the ground filled up, Will's grandfather made Buddy Lee and Ralston (Will's cousins) dig a new hole a few feet away and place the refrigerator over it. They threw lime down the old hole and covered it up with the dirt from the new hole. The refrigerator outhouse had small peep holes cut on each side to let anyone who was in it look out. To keep the door closed, there was a string to wrap around your hand. It was a huge refrigerator. Two people could have sat in it.

As I type, it's eleven o'clock at night and the Buffalo news is on the TV. The big story: CIA director Richard Helms stated that H.R. Haldeman, Nixon's aide, asked the CIA to take responsibility for Watergate.

I'm beginning to think the President might be in trouble.

For a few hours now, I have been angry. Angry at Will. Angry at Ashley. I've been feeling disappointed and hurt by what they did to me. I'm trying to lighten my mood but it's not as easy as turning a switch on and off. I can be light-hearted, but deep within me, the pain won't leave.

Dr. Laighles gave me an envelope containing $250, my salary for the summer. It's sitting next to the typewriter on the porch and is as volatile as a shotgun. On the back of the envelope, he scribbled:

We'll call occasionally. Take good care of the dogs.
Eat up the food in the fridge and cupboards. Don't
break too many hearts this summer.
~ Floyd Laighles

Monday, May 21

United States Attorney General, Harold Titus, said in the morning paper that he is "going to hand down indictments on twelve people." I disagree with the Watergate break-in. It was wrong, but the way government functions, I doubt anyone will ever be convicted and go to jail. Nixon just needs to ride out this storm and help the G.O.P. elect the next president. I like that bad actor from California, whatever his name is. He was on TV one night, talking about cutting taxes, individual responsibility, and freedom. I don't believe Agnew can get elected. He looks mean, like a junkyard dog.

When I was a young boy, Kimberly and I used to sit on the bottom step of the long mahogany staircase in the front of the house, with a map of the United States and talk about places to visit. She wanted to be a doctor. I wanted to be an astronaut.

Now, in 1973, things are not the way I wanted them. Not by myself.

I've always wanted my life to be like Robert Young and his family—eating breakfast together, coming home after school to my mother and an afternoon snack, playing games in the backyard with Kimberly, and throwing the baseball before dinner with my father. Maybe I should grow up. It's never going to be like that. Thomas Wolfe said you can't go home again. I'd like to prove him wrong.

§

Will Croon said once, "If you don't fight, people will hound you for the rest of your life. It doesn't matter if you lose, just as long as you put up a good show."

I don't know how that pertains to anything in my life or what

I've written so far. It just popped into my head.

One summer weekend, Will and I visited his grandfather, who was not much fun because, as I said, he did almost nothing all day long except chew tobacco and spit off the porch railing.

But on one particular day, he said, "The raccoons keep crawling under my house at night to loosen the boards to get in the house. They're causing general mischief. I saw one of those bastards last night drinking from the sink, then skittering across the kitchen floor. By the time I found my pistol, he'd run off. I'll tell you boys what. I'll give you a dollar bill for every raccoon you can catch."

"A dollar for each of us?" Will asked.

"No. A dollar for each raccoon. You two figure out how to split the dollar."

"Dead or alive?" I asked.

"It don't matter. I prefer dead."

We ran off with an old shotgun to hunt raccoons, but we couldn't find one anywhere. We checked the barn, the creeks, and some rotted out trees. Then after about three hours of walking through the woods and along the back roads, Will and I found a dead raccoon lying in the road.

"He looks like he got run over last night," Will said, shooing away the flies.

I carried him by the tail all the way to the old man's shack.

"How'd you get a raccoon in the middle of the day?" his grandfather asked.

"We saw him scamper away and up a tree. Robert was the one who kilt him. One shot. That's all it took," said Will.

"I didn't hear no gun shot," his grandfather said.

"We kilt him way over by Muses' Lake. That's about three miles away," Will replied.

"I know where it is. I reckon it's that far an' with the tree line an' all."

His grandfather gave us a dollar, then we ran off into the woods with the shotgun and the raccoon. When we were about a quarter of a mile away from his grandfather, Will propped the raccoon up against a tree, stood back about thirty feet, and blasted him with the shotgun.

"Two coons in one afternoon," said the old man.

We repeated this throughout the day until all we were able to bring back was the raccoon's tail.

"Where's the rest of the critter?" he asked.

"I got trigger happy and blasted him into a hundred pieces," Will said. "I can take you out to where the rest of him is at. It's a nasty mess."

"Naw. I don't feel like walking all that far. From now on, you got to bring me the whole coon. Not just the tail and an ear."

§

Will's cousins are twins and three years older than Will. They live deep in the woods where they run a corn whisky still with their father—White Lightning. His name isn't White Lightning, but it wouldn't surprise me if it was. Either way, they distill corn into moonshine. Their father used to say that Will was almost named Daiquiri because on the night he was born, Will's father got drunk on daiquiris at The Alibi Tavern. I never heard much about Ralston and Buddy Lee's mother, except one time when Ralston said she ran off with a man, a war hero, with a stubbed arm and a burnt face.

The first night I stayed over at Will's grandfather's house, they tagged along, saying I was the first Yankee to ever set foot in their granddaddy's house, and only the second to set foot in his yard without being plugged with rock salt.

"Being that he was an insurance salesman, he was lucky it wasn't buck shot," Buddy Lee said.

There was only one bed in the house, which the old man slept in, and an old smelly sofa, which Ralston and Buddy Lee fought over, but finally gave in to sharing. Will and I slept with blankets on the dusty floor, which was hard as frozen walnuts.

§

It's late and I'm tired and the leather sofa looks pretty nice tonight. My pillow and blanket are already waiting for me.

Tuesday, May 22

I'm within a few years of my parents' age when they were married. My mother was born in 1928, my father in 1927, just as the Depression was beginning to slam its hammer. It's difficult to picture my parents as children, but of course I know they were. My grandparents were born in 1907, '08, '10, and '13. My great-grandparents were born in the late 1880s, which I find amazing. I wonder who will be the last person born in the 1800s to die? If they die in the year 2000 or later, they will have lived in three centuries. Has that ever happened before? That's twenty-seven years away.

My family has lived in this area since the Revolutionary War. Now, I'm the only person in my family who still lives in Lakewood. The rest have scattered to the winds all over the country.

I told my parents I was attending Chautauqua because the University of Georgia did not have a medical school, but after my first semester, I changed my major to history. I have not told them yet.

§

When my father restored the downstairs bathroom of this house, he found a newspaper dating back to the early 1880s. It was yellow, stiff, and dried out. We tried ironing it, but it crumpled and broke apart.

Today, I watched a baseball game on TV, the Pirates against the Astros. The Pirates mustered only five hits and lost 6—2. It rained all day, so I stayed inside and read from various books on Dr. Laighles's shelves. The phone hasn't rung since I began housesitting. I checked it several times to see if it was working.

§

Late. I just returned home and I'm soaking wet. Harry broke his leash on our walk and ran away. While looking for him, it started raining and I got drenched. I spent more than an hour calling out his name and walking through the backyards of strangers. Bess was holding me back, so I dropped her off at the house, and there he was. Harry was on the front porch, curled up on the cushioned lawn chair. His fur was matted, muddy, and oily, and he had briars stuck to his eyebrows. His eyes were very shameful. Adulterer.

Even after bathing both dogs, it took a while for the chill to leave my bones.

"Go hide," I said, swaying my arms to shoo them away, but they just stood there wagging their tails. So I tossed the tennis ball down the hall. While hiding in the downstairs closet, I found Kimberly's name written on the underside of the stairs, sloping against the back side of the coat room. It was dated March 2, 1962.

Wednesday, May 23

This morning, around 8:30, I mowed the grass. I started in the backyard, but by the time I was half-finished with the front, some guy walked down the sidewalk and sat on the porch to pet the dogs. Once I put the lawn mower back in the garage, I asked, "Can I help you with anything?"

"Is Steven home?"

"No, it's just me and the dogs. Who's Steven?"

"Emily's son. Floyd's son."

His name is Michael Forest, Mike. Something is wrong with him. He's retarded but doesn't look retarded. He's slow and has a hard time getting his words out. I didn't know he was retarded, of course, until I talked to him.

Mike volunteered to trim the hedges.

"Naw. That's more work than I want to do today," I said. But really, I didn't want some retarded guy using the electric trimmer and cutting off his fingers. That's all Dr. Laighles needs when he returns, a lawsuit.

Afterwards, we ate peanut butter cookies and drank some milk while playing pinball. I lost 26—12. Then at eleven o'clock, he shot out of his chair and said he had to go home. He asked several more times where Steven was. I had no idea who he was talking about, except that I guess Steven is the Laighles' kid. He must be the kid in the pictures they have on the walls and tables.

§

Last year at graduation, people hung around in the high school gym before the parties began later that night, just milling around drinking punch and taking photographs. Will's father showed up drunk, but since most of the kids had never seen or met him in all these years, they figured he was a bum off the street.

Mr. Croon jumped up on stage and stumbled to the microphone.

"Hey, ain't it great?" he slurred. "These kids are high school graduates and now they're one step closer to getting the hell out of the house."

"Get down from there," someone yelled at him.

"Hey, kiss my ass."

"You're drunk," someone else yelled.

"You're ugly, but I can sober up," he yelled back.

I stood a few feet away and watched as Will and his mother exited near the library, quickly getting out of Dodge before anything worse occurred.

"My kid graduated today, somehow, and I just got to say thank you. He's like his momma, cute but not the smartest bulb in the lot."

"Get out of there," Mrs. Huckleby said. "You're a disgrace."

"You're a pretty number, sweetheart. Come on up here and give me a kiss." Just then, three men hopped up on stage, and when they approached Mr. Croon, he hit the first man in the jaw and sent him tumbling to the floor.

He reached for the microphone and yelled, "I got something else for you, ladies. Where's that bitch wife of mine?"

Then the other men tackled him to the ground, placed him in a full-nelson around his neck, and escorted him through the boys' locker room. As they dragged him away, he kicked his legs like a trapped animal.

I did not see it but was told that they beat up Mr. Croon in the boys' room before the police arrived and took him to jail.

My mother and father asked Will and his mother to join us for a celebration lunch that afternoon at our favorite restaurant, Anne Marie's near Lenox Mall. We had a nice lunch and never once mentioned the incident, though I know it was churning in Will's stomach. Afterwards, Will and I went to Kyle Onderdonk's party.

Thursday, May 24

The sun rose up this morning to an isochromatic canvas of apricots and peaches painted in one slow, firm stroke. A solitary motion glowed over the hills and broke the tops of the trees. The air warmed up today and honeysuckle floated through the air. I smelled pine trees, too. I walked the dogs to the park across the street, then along the lake. There were a number of small boats out early, with people's fishing lines cast outward with hope.

In the afternoon, while I was sitting on the porch, I heard the ping of a basketball being dribbled in the park. I walked over and there was a man there dribbling and shooting hoops, Eric Storm-Tammus. I remembered him from a few Eagles' basketball games this past winter and when I mentioned it to him, he laughed and said, "No one remembers the basketball refs."

We played several games of HORSE and 21, and though I came close, I lost every game. The best I did was 28—26.

He lives down the street and played minor league baseball for four years.

"I couldn't hit. It's that plain and simple. I was a good defensive player. Just couldn't hit big league pitching. I played with Dick Stigman, who went on to pitch for Minnesota for a few years."

§

I watched public television this evening, a show on Albert Einstein. One man gave his account:

> The one time I met Albert Einstein, I was riding on the same train to Chicago and sat across the aisle from him, but I did not bother him at all. The conductor asked Mr. Einstein for his ticket, but when he couldn't find it, he became quite upset with himself. Frantically, Einstein searched every pocket several times, but was unsuccessful. He rifled through his books and papers, and his briefcase. He couldn't find the ticket and became quite nervous

and distraught. The conductor told Einstein not to worry, he knew who he was. 'You're very famous, and I'm certain you have a ticket.' Einstein said, disheartened, 'No. I must find my ticket. You don't understand. If I don't find my ticket, I won't know where to exit the train.'

In my psychology class this past spring, my professor, Dr. Walton, said that when she was a little girl, she lived in Princeton because her father taught there. She met Einstein several times.

"I've always been fascinated with his ideas on reverse dynamism," I told her.

"He loved the little children and always liked picking us up," she said. "But he smelled. He didn't bathe too often."

Upon deciding to attend Chautauqua University, I figured I would run into a childhood friend or two, but I have not. They've probably moved away or run in different circles. I'm a stranger in my own town. I had decided not to contact them, but that was easy enough—no one I used to know is here anyway. The one person I looked up was Peggy Weislogel because I had a crush on her. She lived on Maplecrest and had an in-ground swimming pool, where Kimberly and I went to swim for her birthday party one summer. During my first semester at C.U., I drove to her house and there was a woman planting flowers around the mailbox, which had "Smythe" painted on it in white letters with daisies around them.

"Do the Weislogels still live here?"

"No, not anymore. They moved to California back in 1967 after their son was killed in the war."

That would have been Ricky. He was a lot older than us, and I remember he was always working on his car. He let me look in the engine the day of Peggy's birthday party. I guess that was 1960 or '61.

"I looked them up in the phone book and it shows they still live here."

"I know. I've tried getting that changed, but the phonebook people can't seem to get it straight. No, they moved. We've been here for six years."

Mrs. Peterson still lives next door to our old house, and I have on several occasions stopped by to say hello. She used to give me cookies when I knocked on her door. Her husband died three years ago, and now that she's in her nineties, I think she may not be as sharp as she once was. I don't think she realizes I moved away years ago. When Kimberly and I were little, we'd knock on her front door and ask for a cookie. She always had freshly made cookies, not store-bought. They were Norwegian cookies like butter cookies and Pepper cookies. Kimberly liked Pepper cookies the best. I didn't—not at all. I liked the Fattigmann, which we always called Fat Man Cookies.

After breakfast this morning at The Big Tree, I walked to the pharmacy where I bought five packs of baseball cards for ten cents each. Mr. Barone, who was wearing a Notre Dame sweatshirt, rang me up.

"You must like baseball?" he asked.

"Yes, sir, but I can't throw it straight to save my life."

"It's my favorite sport to play or watch."

"Did you play at Notre Dame?" I asked.

"No, I was too busy studying. I bet you didn't know that Nellie

Fox played here in Jamestown. So did Irv Noren. He was born in Jamestown."

"I didn't know that."

"As a matter of fact, Ray Caldwell, an old-timer used to live not far from here. He died in sixty-seven. He used to work at the Rod and Gun as a bartender."

In the packets of cards I bought, I got a Sonny Jackson and Hank Aaron (both from the Atlanta Braves), Roy White, Nolan Ryan, Tom Seaver, and Roberto Clemente, which I suspect will be his last card since he was killed not long ago. I like Nolan Ryan because he has a no hitter, but how he ever got traded to the California Angels, I'll never know. They stink. His career is over. He'll be lucky to last a few more seasons in the big leagues in that abyss.

Most people probably don't remember this, but on the first episode of the television show, *Lost in Space*, when Will Robinson was listening to the World Series on the radio and the spaceship was ready to blast off, the year was 1986, twenty-five years in the future. The two teams playing in the World Series were the New York Mets and the California Angels. I doubt Nolan Ryan will hang around to play baseball that long. I saw him pitch twice last year on TV, though he didn't do so well in either game. One game was against the A's and the other game was against the Red Sox. It will be interesting to see who's in the World Series in 1986, thirteen years from now.

§

I called home this evening, after seven when it was cheaper.

"Mom, I'm staying here for the summer. I got a job in Bemus Point working at the Hotel Lenhart."

"Maybe your father and I will visit you."

"Mom, I kind of want a summer on my own. I'm working hard and I'm taking a watercolor class."

I'm not sure why I lied about the watercolor class or where that lie even came from except if I tell them I'm at the old house, I'm not sure what would happen. They'd be upset. It was nice hearing my mom's voice. I miss her. When I called, my dad was at the golf range working on his swing.

§

Outside the school post office, I ran into Caroline DeBauché, who returned from her vacation in Bar Harbor, Maine.

She told me she failed her biology class when she didn't show up for the final exam.

"Dr. Stephenson called my parents saying that if I came back this week, I could take a make-up. If I pass, he'll forget everything."

"Too bad you had to fly all the way in from your vacation."

"I was in Bar Harbor only one stinking day when I got a call from my parents to fly home immediately. I thought someone died."

"Are you doing anything tonight?"

"Yeah, studying. My test's on Friday. I have two days to prepare."

"Let's go see *Paper Moon*. It's playing at The Lakewood Drive-In."

"I'm not going to the drive-in with you."

"Just come over for dinner. I'll cook something up and I'll quiz you. Bring your books."

§

I felt guilty for having lied to my mom earlier, so I bought a watercolor set at the university bookstore after talking with Caroline. Nothing fancy.

I did not read Ashley's letter that was waiting for me in my college P.O. box. I put it in a binder with the others, #7. I'm sitting on the porch with the typewriter and the dogs, who are so relaxed. They just sit and watch people walk down the sidewalk near the park. I need to close the windows on the front side of the house. It's beginning to sprinkle.

Friday, May 25

Late night. I am in a heap of trouble.

I wrecked Dr. Laighles's Corvette. I am as good as dead. I've been on the job less than a week and already I've destroyed their property. What's next, burning down their house?

§

When I picked up Caroline at the Hotel Jamestown, she was wearing a pink jumpsuit with a gold looping belt that nicely revealed her shape. One thing I always liked about her in school is that she is not gaudy. She never wears too much of anything. Nowadays, everything is big and bold, and oftentimes it is too much for my tastes. She keeps everything simple, and tonight, she was wearing small pearl earrings and a bracelet.

"I'm not getting in that thing," she said pointing to Dr. Laighles's old pickup truck.

"It's that, or I go back for my motorcycle."

"I'm not riding that, either."

Caroline was actually nice and except for hating the truck, she was not as bitchy as usual. I finally convinced her to jump in the truck and ride back to the house.

She's twenty years old, and a year ahead of me in school. What does she offer the world? I can only think of this now after the fact. She offers the world her demands.

I cooked dinner, though I didn't really. I bought a variety of fish dinners and seafood from Davidson's Restaurant, enough for four people. I didn't know what she'd want. It was delicious and afterwards she helped me clean up the leftovers and plates.

We sat in the "old" music room, on the floor in front of the fireplace, which has gas logs. I turned them to low and with the lights off in the house, it was romantic. We snuggled together and talked a little about her life in Boston and mine in Atlanta and moving away when I was a kid. I wanted to make a move on her, but I did not.

We drank some wine and I tossed out biology questions to see what she knew. She only missed a few. She nailed the light and dark cycle of photosynthesis.

After studying, that's when I made a move and kissed her. We started making out a little, but she stopped only after a minute of kissing.

"Show me the house."

"It's just a house, like any other."

Harry and Bess followed us up and down the stairs and into each room. When we got to Kimberly's old room, Caroline tried the knob.

"Why's this one locked?"

"I don't know. It was my sister's room when we lived here. I think Emily is an artist and this might be her fortress of solitude."

"You got a key?"

"No. I don't think we should go in there. It's locked for a reason."

I took her into the garage and pulled back the dust tarp to reveal Dr. Laighles's 1961 Corvette, Roman red with white coves. It was parked next to Emily's blue Volvo 144. It was as square as a shoebox and boring.

"What do you think about that?"

"In the first place, my father has a Porsche, so I'm not impressed by fast cars. Is it yours?"

"No, it belongs to Dr. Laighles."

"That's what I figured. You know, he gave me a C in his class. I deserved an A."

"Want to go for a spin?"

And with those six words, my world, my life, has been completely destroyed.

§

We drove around the county, just cruising for an hour or so. Although it wasn't raining, the roads were still wet and it was cool outside. With the top down, I blasted the heater. Near twelve-thirty, I stopped the car and we got out in Bemus Point, in front of the Hotel Lenhart. A man and a woman were sitting on the front porch in rocking chairs looking out over the lake, but except for them, we were the only people around and the only sound was the lapping of water against the shore. Near the dock, we kissed under the moonlight, and for a moment, I imagined that more might happen later.

When we walked back up to the porch, the man said, "Have you seen the paintings inside?"

Caroline and I walked inside the lobby of the Hotel Lenhart. It was so quiet that I did not dare speak above a whisper, but on the walls, there were some beautiful paintings by Charlotte Lenhart Johnson. I scrutinized over them, but Caroline said she was bored. Somewhere in my mind, I remember Miss Charlotte back when I was a kid. She was old by then, having been born in the 1800s, but when I was young, my parents brought Kimberly and I to the hotel to take art lessons one day. I remember a very old woman who was kind and patient. I wanted to paint like Jackson Pollack, which made her laugh.

I asked the woman at the front desk about the paintings.

"Those were done by Miss Charlotte back when she was younger. She died five years ago. She was the owner's daughter."

Caroline did not care about any of this, but I was intrigued and have decided I will return this summer.

At one o'clock in the morning, the disc-jockey at WJTN was going to play *Tubular Bells* by Mike Oldfield, which Caroline wanted to hear in its entirety.

"Here it is," the DJ said, "just released today, although I've had this album in my hands since Wednesday. From start to finish without interruptions, WJTN, and sponsored by Mose's Accordion School, Mike Oldfield's *Tubular Bells*."

We drove around the lake to Long Point, Midway Park, and all around, listening to this new album. Both of us were quiet and enjoying the music and ended up in Busti and driving by Stateline Raceway.

Once the music finished, Caroline randomly yelled, "Don't touch me. Ever!"

"What are you talking about? I'm driving the car. I didn't touch you."

"Don't touch me!"

"Hey, hey, stop screaming."

"I'll scream my Goddamn head off if I want to. Don't touch me."

"What'd I do? I'm driving."

"I'd never do anything with you."

"I thought we were having a nice time."

"No, I hate you."

She reminded me of Elizabeth Taylor in *Who's Afraid of Virginia Woolf*—just screaming and screaming with venom. She screamed so loud and said so much, I don't even remember all that she accused me of.

"Hey, shut up. Stop screaming for Christ's sake."

"You listen to me." She shook her finger in my face. "My father says the same thing to my mother, and I hate him for it. Do you hear me? Don't ever tell me to shut up. Where do you come off assaulting me? I'm going to the police. I'm going to tell them how you got me drunk and raped me. I'm still a virgin. You tried raping a virgin. I hope they put you in jail for fifty years."

"What the hell are you talking about? All I did was kiss you by the lake."

"You tried raping me!"

"I bet you haven't been this angry since Dorothy threw water on you!"

Her arms just started flailing at me like Joe Frasier. I blocked most of her punches with my right arm then grabbed her wrist. She bit at my hand. When I pulled it away, she caught me in the upper jawbone with a closed fist.

At the corner of Cowing and Winch Road, I lost control of Dr. Laighles's Corvette and slid on the wet tar and cinders. The car fishtailed and took down a stop sign before sliding off the road and over a ditch. There was a massive thump when the car hit all four tires on the ground then ran a gauntlet through the cornstalks.

In the commotion, Caroline hit her face on the curvature of the glove compartment, and I hit my head on the metal windshield trim. Her left eyebrow was cut open and blood ran down her cheek, around the curve of her nostril, and over her lips, spreading out in the crevices.

"Where the hell are we?" she asked, spraying blood off her lips as she spoke.

"Nebraska. Where do you think? It's a cornfield. Here, put this handkerchief over your eye."

It took an hour to drive out of the cornfield, a task that had me turning around in a complete circle before heading down a tractor path to Cowing Road. The cornstalks were dry and hard and brown and torn in shredded parcels, left over cow corn from last year's harvest. They were gummy as glue, which smeared the windshield.

"Do you need to go to the hospital?"

"Just take me back to my hotel."

The blood on Caroline's face had dried by the time we were out of the cornfield, but her face and right eye were swollen. The ends of her hair were brittle sticks where the blood had coagulated.

On the road, the car whined like a coyote caught in a trap. The front bumper fell off on Southwestern Avenue, scraping and sending sparks in all directions as it slid into the curb where it lay broken like a fibula. How did it not wake up the neighborhood?

"I want ninety-five dollars for my outfit!" she yelled.

"I'm taking you to the hospital."

"I'm not going anywhere, except to the hotel to call my brother. You're going to wish you'd never touched me."

I pulled under the brightly lit hotel portico. The oval bulbs glared overhead against the dull shine of the car's body. The night clerk rushed up to the car and stared at the grillwork.

"You know you've got corn all over your car?"

Not long ago, this car was a collector's item, but now it's been reduced to a Flintstone-mobile. The windshield is smashed and the right fender and headlight are busted up. I'm sure the frame is bent, and every place the corn hit the car, there's a crack in the fiberglass.

Under the glow of the hotel lights, Caroline clutched her small purse. Her outfit looked like it had been tie-dyed with blood.

"Are you guys okay?"

"Take your hands off me, you idiot. I'll have you fired."

"I'm just trying to help you."

"I don't need your help. Of course, I'm not okay. My outfit's ruined. Robert! Robert! Do you hear me? I want a hundred dollars. Are you listening to me? I never want to see you again."

The desk clerk opened her door, then trotted up the steps in front of Caroline and opened the glass door, but she tugged open the other one and walked in unassisted. He ran behind the car, then up to the window and leaned on the door.

"Hey man, what happened to your car? It looks as if you drove through a farm. Your front bumper's gone. It'll cost a couple thousand bucks to fix this mess."

"Think about it for a second," I said, "I went out with a girl I don't really like, then I drove my car through a cornfield at two o'clock in the morning."

§

It's five thirty in the morning as I type this. Nothing can make me sleep. I parked the car back in the garage under the tarp.

Like the snake said to the man after he was bitten, "What did you think I would do? You knew I was a snake."

Saturday, May 26

Mike woke me up at seven o'clock this morning, playing with the doorbell. One hour and five minutes of sleep—that's all I got.

He had his work gloves and a black lunch box. I let him trim the front bushes while I mainly stretched out in a lawn chair. As a result, I got nothing accomplished on the car. I thought I could take it in for an estimate on a Saturday. No dice, because I did not want Mike to see or know. I'll have to wait until Monday. I don't have insurance, so this is going to all be out of pocket.

Mike ate lunch, then we played World Series pinball. After he left, I went into the garage to see if it had been a dream.

Sunday, May 27

Again, Mike was here early. I felt physically better, but I made Mike watch an hour of Garner Ted Armstrong with me. I felt the need to center myself with the Good Word.

We played World Series pinball until church let out. Mike now leads me, 7—1. In the backyard, we ended up tilling nine small rows in the garden this afternoon. Mike chopped and hoed the clumps of dirt into small workable bits as we cut a seven-by-nine plot. While we were playing more pinball, we soaked the seeds in water on the back porch. Later we dropped them in the dirt and covered them into darkness: lettuce, green beans, watermelon, squash, carrots, radishes, and cabbage. A little of each.

That was a lot of work. As I type this, I am exhausted!

§

This afternoon while taking a break, I made a list of things I need to do this summer to stabilize my life:

* Go grocery shopping for nutritional foods (no junk food) until the garden comes in
* Weed the garden when it grows
* Take good care of the house and dogs
* Respect others' property
* Read five to ten novels
* Change my name to something interesting. R.C.E. is

as dull as dishwater. I need an alter ego, like Liam Breathnach. That sounds like a name for a writer.

* Paint with my watercolors
* Remain as quiet and reserved as possible
* Listen to calming music
* Write my novel about Isabella and Vincenzo
* Go one day per week without talking to anyone so as to savor the words I speak on other days
* Fix the car
* Above all else, get to that place in my life where I can get things together.

Monday, May 28

It's 1:30 p.m. I realized this morning that I cannot have the car fixed in town or anywhere within thirty miles. This is probably the only 1961 Corvette in the county and everyone knows Dr. Laighles. I drove over to Dick's Auto Body in Celeron, where he gave me the name of a shop in Buffalo.

"The man to talk to is Jerry Scott. He's the best body man in Buffalo and he's nuts about Corvettes."

While I was there waiting, I watched a man fixing his race car. It had *4 Jr* painted on the side.

"You ought to come out to Stateline to watch the race."

"I drove by the other night. What are you fixing?"

"The axle. I need to replace it. I cracked it last week. You said you messed up your Corvette?"

"Yes, sir."

"How'd you do that?"

"Because of a girl."

"It always is."

"It's gonna cost a ton of money, isn't it?"

"The girl or the car?" he asked, which made me laugh.

Ronny Blackmer was the race driver's name. I am going to go to the races one Saturday night and cheer for him.

I drove from the garage to the university and called Jerry Scott long distance from the library, which is one of the few places on campus open during the summer. Dave Edwards, who was in my English Comp II class, worked with me at Chautauqua Indoor Advertising before I quit. He's majoring in Library Science (for some reason). A while ago, he told me about this little trick on the third floor in the archival room—you can call anywhere in the country and no one will know. Free long-distance.

"Depending upon the availability of parts and whether you bent the frame, I'd guess four to six weeks. Maybe longer," Jerry Scott told me.

"Take your time. I've got all summer."

"Bring the car in on Wednesday at seven o'clock. I'll get you taken care of."

While at the library, I learned a few things I should not know. I discovered that the library has a computer on the second floor that you can use to search someone's name or a subject. It's like a typewriter with a TV screen, and if they have your topic, like 20th Century Russian novels, the computer screen will list books and articles they have in the stacks. It's in monochrome letters—so cool. If they don't have it, a list appears of university libraries that should have it.

I typed in Kimberly's name and her obituary was listed as being in the *Jamestown Post-Journal*. If I want to read it, I can ask the librarian for the microfiche, which I did not. I did not feel comfortable doing so. In time perhaps. When I typed in my parents' names, her obituary reference appeared, along with three articles on my dad and two on my mom from years ago when they were kids. This IBM computer is pretty cool. I wish the articles would appear on the screen—that would be awesome, beyond awesome. I typed in "Dr. Laighles." A bunch of stuff popped up, but so did an obituary for Steven Laighles in the *Chautauqua University Eagle*, which is the school's quarterly magazine, which the computer said were on the third floor, in the stacks not far from where I was standing when I called Jerry Scott about the car.

I searched the stacks for the correct *CUE*, and after finding it, pulled it from the stacks. The Laighles' only son, Steven, drowned in 1968 at Kinzua Dam in Allegheny State Park on Labor Day, just a year after the lake was at full capacity. There was a reference to his obituary in the *Jamestown Post-Journal*, but I did not pull it from the microfiche. The *CUE* showed his picture. He had blonde hair. It also mentioned Mike and how he tried to rescue Steven but was pulled under by the current. It did not provide any details into his injury other than saying that Edward Proudfoot, a Seneca Indian, drove by the scene and pulled Mike from the water. Otherwise, according to local authorities, he most likely would have drowned alongside Steven.

Tuesday, May 29

Vice-President Agnew expressed a renewed faith that the outcome in the Watergate conspiracy would demonstrate that Nixon was untouched by "these matters as far as any direct involvement is concerned." I agree. Nixon will be exonerated.

§

Mike came over late in the evening. I was not tolerant of him as I was in a bad mood for no reason. We played some Crazy-Eights, then he left. I wish I had been more pleasant. I can't let him know about the car.

Earlier, I rented a U-Haul trailer from the folks who live in the same building as the Lakewood Supply Company. In the back, a man runs a rental business. He helped me hitch the trailer to Dr. Laighles's pickup truck, which I parked in the backyard so no one on the street would see it and get suspicious.

Wednesday, May 30

I was up by 3:00 a.m. I had the Corvette loaded on the trailer and was on the road by 4:30 with a cup of coffee and a stack of buttered toast. It was a two-hour drive to the mechanic's garage on Kenmore Avenue in Buffalo. While driving there, I drove past the Buffalo Psych Center and almost stopped in to ask them what's wrong with me.

I arrived thirty minutes early to the repair shop, but that was fine. I did not want to be late.

"It looks pretty bad," said the mechanic as he looked over the damage. His thick-muscled arms were like round, pale dumbbells splattered with freckles. "That's my first impression."

"When do you think it'll be ready?"

"No telling. Several weeks, maybe a month. Depends on how much trouble I run into." He scratched the inside of his nose with one of his sludge-filled fingernails. "Give me a call around lunch time next Thursday. I'll know by then."

"How much is it gonna cost?"

"It'll take hours to get at the damage. It's not going to be cheap, but it won't cost you your balls, either."

§

This afternoon, after I returned the trailer, the *Post-Journal* had a picture of a farmer, W.S. LeBaron, standing in front of his corn field where an eight-foot-wide gap had been cut through. The caption said: "Full Moon Raises Havoc in Corn Field." A local man who did not wish to be identified speculated it was aliens.

I stopped by to see Roy Paterson at Chautauqua Indoor Advertising this afternoon about working this summer. Back in April, I told him I was going home for the summer, but I actually quit without notice. I felt awkward returning to the scene of the crime and then asking for my job back with a requirement—I would only work nine to five, no second or third shifts, because my body and mind just can't take those hours. I was prepared for him to kick me out of his office, but he said, okay.

I told Roy about the Corvette.

"Minimum wage is a buck-sixty. I can pay you two-twenty. Overtime is time and a half."

I figured it out—that's seventeen dollars per day, but if I work all day Saturday, it's twenty-six dollars. Before taxes.

§

Dr. Laighles called at four o'clock my time, ten o'clock his time. How appropriate, as if he knew I had destroyed his car.

"Everything's been smooth sailing so far," I lied.

"That's good. How are Harry and Bess doing?"

I told him about Harry breaking his leash, and how I found him when I returned to the house.

"A friend of ours might stop by if he hasn't already."

"Yeah, I've met him. Mike, right?"

"Great. Great. About Mike," he paused, "he wasn't born retarded. He was injured in an accident several years ago and has irreversible brain damage. Be patient with him. He's a good kid."

The line crackled and he began shouting into the receiver.

"Look for a postcard. The weather here has been horrendous. It keeps raining. That's expected. Emily says hello. We'll talk in a few weeks." He was shouting through the static, but I could barely hear him.

I'm sitting at the kitchen table looking out the window into the backyard where the treehouse used to be. I moved the typewriter in here. My garden is being rained upon quite heavily. Of course, nothing's begun to grow, yet. I'm listening to a baseball game on the radio—the Yankees are defeating the Oakland Athletics. The Atlanta Braves are in the basement. At least we have Hank Aaron.

The Senate voted 63 to 19 to cease funds for bombing Cambodia. Wake up, people! It's been a long-time conclusion that this war is in vain. Look at the numbers. Listen to the people. Look what happened to Ricky Weislogel.

Thursday, May 31

There's a chill in the air, so I turned up the heat and fired up the gas logs. The temperature says fifty, but it feels colder. I'm sitting next to the fire and looking out the big window at the lake. I have the typewriter on my legs. Every once in a while, a sheet of rain moves across the lake that I can track until it hits the house. I kind of like that and am waiting for the next wave. The weatherman says it will clear soon and we'll have sun all next week.

I was looking around in the attic today when I found Kimberly's name written in crayon on a support beam, along with a picture of the sun and a flower, dated July 29, 1961. We never played in the attic because we believed we'd be attacked by ghosts as soon as we opened the door, or worse, eaten. I've been thinking about that ever since and I don't know what to make of it.

I took several books down from the shelves and thumbed through them, looking for something interesting to read. Dr. Laighles has a card catalog of his books and keeps them in keen order. I studied a surveyor's book on Chautauqua County. I read a little of *The Illustrated Jamestown* (a history book from 1800 to 1902), *140 Years of Methodism* by Helena M. Stonehouse (a very interesting book), *Early Post Offices of Chautauqua County, New York* by C. Malcolm Nichols, *History of Lakewood* by Lucy Darrow

Peake, and *Chautauqua* and *Nineteenth-Century Houses in Western New York* by Jewel Helen Conover. I didn't actually read each book cover to cover. I skimmed and flipped around. *The Illustrated Jamestown* was published in 1902 and was very worn and fragile. My house was not in the Conover book.

With the exception of the houses and the internal city of Jamestown, very little seems to have changed since the Second World War when most of the industries moved out.

I love driving through town because the streets are still mostly cobblestone, and the sound of the stones emanate into the wheel wells and vibrate throughout Dr. Laighles's truck.

Dr. Laighles has a large map book, and when I placed it back on the shelf, I found something I had not seen since I was seven. Sitting on the shelf was a book my parents gave to Kimberly on her birthday, *Little Girl's World* by Ellen Ballensperger. I received one called *Little Boy's World*. Mine had doctors and astronauts on it. Kimberly's had nurses and schoolteachers. It was listed in the card catalog as a book Steven found in the "secret room" on August 25.

I don't know what's meant by the "secret room." He must have found it underneath the spiral stairs in the small closet.

As I read Kimberly's book, I was deeply saddened, while at the same time joyous to see it again. I remember when we received them for our birthday, we sat on the porch and gave a private reading to one another. We had lemonade and pretzels and pushed our cushioned lawn chairs next to each other. I liked my story more, but Kimberly was a better reader. There's an inscription in the front in my mom's handwriting: *To Kimberly, for your seventh birthday. Love, Mommy and Daddy.*

A long time ago, I either lost my original book or threw it out. I don't remember.

What secret room was Dr. Laighles referring to in his card catalogue? Kimberly's book must have been left behind by accident when we moved.

I walked through the house, trying to determine where a secret room might be located. As I did, a cool gust of wind hit me in the face when I was upstairs in the hall. It felt like air-conditioning and made me shiver. I don't think the attic constitutes as a secret room.

Friday, June 1

I spent today reading portions of *Gravity's Rainbow*, which I only half understand. The sun was out, and a brisk wind was blowing off the lake from the north when I walked the dogs.

William Faulkner once said, "Man must lose something of value, man must learn to be afraid."

I have lost and I have been afraid. I fear being alone as I get older. That does not sound like the words of an eighteen-year-old kid, but if my parents died, there is no one left for me. My grandparents are all dead. My father's older brother was twenty-two when he was killed in Italy during World War II. My mom's sister lives in Australia. That is it. I have no one else. Kimberly is gone. Ashley is out of my life. If my parents were gone, I wouldn't have anyone to spend Christmas with. I have thought about this a lot throughout the years. Yes, even when I was younger. I always wanted to start a family early, maybe in my early twenties. I want a wife to love and who loves me, and I want children. I want to be surrounded by people who love me.

I must shake off loneliness like a dog shakes off the rain.

Besides holding the lifetime world record for home runs, Babe Ruth also holds the world record for striking out the most. The baseball commentator on the radio just mentioned this.

Saturday, June 2

I was up early this morning and had my first cup of coffee on the porch. The streetlights turned themselves off one by one down Terrace Avenue, as though someone walked to each of them and snuffed out their flames with a long pole. The lake was bucolic this morning. On the other side of the lake, from the shoreline and up the terrain, there are rich pastoral greens. Bucolic is a word I like. It sounds like a brand of English tea. I walked to my old job (now new). My first day back.

§

"With you working so late at night, I rarely got to talk or see you except for when something went wrong, or when you got locked out of the building," Roy Paterson (my boss) said, as we sat in his office as I filled out some papers.

"It was hard for me to work those late-night hours."

"Well, I'm a firm believer in working as little as possible for the maximum return," he said, tossing some papers on to his desk. "That's why computers are going to revolutionize the world. Just wait and see. Things will change so fast you won't hardly be able to keep up. Computers will maximize your return with the least amount of effort. Profits will rise. It will cut down on the amount of paperwork we'll have, meaning less storage, too. Look at how much we do with computers here. Let the machines work hard. If hard work is so great, don't you think rich people would have kept it for themselves?"

Before I left, Roy handed me a wooden box about the size of three shoeboxes.

"I heard you like playing chess?"

"I haven't played since last year in high school, but I was on the chess team."

"This box is a prototype from a friend of mine at Bell Labs. It's a computer chess game. It's just you against the computer. We have one on our Unix system, but this prototype is going to hit the market in a few years. They're working out the bugs and patents and all that horseshit."

"Have you beaten it?"

"Only on levels one and two. There are five levels. The rest are impossible unless you're a grand master. Take it home. Play with it. It doesn't think like we do. Every move is based on a numerical formula and the highest probable outcome. Unlike us, we think and calculate the risk, then act upon it."

"Really? I can take this home?"

"Yeah, yeah. Don't worry. This isn't the only prototype. There are at least twenty out there being tested. That's why they gave it to me to play with. They want our opinion and suggestions on how to make it better."

§

Mike came over after I got back from work. He had a large bag of apples. We played two games of World Series pinball. I won 7—6 and 12—8. I showed him Roy Paterson's computer chess set. I turned it on and showed Mike how to use it. He played a few games but lost quickly. Roy and I have a big chess match coming up, or so he warned me to be ready.

"Bob, I used to play chess."

"When was that?" I said, half ignoring him as I stirred some chicken noodle soup.

"A long time ago. I remember playing with my uncle." He giggled and laughed at how the computer lit up and beeped each time a move was made.

Sunday, June 3

I thought about going to church today but changed my mind at the last moment. There is no salvation quite right for me these days, as I am having a difficult time with organized religion. However, I watched Garner Ted Armstrong and felt much better about the world and myself after he spoke about ridding oneself of guilt. I think that is hard to do, but there is the prospect of purging guilt.

There is the old joke: How to have guilt without sex.

§

I have not heard a word from Caroline DeBauché, nor from her brother. I thought about buying a gun, but that's stupid, as well as unnecessary. She probably forgot everything once she got back home. Besides, I never touched her. I rubbed her tits a little bit that night while kissing her, but big deal. I never raped her, that's for damn sure.

I didn't mention it yesterday but working at Chautauqua Indoor Advertising on a Saturday is pretty much how it was at night, except there are other people running around. I have my own cubicle in the back and am pretty much left by myself, meaning, no one bothers me.

After talking with Roy, he and a man from Virginia installed a new computer monitor in my cubicle. It's a Wang 2200. The only way to describe it is to say that it's a spaceship TV with a cassette player and a typewriter. Once they got it connected and running, all I did was type in my responses to what I am reading. All of that is fine. It takes me a few hours to fill out my reports once I've finished reading. The best part is, as Roy calls it, "free writing" and expressing my opinion about the book or magazine in as much or as little detail as I want.

I think most people would think reading and writing reports about what I read would be a dull job. However, I find it exciting because they use the computers and what we write to determine trends in advertising and what people in five to ten years will want to buy. Especially stuff that hasn't been invented yet or on the market, like the computer chess set.

I read a story last year when I was working at night where this man murdered his wife's lover. This was in a novel. He bought batrachotoxin on the black market, which is produced by a specific poison dart frog. The main character took a Q-Tip and rubbed the poison on the door handle thumb button of the Chrysler owned by his wife's lover. He added less than a drop. Once the man pressed the button, he had a heart attack less than a minute later. I read where the same result can happen from a puffer fish. It has some sort of toxin that kills almost instantly. I'd never heard of that before. The murderer was caught when his wife found her lover slumped over in his car and when she opened the door, she was poisoned, too. She didn't die immediately in the story but there was no antidote. That was the best thing I've read.

In addition to the computer chess set, Roy gave me a pile of books to read, none I'd ever heard of before. I can read them at the office but also at home if I want. I took them all home.

"I'll pay you your hourly rate if you read at home, but it's on the honor system. I can't police you at home. In fact, I don't want to. That's not how I operate. What I want is for you to read everything and do a good job. I don't mind paying for it."

"You know I read slow," I told Roy, worried that he might pay me less.

"Slowly. It's an adverb. Slow is an adjective. It's like when people say, 'Drive safe.' No, it's drive safely."

"I read slowly," I corrected myself.

"I want your reports to be grammatically correct. No lazy-ass writing."

"Okay, but I read slowly."

"Can you do anything about that? Maybe speed it up?"

"No, but I comprehend everything. I may read more slowly than the others, but my reports are more thorough and detailed."

"That's true. You know how to write."

The books he handed to me are:

- Watership Downs

- Tales of a Fourth Grade Nothing
- The Great American Novel
- All Creatures Great and Small
- The Woman's Bible
- Sula
- The Odessa File
- Rubyfruit Jungle
- The Earthsea Trilogy
- Burr
- The Water is Wide
- Clockwork Orange
- The Optimist's Daughter
- Love
- The Fear of Flying
- The Happy Hooker
- Child of God
- Breakfast of Champions
- I Never Had It Made
- The 158-Pound Marriage
- The Princess Bride
- P.S. Your Cat Is Dead
- Theatre de Situations

God Almighty! I brought home twenty-three books to read and write reports on. It took two trips from the car to the house to carry them all in. I had actually heard of one of these books: *Love* by Leo Buscaglia. Ashley read it last year. She took it with her everywhere and said it was the best book she'd ever read. Maybe she should write the analysis. Or the sequel, *Screwing in the Back Seat*.

Monday, June 4

Most of the time when I'm not in my cubicle, I'm in the computer room learning how to write COBOL and FORTRAN computer code and using the IBM punch cards. Brooke and Carl are teaching me the basics. They are both so smart, but I think Brooke is smarter than he is. She knows how to teach me this stuff better, that's for sure. I have one goal—make enough money to pay for the car. After that, I plan to quit again.

At lunch, Roy and I played a game of chess in the breakroom. He won.

I can't begin to wrap my mind around all these books, so after work I took Mike for a ride on my motorcycle around Lakewood. I hadn't ridden it in more than a month and it felt great. Mike pointed out all sorts of places and interesting facts about them. Some were so wild, I figured he was making stuff up.

When Mike plays chess, he stares at the chessboard and concentrates on each move as if it were a breath of air he's tasting for the first time. When the computer chess set beeps, he giggles.

Though it was late in the evening, I watched a strange television show on PBS about how television is going to change in the next decade. There will be hundreds of TV channels, but viewers will pay for only the channels they watch. No more free TV. I doubt that. Who would pay for television? There's supposed to be a channel just for cooking, sports, movies, and all sorts of other things. The stupidest one I heard of was about a channel where people would shop by watching television. They would just pick up the phone and shop. No more malls, they said. No more driving. The mailman will deliver all your purchases to your house. That's total bullshit. I think they should call that the Reclusive Channel.

I have a hard time believing in this. People are much too interested in interacting with other people. All I can imagine is a lot of fat people sitting at home, ordering food and beer. The commentator said crime will get so bad no one will want to venture outside their house. The spokesperson said that the malls would be torn down some day. I like what one salesgirl at J.C. Penney said, "I'm not going to worry. I don't plan on working here past the summer." My sentiments exactly.

Emily and Dr. Laighles have cable television, but there is nothing but crap showing. For instance, in today's TV listing at 12:30 a.m., Seymour Schartz and Irving Chin for Civil Court 3rd District. That must be a local debate out of NYC, I believe. Who can hold back that tide of interest?

Life is binary. You work towards a goal or you don't. What else matters? Otherwise, you become a mass of globular cells lamenting over game shows, cable television, soap operas, and shopping malls. I have no excuse for wrecking Dr. Laighles's car. I did it. I shouldn't have, but I did. I accept my fate—and punishment. I expect to pay for it in many ways.

I am on the front porch as I type this, drinking a cup of tea to relax. It is well beyond my bedtime. The rose bushes my mother planted so many years ago are in bloom and their fragrance has me dizzy with pleasure.

The night air is warm like a basin of water. The typewriter clicks. A few cars rumble down the street. Their sound fades. Lights flicker across the lake in the windows of other sleepy houses.

Tuesday, June 5

It's very late as I type this. Mike left a little more than an hour ago. We played World Series baseball the entire time the game was on the radio. The game went into extra innings, so we kept playing. He won 9 games to my 4.

Wednesday, June 6

The newspaper reported on the back page that the Greek Government defended the abolition of the monarchy six years ago. They appear to be denying the king a return to power. The king said a monarchy was more realistic than a military dictatorship. I think I agree with him, although I know next to nothing about their politics.

I met a woman this year who is married and lives with her husband in Bemus Point. They are both from Greece. Cyprus, to be exact. I shall ask for her opinion when I next see her. She was in my English class with Dr. Leibrandt. She's one of the most beautiful women I've ever met, and I was in love with her until I found out she was married. That sort of dimmed the fire. If she ever left her husband. . . . I have met him and found him to be very nice. He is a good-looking man. Much better looking than me. He has kind eyes and a pleasant smile.

I bet that someday when she is forty years old, she will look like she is only twenty-five. She will probably cut her hair short and be more beautiful than anyone can imagine. As I sit here typing, I can see it in her. I could never tell her this, of course. The typewriter keys are whispering softly upon the white paper: I am a fool.

I would be embarrassed to tell her how I feel. She would think that all I want to do is sleep with her, and maybe that's true, but is that so bad? What's wrong with desire?

Mike came over after I got home from work. I was curt with him yesterday, so I took him for a ride on my motorcycle again. We skidded out of the driveway toward Panama Rocks, like Peter Fonda in *Easy Rider*. I drove while Mike navigated. We went to an old railroad track grown over with grass and bushes and a washed-out bridge. We rode through the hills, down dirt roads, past shanty houses with refrigerators on the porch. I saw Amish children playing in their yard, kicking a ball. In North Harmony, we stopped at the "Old Checkered School House" and just looked at it. It was built in 1894. It's now been renovated into a house.

"My grandfather went to school here," Mike said.

We rode up a flat trail wide enough for a small car but is now grown over with foliage, a forgotten place. The trail wandered uphill for a couple hundred yards then tapered off flat. For thirty or forty feet, the path narrowed with enough space for the motorcycle. We twisted and turned around trees, and dashed down gullies, under hanging branches, over mounds of dirt, and through the dark woods. We left a trail of two-stroke motor oil smoke hanging stagnant in the air. I did not know where we were, but then we exited the woods and entered a dirt road. Mike might have known where we were, but I did not. We rambled about.

A few miles down the dirt road, Mike yelled, "Stop here."

I slowed the motorcycle and revved the throttle to keep the bike from vibrating too much.

"We used to come here after football games," he said.

Mike hopped off the motorcycle and removed a thick steel cable stretching across the dirt drive. There were several "No Trespassing" signs. He motioned for me to drive up.

"Can we go in there with these signs posted?"

"Sure."

"No one's gonna shoot us, are they?"

"My grandfather owns this land."

We rode down the dirt lane as it curved back and forth, then as if driving from out of a tunnel into daylight, we broke out of the woods into a golden field of high grasses. For hundreds of yards in all directions, as far as I could see, there was an open, flat field of grass surrounded by tall, dark trees in the distance. Through the middle of the field, a small creek babbled out one end of the woods and into the other as if it was connecting two worlds.

I brought the bike to a complete stop and took off my helmet. Mike took his football helmet off and jumped to the ground.

"Pretty, isn't it?" he asked.

"Yeah. Very peaceful."

"I know, Bob. I been here before. Lots of times. When I was in school, we came here with our girls after the games, Steven and me," he said as he walked around.

When the sun struck his face, he looked younger and had I not known about his issues, I would see nothing but a strong person with a future. I stretched out in the tall golden grass and stared at the clouds, while Mike wandered off. I closed my eyes and nearly fell asleep.

When I caught up with Mike, he was wading in the water up to his knees.

"You're getting your pants wet."

"I don't care."

"Just be careful you don't fall in."

"I know how to swim. We used to come here all the time. Once I brought my girlfriend here to swim. So, I know how."

"Okay. Just checking," I said, though the water was no more than two or three feet deep. He picked up a crayfish and held it up as it squirmed its legs and feelers. Then he laid it on the surface of the water, and it sank.

"You'll find bigger crayfish under the rocks," he said.

"Who was your girlfriend?" I asked.

"Julie."

"Julie who?"

"My girl." He ran his hand across the top of the water, spraying a wave over the bank. "She lives in New York City. She's a model."

"Got a picture of her?"

"At home on my dresser."

§

My parents sent me a letter, which arrive today. Again, my mother asked me to call Ashley. At this point I don't think I'm ever going back to Atlanta. Colorado sounds nice. John Denver. Coors.

According to my mother, Marty Christof, who lived down the

street from us, and was two years older than me, fell into a bad crowd and punched a cop. He's always been a dick.

My mother hasn't seen or heard from Will since I left for school. I don't think she's going to.

A friend of mine, Scott Brewer, has been promoted in the Army, but my mother could not remember what rank. She read it in the local paper but forgot to cut out the article. Good for him to be on the move.

My father is taking a computer programming class at the college. He will be surprised when I come home knowing more than he does.

"The house is quiet without you," Mom wrote.

Thursday, June 7

After work, I read until ten o'clock when the news came on. I have a ton of work to do but feel as if I am not fulfilling my job. There's just so many books to read.

Although, late afternoon, post-work, I walked the dogs to the lake and to the beach house where I watched the boats roll by for about ten minutes.

Friday, June 8

I read again until about eight-thirty when Mike stopped by. We walked the dogs to the lake. Mike did most of the talking as we walked. I grunted a few replies back to him until he asked, "What happened to Steven's car?"

"How'd you know about that?"

"I shouldn't have said that, should I?"

"That's okay. How'd you find out?"

"I went in the garage," he said. "I like to sit in Steven's car. I'm not supposed to. Floyd said not to. I went there and his car was wrecked. How'd it get wrecked?"

"Listen to me. You haven't told anyone, have you?"

"No. I didn't want to get in trouble. Floyd and Emily don't want me in the garage, and I knew they'd be mad."

"They might even blame you. So, it'll be our secret."

"Sure," he said.

Across the lake, there is a small mountain of land that caught the last glimmer of sunlight at about 9:10. I have always had my eye on that parcel of property, even as a child. It's in Greenhurst, which sits up high overlooking the north-eastern portion of the lake. I have walked to the lake many times this year just to look at it. The land I'm talking about is covered with trees, thick tall woods, and in the middle, there is a large plot of acreage that is clearcut. I have always wanted to buy that land, build a small white farmhouse, and surround myself with cows, dogs, horses, and a barn full of hay.

Mike and I finished by walking the dogs down to Packard Field, the old football field and park that was donated years ago by Mrs. Packard, the wife of the famed car manufacturer.

I spent the last half hour of my day in bed reading *The Water Is Wide*, which I'm enjoying. I need to finish tomorrow and write my analysis. Reading this Conroy-guy, I realize I will never be a good writer, not like him. He has flare and a wildness. I have nothing.

I have moved the typewriter to the bed with me and it is resting on my legs.

A Soviet Supersonic TU-144 crashed at the Paris Air Show, killing at least fourteen people. It exploded in midair in full view of the air show. Seeing that would have been so damn cool, provided no one was hurt.

Saturday, June 9

I worked hard today, all day. Seven to six-thirty. I worked twenty-three and a half hours overtime this week. Except for today, all of my reading was at home. I earned an extra seventy-seven dollars. After I wrote my analysis on *The Water Is Wide*, I read an article about a girl who rode a bicycle around the circumference of the United States by herself. She had thirty-four flat tires and took seven months. She wasn't a girl. She was twenty-four, so I should say woman.

I would like to go to New York City and throw a baseball, then pick it up from wherever it stopped, and throw it again. I want to throw a baseball across the country. Just throw the ball, pick it up, and throw it again, and just keep going until I am in San Francisco where I would throw it off the Goldengate Bridge. From one side of the country to the other, east coast to west coast. I bet no one has ever done that. Not even Bob Gibson.

Margaret Court won the French Open. It's in the paper this morning. I didn't watch any of it, but I read that she beat that little American girl. I've forgotten her name and I'm too lazy to walk into the kitchen to look it up. I don't think this Conners-guy is very competitive. Either that or he doesn't play well on clay courts. He lost the doubles final, but because he's an American, I pulled for him.

§

Again, it's late at night. I am on the porch with the typewriter, slowly clicking away, and reading the newspaper. *The New York Times* front page says that Nixon approved a partly illegal 1970 security plan. I cannot imagine him being in on something so damaging and trivial in its conceit.

I worried a lot today about the car. The money. Getting caught. The deceit. I do not like the feeling of being broke, poor, and owing money. My life feels chaotic. Out of control.

Sunday, June 10

I mowed the yard this afternoon, read a little bit of *Watership Down*, baked a dessert (apple pan bars that burned at the bottom), and walked through the house several times. I found Kimberly's name written in one of the downstairs closets near the spiral staircase. It was written in blue ink. This was after I walked to the Bucket of Blood to play pool. It's a bar inside the Victoria Hotel, but the pool hall was closed for renovation. A sign on the door read: Reopening on July 1st.

I walked to Packard Field and sat on the wooden bleachers and watched a little league baseball game for two innings. I saw some boy named Johnny (everyone was yelling his name) hit a triple then steal home when the catcher threw the ball back to the pitcher. The pitcher was so startled that anyone would steal home, he threw the ball to the umpire, hitting him in the ankle.

Monday, June 11

It is late in the evening, warm as the day winds down. I am home, typing, of course, and on the radio, I'm listening to WJTN and the entire album of *Goodbye Yellow Brick Road.*

The *Post-Journal* had an article on page two that caught my interest:

> Retired high school teacher, Harold Scruggs, has had the problem of plastic pink flamingos occasionally popping up in his front lawn. Thursday's episode was the third such occurrence in the last five weeks. Scruggs says he doesn't know where the flamingos are coming from, and though at first, he thought it was a spur of-the-moment prank, he has now become irritated, because the metal stems poke large holes in his lawn. Each time the flamingos have been found in his yard, they have been in groups of five. When asked how he thought the plastic flamingos got there, Scruggs said, "I know they didn't fly."

The article went on to say that the police have been looking into this incident; however, no other flamingo sightings have occurred in the area. Police Chief John Milner called it "malicious mischief."

Scruggs said that he tossed out the flamingos with the trash, but by the next morning, the birds were gone.

See, I'd have had a yard sale and sold the birds.

Around six o'clock I was restless and hungry but did not feel like cooking dinner, so I drove over to the Chadakoin Restaurant. Afterwards, I walked across the street to the Keg Room for a beer. Two young kids were singing, a boy and a girl, and I swear they were no older than ten or eleven. The boy played the bass while the girl sang and twirled around. She twirled around so much, I thought she might get sick and throw up, but she didn't. She called herself The Bunny Girl and kept singing. She sang a few songs by The Beatles, Petula Clark, Mavis Staples, and Al Green's "Let's Stay Together." What a good voice.

Tuesday, June 12

I have painted several watercolors. I feel as though watercolors are too thin, that I prefer a thicker textured paint, an acrylic perhaps.

I played chess against Roy at lunch. He won both games.

After work, Mike and I went to the Lakewood Library. I wanted to look up information on the history of this house. I read somewhere that it was built before the Sorg House, which is down the street. Mrs. Parker was there and helped me research the house's history. We found some records proving it was built in August 1860, just before the start of the Civil War. The man who built it was Thomas Fleek. Mrs. Parker is the librarian at the elementary school and was so when I was a kid. She doesn't seem to remember me.

While at the library, I saw a beautiful woman reading *LOOK*.

Her hair was slinking down her shoulders like a sheet of gold. When she stood up, her hair dropped in a full bounce. Her indigo blue Levi's squeezed tight over her hips. Her small sneakers were bright white and new looking. She wore no bra under the white crew neck t-shirt.

"Mike, look at that girl," I said. "Look. Look."

"I see her."

"God, she's pretty. She's absolutely gorgeous."

"That's Annie."

"You know her?"

"She's a friend of mine."

I watched as she moved around the library without a clue in the world that she is a goddess, floating from place to place like an angel. If there had been more people in the library, I might have followed her around a little; otherwise, it was too conspicuous.

"I've got to talk to her," I told Mike.

"What do you want to talk to her about?"

"Anything. It doesn't matter. I've just got to meet her."

"Okay. I'll go over and get her."

"Don't say anything stupid to her about me. Just have her come over here."

Mike walked to the far right-hand side of the library, near the checkout counter, and looked back and forth to me then to this divine creature, until he had fully circled up behind her about twenty-five feet away. He stood at the stacks and pretended to be looking through a book, but kept pointing at her as if to ask me, "This one?"

Before Mike walked up to her, she placed the magazine back on the shelf and left.

"Look at that," I said. "You let her get away."

"I did not. You did. You wouldn't even talk to her. She's just a girl."

"No, she isn't. She's not just a girl. That's a woman. I know a woman when I see one, and she's a woman. You need to listen to me where women are concerned."

"Yeah, I know where she lives. We went to high school together."

"No kidding?"

"We can drive over to her house, but she doesn't live there anymore. She moved. I don't know where she lives now."

Mike and I hopped on my motorcycle and slowly drove down the street, and there she was walking, her tight blue jeans and her hips slightly popping in motion with each step. She has such great posture.

"There she is!" Mike screamed as we passed by her.

As we stopped at the stop sign, she caught up to us and stood at the crosswalk.

Mike shouted in my ear, "Hi, Annie!" He took off his football helmet. She waved.

"Hi, Mike."

"This is Bob. He's my friend. He really likes you."

"No, I don't," I said.

"He called you a real woman."

"Thank you. I will take the compliment."

A part of me was angry at how stupid I sounded and acted around Annie. The only positive is that it all happened so quickly, maybe she didn't notice I was an idiot.

"He wants to go to the movies with you," Mike said.

"Thank you," Annie said, as I gunned the throttle and blasted past the stop sign, with the force of the engine pulling us away.

§

Per the newspaper, the average cost of a house in Washington, D.C. is $67,500. The cost of houses throughout the country has risen 91.7% in twenty years. If that trend holds true, in 1993, the cost of a house in our capital should be about $130,000. I find that hard to believe. Who can afford that?

Secretariat, by winning the Belmont Stakes, won the Triple Crown the other day, the first horse in a quarter of a century to do so. What a charmed life he can look forward to.

Wednesday, June 13

"Is it spooky living in that old house by yourself?" Roy asked me at lunch in the breakroom. "I heard that it was once a brothel and a speak-easy."

"I don't know about that, but at one time it was a hotel and a boarding house. All the bedrooms have old-fashioned locks."

"About three years ago, there was a tour of homes and I got to walk through it. It cost five bucks per couple to walk through three houses, so Louise and I took the tour. The old Fleek House was one of them. I remember the button light switches because you rarely see them anymore."

"For being so old, they still work," I told him. "On the side of the house, there's a tiny door leading to the basement. It's a coal chute. There used to be a brick bin for the coal, but it's gone. If you stand in the middle of it, you can still smell the coal."

It was an absolute hurricane late this afternoon right after I returned home. It rained so intensely that I couldn't see across the street to the lake. The lights were lost twice, which delayed the World Series Pinball Tournament we were having.

When it was time for Mike to go home, it was still raining, so I drove him home.

The dogs followed me around the house, though I don't know if it was for their protection or mine. The thunder scares them. It used to scare Kimberly. She would always hide.

The thunder gives me power. I love the crackle across the sky.

With candles burning until the power was restored, I read and then typed.

Of note: Everyone was streaking naked this year across college campuses, down Peachtree Street, on Johnny Carson, and some people even streaked at our school during a football pep rally. They never caught the guys and girls, either. I went streaking with Ashley in Stone Mountain Park late one night in the tenth grade and ran down the manicured lawn.

§

It's still raining. The National Weather Bureau issued a warning about flooding in many areas. My garden is gone. It's a pond now. It'll take a week to dry out.

Thursday, June 14

Roy called to say the power was out at the office and for me to work from home. That was perfect. I rolled back over and slept until nine o'clock. The dogs and I have had a lazy day reading. Got paid for it, too. Me, not the dogs. Smart as they may be, they cannot read.

§

9:50 p.m. Mike and Annie just left. Mike brought Annie over to the house unexpectedly. My nerves are still shaking because the woman I have fallen in love with has asked me over to her apartment tomorrow for dinner. Lord, what wonderful fate has come my way?

Mike and Annie went to high school together—just like he said—and she asked him to introduce us.

What did we talk about tonight? I can hardly remember a single word, but she was dazzling. And, she likes games and has a playfulness about her. It's sexy. The three of us took turns playing baseball pinball.

Friday, June 15

I'm home for lunch: a peanut butter sandwich and a large glass of milk. Oreo cookies. Pringles. I'm on the porch watching a sailboat zip by. The wind is brisk under the blue skies. There are a few big clouds and the air is clean, like when you stick your head in the freezer and suck in air through your teeth.

Back from work: I feel swallowed up in the house, but I'm not sure why, except that I'm anxious to see Annie and I have ninety minutes before going to her place, so I'm typing. I shaved again after work and took another shower.

Perhaps of interest to myself: My favorite biblical passage is as follows:

> And God said, "Let there be light," and there was light. God saw that the light was good, and he separated the light from the darkness.
>
> Genesis 1:4

§

It was sunny all day and everything seemed to dry out; however, around 5:30 p.m., it rained again. Not hard. A sprinkle, but it lasted for an hour, just enough to curtail a picnic.

"I brought these for you," I said, holding out daisies. Annie had planned to have a picnic on the front lawn of her apartment building. She lives in the Red Door Apartments. Each apartment has a red door. It's right on the lake near the Yacht Club. She had a bottle of wine and a picnic basket set out on the floor of her living room on a red-and-white-checkered cloth. It stopped raining, but the ground was soaked, so we stayed inside.

She cooked everything herself: sesame chicken, French bread, homemade farm butter, and baked zucchini and squash casserole.

"I churned the butter myself," she said, showing me the small hand-held butter churn.

"All you do is warm whipping cream to room temperature, then you churn it until it thickens. I used to work at the Fleek Seed Company, and they had a dairy. Once you have butter, just add salt.

There's always some liquid left over. You can drink that."

The butter melted into the French bread, and as I pulled it apart, I nibbled it and sipped the wine. It was a chardonnay, which I had never had before, but Annie said it goes with any food.

I learned something very exciting about Annie, but she made me promise to keep it a secret. I won't tell anyone except the typewriter.

Annie posed naked for a photographer once. She showed me a few pictures. I didn't say too much about the photos, nor did I stare too long, figuring she might think I was a pervert if I asked too many questions. The picture I remember most is of her nude body stretched out on a rug in a tight perpendicular yawn, her arms pulled over her head, her hands clasped together in a ball, stretching her breasts high towards the powdered white valleys underneath her arms. I'm certain I was a dumbstruck idiot. I started to get a woody so I thought about baseball but kept looking. "Can I have this one?" I asked her.

She didn't answer.

I had asked so quickly I thought maybe she didn't hear me. I didn't dare ask again.

"Did you go to college?" I asked instead.

"Oh, sure," Annie replied. "I went to Cornell, then got a master's at Chautauqua. This fall, I'm starting my Ph.D."

"What're your degrees in?"

"English undergrad and psychology as my minor. I did my master's in shrink-think, and that's what I will do my doctorate in. I'm going to be a counselor, a shrink, maybe focus on family therapy."

Her eyes are blue. Her lips pink, and fleshy. Annie is carefree, not like a Flower Child, but in an innocent nice way.

"If you have a master's degree, why would you have nude

pictures taken?"

"My degree has nothing to do with posing nude. A Ph.D. can't keep you from getting old. I'm twenty-six, and if I'm lucky, I have ten more years of youthful looks. Maybe fifteen years. I'm proud of my body. I work out all the time. I walk, run, and ride my bicycle all over town. I want to look back and remember my body being in great shape."

"Marilyn Monroe used to ride her bicycle. My mom told me that."

"I know. She was into physical fitness, too."

"Aren't you worried about people seeing you?"

"I don't want just anybody looking at me. I mean, I'd never pose for a magazine or anything. I'd never show anyone my pictures. You're only the fifth person who's seen them. My sister and her friend have seen them, the photographer who took them, and my best friend in high school, who lives in New York City. And now, you."

"Does it bother you that I saw them? Isn't that strange?"

"No," she said.

"I mean, here we are and the only difference is we have clothes on."

"I showed them to you because I wanted you to see them. You can look at them whenever you want. I'm proud of them."

"What about the guy who took them?"

"He's an artist friend, a photographer and painter."

"I'm a painter! I didn't show you my watercolors last night but I've painted a lot. I'm looking for a new texture, acrylic or maybe oils. I'm not very good, though."

"I trust my friend," she said. "Plus, I have the negatives. And, he's married. I absolutely love him, but that doesn't mean I'm in love with him, because I'm not. There's a big difference. You can be friends with someone, but that doesn't mean anything's going on. No hanky-panky stuff. People make the assumption that if you're off with someone else's spouse then you're in bed with them. That's just not the case. I'm not like that at all."

"I wouldn't think that."

"I don't believe in fooling around until you're married."

"I've never thought about it too much," I lied.

"I don't tell just anybody this, but I can tell that you can keep a secret."

"I'm great at keeping secrets."

"Here's our second secret. I'm still a virgin."

"I have a tough time determining that with women."

"I know that's weird because of the flower children and hippy-dippy craziness you see all around. All that free-love, it's not free. I want to get married and I want to be with my husband. I tell men that right away that I am waiting until marriage, no exceptions. I don't believe in free-love. Nothing's free. If it's free then what value can it have? When I fall in love and get married, that's who I want to give myself to."

"Don't you believe in pre—"

"Pre-marital sex? Sure, but not for me, I guess. I decided a long time ago to wait."

"Isn't it hard not fooling around?"

"Not really."

"What about your boyfriend?"

"I don't have a boyfriend. I've had several but they all wanted to get married. I never wanted to marry them. They all wanted to fool around, but I didn't."

"That's the only thing on everyone's mind."

"It's sort of like bowling. I don't like to bowl, so I just never think about going bowling. It doesn't distract from the quality of my life even though many people love to bowl. That's great for them. For me, I just never think about it. Same with sex. I obviously know about it, know that it's there, but I've made a commitment. Every day I feel good about who I am. It's a gift I give to myself. If I can't keep a commitment to myself, how can I commit to marriage?"

"I thought everyone in college was having sex."

"Not this gal."

I have fallen insanely, and instantly, in love with an older woman. She is so smart about so many things. How does a man choose a wife? Annie would be my type. Or someone like my mom. A good cook, too.

Annie is twenty-six and I am eighteen. I will be nineteen on August 20th. She's eight years older than me. I'm sure this could never work out.

"Since I've told you two secrets, you owe me two."

"I can't think of any to tell you."

"Next time, have them ready."

NEXT TIME! Date #2. I'm assuming she thought this was a date. Probably not.

NOTE TO SELF: Do not take Annie bowling.

§

Annie's been engaged twice, but the guys turned out to be too constricting for her. The major problem: once she was engaged, her fiancés figured she would stop hanging out with her male friends.

Annie said she had some funny stories about her old boyfriends, but I didn't think they were funny, mainly because she couldn't get the story straight.

"I have a medical joke," I said. "What do you call a girl with one leg?"

"Peg," Annie laughed.

"No, Ilene," I said.

When Annie laughed, her breasts jiggled up and down like water balloons. Nothing happened between us, but I did not leave until one o'clock. I had a great time talking. That was all. And now I'm home, typing this up at 2:22 a.m.

Saturday, June 16

I worked all day, reading and writing my analysis reports. I listened to Casey Kasem's Top 40. My favorite song was George Harrison's "Give Me Love."

I stayed up way too late thinking about Annie. I drank too much last night and that makes me feel guilty, as if I shouldn't have too much fun or feel too good about my life. There is a loss of order when I have too much fun. Dr. Laighles said in class one day that guilt is an Irish curse.

Of note for today: Nixon ordered a price freeze. I think that's a bad idea. Prices will skyrocket when it's lifted.

Sunday, June 17

Nothing to write today, save that a new Vietnam truce is on and the fighting is down considerably. Somehow, truce seems to rhyme with ruse, or is close enough. But, all in all, I'm becoming less scared of my friends being drafted. I'm 1-A so I have fewer worries.

I went to an anti-war demonstration on campus during my first semester, thinking it might turn violent, like at Kent State, but it did not. I stood in the background, listening, but the sound system did not entirely work, so people became restless and left. It was anticlimactic. I drank a few beers before I went there, and I was buzzing a little. I thought I might meet a few girls or know someone from my classes, but I did not. It was like a rock concert—all the dregs I never knew existed crawled out of the woodwork, most of them unaffiliated with the university, or so it seemed.

§

I weeded the garden. If only weeds tasted good and were nutritious, the world would never go hungry.

Monday, June 18

The alarm clock has no respect for the dreams we fall into. The morning fog off Chautauqua Lake hung in the air and was like a call of reveille for the troops to battle the new day on Kennesaw Mountain. I have camped there in the Boy Scouts. We hiked to the top of the mountain and looked out over the entire region, and we could see Atlanta from there.

My bed was soft and warm this morning. Bess was curled up at my feet, while Harry was stretched out on the bed. He had his head on the pillow. I'm now in one of the upstairs bedrooms, which was a guest room when I lived here. I don't remember anyone ever staying at our house, but I'm sure someone must have. It's more comfortable than the couch. I have permanently moved to this room. Although, one night I threw down six blankets on the floor in my old bedroom, which is Emily's sewing room, because I wanted to sleep in there at least once. It was not comfortable being on the floor.

At the office, Roy asked if I'd like to see a baseball game on Friday. The Pirates are hosting the Cubs.

"Can I bring two friends?"

Mike and I rode over to Annie's to ask her, but she's going home to a wedding and can't go with.

When we were there, about to go get ice cream at Jenkins Dairy, Annie's mom called. She was in the kitchen while Mike and I sat on the balcony, but I overheard her conversation.

"I know, mom. I'm not bringing a date. I'm coming by myself. I'm looking. No one escapes love, death, or taxes," Annie said. "I said taxes. What's it matter? Well, I don't want that. I want it to be right the first time."

After she hung up, I did not ask any questions.

Annie had a big bluish-green bruise on her thigh where she'd run into the countertop corner.

§

I read an article from a scientist in Oregon who posed this idea:

> If a man and a woman conceived a child outside the
> earth's atmosphere, like in outer space in an Apollo

craft, and if the woman gave birth to the child in space, that child would be born away from the planet Earth, thus proving that life can exist beyond our planet.

I guess she would need a team of physicians in space when she gave birth to the child. I can see something like that happening.

Has anyone given birth in a 747 jet at 30,000 feet? My question—not the scientist's. Surely this has happened. Why not in the Apollo spaceship?

§

When I told Mike he'd have to get permission to drive with us to Pittsburgh he became irritated. I didn't know what else to do. Pittsburgh is almost one hundred and fifty miles away.

"I don't need permission to go see the Pirates. I'm old enough to do what I want."

"Ask your dad if he wants to go."

Mike lives on Lakeview Avenue in a white house with a light blue wooden porch with no railing. There's a picture window centered in the front living room facing the street. There's a gravel driveway and double garage, which is separate from the house. Off to the right side of the garage, there's a row of blueberry bushes. I'm not sure why I'm detailing this information except that it is quaint, and I like the look of his house.

During our conversation, Mike's father said, "Mike owns Bear Mountain."

"He told me his grandfather owns it."

"No. Mike owns the whole mountain, all seventeen-hundred acres. His grandfather, my father, purchased the land three months before he was drafted into the Army. He was going to build a house in the center of the mountain where the creek runs through, but it never happened. He was killed in Canada in a car accident. He hit an icy spot in the road and went over a cliff. Mike was about six years old at the time. That was my father, Hoyt. Mike's momma died just a few years ago. Cancer."

I couldn't help but wonder what's in the water. Everyone in this town dies. Eventually, I suppose.

"Some people call it Bly Mountain because the road runs through it, but we've always known it as Bear Mountain. Mike has it posted, but I still hunt over there. One night, a big cat started tracking me. That gave me a fright."

"How'd you know?" I asked.

"I saw him jump over a small ravine. He hunkered down when I stopped moving. I held my sights on him and zeroed in, but I didn't shoot. I was only a few hundred feet from the road, and once I was out of the woods, I figured I was okay. But they've been known to attack if they're hungry enough and there's no other game around. Many years ago, a big cat carted off a kid over in Findley Lake."

"What happened?"

"A group of men tracked him down and killed the cat, but the kid was already dead. His father carried him home."

Mike's father, Monroe, said "Developers have tried buying the land, but Mike refuses to sell. All the farmers around that area know him and they keep a lookout over his land. He's had two hunters thrown in jail for trespassing. Yeah, Mike went out and hired himself a lawyer one day, and they had Jack Milner serve up the warrant. My father willed all that land to Mike because he knew Mike would cherish and protect it."

I'm typing everything I can remember, all the stuff his father said. It's probably not in any coherent order. I think the most important thing he said was about Steven.

"Steven's dead, and Mike will never be the same. Mike's high school sweetheart, Julie, married a guy from Albany and they have two children. I still hear from her at Christmas. She sends a card every year."

Mike sells apples in the summer, and in the winter, he sells hot chocolate at the lake to the skaters. Six months ago, he took a cab all the way to Warren and wouldn't say why. He just said he might do some business.

"Two days later, a junk dealer delivered over two hundred pink flamingos to our back door. They're down in the basement," his father said. "Hell, I read the newspaper. I know what he's doing, but I learned years ago not to stop him. He gets something in his mind and there's no changing it."

On the ride home, as I passed the elementary school, there was a kite flapping in the telephone lines, twisting and turning like an animal caught in a snare.

Two things caught my eye in the newspaper today: Johnny Miller shot a record 63 to win the United States Open, and Marc Chagall returned to Russia after a fifty-one-year absence. I had always thought he was French. Chagall, not Miller.

Tuesday, June 19

It was a quiet day all around. Warm and sunny. Later on, after work, I sat on the porch and began reading *The Odessa File* by Frederick Forsyth. It makes me wonder how much of this is based on fact. Dave Edwards, who was in my Comp II class, told me that Hitler got away and that the U.S. intelligence forces are still looking for him in Argentina.

"Both Hitler and Eva Braun escaped," Dave said. "We know that as fact. Half of Hitler's staff escaped to Argentina. You just wait. They'll be caught."

"Why doesn't anyone report this?" I asked.

"Look, the secret is that a lot of big companies made a lot of money during the war, companies like IBM, General Electric, Kodak, Ford, and Chase Bank. They made money helping the Germans. Hell, Coca-Cola invented Fanta so they could sell it to the Germans during the war. Look it up. Go do your research and you'll find out I'm right."

"How'd you figure this out?"

"I didn't. I read about it. I also read about how the intelligence department determined how Hitler escaped and who helped him. It was the Catholic Church, the Pope. They helped all the Nazis escape. It's documented. The Red Cross was also involved with creating new identities for everyone."

"Why'd they help the Nazis?"

"Because Nazis hate Communism, but they like religion. If you are the Catholic Church, you have to grab the bull by the left or right horn. The Pope figured the Nazis were better than the Commies. The U.S. knows exactly where these people are in Argentina, but the reason we don't go get them—too many big companies would be implicated. You can't have Ford Motors or Coca-Cola's executives being friends with the Nazis. All that shit would hit the fan. You think Watergate is news. If *The Washington Post* reported that Hitler was alive and that American companies were helping the Nazis during the war, people would riot in the streets."

Wednesday, June 20

The divorce rate is skyrocketing, the news anchor reported. It's 39% and expected to reach 50% by 1980, which is only six and a half years away. The 1980's sounds so improbable, almost impossible. I don't think I will ever get married.

Divorce is fine if two people don't want to stay married. Why should anyone else tell them what to do or judge them? Isn't divorce better than remaining in a marriage that is dulled or loveless? Too much of the world is loved in silence.

I have not seen Annie in a few days. Should I call her? I think about her all the time. Is this how women operate? They already have power!

Thursday, June 21

Mike woke me up this morning at 5:30. He asked if he could come to work with me today. I said no.

He came back this afternoon after I got home from work to help me wash the dogs, then tagged along when I went grocery shopping. I let him push the cart.

Late this afternoon, before Mike arrived, I sat at Dr. Laighles's desk in his robust leather chair in the library, my feet propped up. The smell of cigar smoke still lingers in the air. I could have mistaken today for a lazy Sunday afternoon if I didn't know any better.

I tried imagining myself living here at the turn of the century, the sound of a horse-drawn carriage trotting by on the cobblestone, the clanging metal sounds of the trolley skipping over the tracks from Ashville down to Lakewood. Maybe I'd take in a baseball game, with the old South Sides team in their puffy, baggy pants and loose awkward catching mitts. The women would be twirling umbrellas in the sun, the frilly edges spinning like a carnival ride, and the skies would be free of planes buzzing overhead for many years to come.

That's how quiet the room was, but even still, I could not bring myself to dream in color, the pictures I see in my mind are black and white.

The street in front of our house was red cobblestone when I was a kid. Sometime in the last eleven years it was paved over with blacktop.

A note: Babe Ruth once played baseball at the fairgrounds in Celeron, which is the town where Lucille Ball grew up. My mother says that my grandmother grew up with Lucille Ball, and that she was poor and used to borrow my grandmother's ice skates.

Friday, June 22

It's 4:20 a.m., and actually June 23rd. Roy just dropped me off a little bit ago. The Pirates' game ended a few minutes before eleven o'clock, but there was an accident on the highway leading out of Pittsburgh.

Mike counted nine cars. It didn't look as though anyone was injured, but the cars were banged up. It took forever to get home, and at one point we thought about staying the night, but we drove on instead.

Roy drove back, and the last thing I remembered before falling asleep with my head against the window, he and Mike were talking over and over about Willie Mays hitting three doubles. A foul ball came very close to us. Mike almost caught it, but a woman six rows up caught it when it bounced off the cement floor, over everyone, and into her lap. Mike and Roy brought their gloves. We also invited Mike's dad, but he didn't want to go to the game.

When I woke up, just on the northern side of Erie, Roy was teaching Mike a song, "She was a red-hot momma 'til the ice man cooled her down."

I had a great time at Three Rivers Stadium. The Mets won 5-4. George Stone beat Steve Blass. The Mets scored all their runs in the second inning. Al Oliver, Rennie Stennett, and Gene Clines each went 2 for 4, but it wasn't enough. John Milner hit a two-run homer for the Mets. He's no relation to the sheriff in town, Jack Milner, according to Roy. I'm not sure how I thought the Pirates were playing the Cubs, but I did. I must have looked at the wrong day. It was George Stone's first complete game since last year when he played for the Atlanta Braves and beat the Houston Astros. I was at that game with my dad and Will Croon, so maybe I'm a good luck charm for Stone. Of course, he doesn't know it. He's a lefty, like me. His record went to 3—2, while Steve Blass dropped to 3—5.

Tonight, Dock Ellis is pitching for the Pirates. I'd like to see him pitch. He's one of my favorites. Although it looked like a packed house, only 21,129 attended the game at the Three Rivers Stadium.

I have now seen Hank Aaron, Willie Mays, Pete Rose, Johnny Bench, Willie McCovey, Willie Stargell, Nolan Ryan, and Carl Yastremski play in person. I have also now seen my two favorite players of all-time, Roy White and Al Oliver. I saw Roy White and the Yankees play the Chicago White Sox in Comisky Park two years ago when me and my parents were on vacation. They lost 6-9, but White had a hit, scored a run, and had an RBI. Bobby Mercer hit a homer.

I'm sitting in the sunroom looking out over the darkness of the lake. I've decided this is the spot I enjoy the most when typing. A light misty fog is hovering over the front yard, and it is casting a texture of mystery over the lawn. I've gotten into this habit of typing at strange hours.

The WJTN weatherman said to look for warmer temperatures throughout the weekend and probably into next week. I will sleep out here tonight. I will lay down blankets for the dogs. My hot chocolate is smooth going down.

I did not go to work today. Instead, I spent the day stretched out in the long lawn chair reading. I kept track of my hours, and when my eyes became tired of reading, I took a break and walked across the street to the park and played basketball with a kid named Ronny. He was a good shot. He was only thirteen, and when he tried driving the basket, I could stop him most of the time, but he hit nearly all his shots from outside. I won two games of 21, but he smoked me in Horse.

Saturday, June 23

From work, I rode my motorcycle slowly past Annie's apartment. She wasn't home, of course. It would be weird if she was home and saw me.

Sunday, June 24

I did not go to church today. Oh, but probably I need to. I watched Garner Ted Armstrong. He is the messenger for me to receive the savior. Somehow, I feel more connected to him through the TV than if I went to church, which is too organized. I don't like that in my life. I can sit and watch G.T.A. and feel as if he is talking to me on a personal level, but not structured to the point where I feel that everything I do and think is a sin.

The New York Times reported: Four men are trapped in a submarine 360 feet below the surface in Key West, Florida. They have enough air until tomorrow at noon. They are caught in the wreckage of the destroyer Fred T. Berry (a stupid name for a war vessel), which the Navy scuttled last May. A war ship should have a name such as the U.S.S. Ass Kicker or the U.S.S. We Don't Fuck Around. They were observing fish around the destroyer. I can bet all four wish they could be in church right about now, and I am certain even the least religious of them is praying for God to help them.

§

Art is the attempt to imitate life, or what the artist believes life should be. If it's true art, it will be true to the artist's soul, true to life. Only through art can the purest form of one's "self" be revealed.

I want to achieve immortality and create something that says, "I was here." Therefore, I paint.

Good thing I didn't type immorality.

Monday, June 25

During lunch, I rode to the Pearl City store on Cherry Street to buy several tubes of acrylic paint, one of each primary and secondary color. I bought new brushes, too.

"This is real horsehair," the woman said, stroking the brush against my chin. "See how fine that is."

I could not carry any canvasses, so I didn't buy any. I'll return another time with the truck.

The sun, along with the cool air, felt good as I rode down the streets on my motorcycle. I slid back the face plate of my helmet to allow the wind to hit me.

When I returned to the office, Roy and Brooke Spearman were in the computer room arguing. She's a programmer, and that means she writes all the computer programs that keep this place running. She was arguing about how she was making less money than Carl Weeks, who does the same job, and she's been employed longer.

Roy said, and I quote, "He has a family to support."

Roy was wrong. Brooke is very smart . . . and, to me, smart is sexy. She's not married but she has a boyfriend, who might be her fiancé. I'm not sure. I think she is paid less because she is black. That never came up in the argument. Carl is an okay guy, but he has horrible breath and likes to stand close to you when talking. Someone should say something to him.

§

Leonid Brezhnev left the United States yesterday to go back to the Soviet Union, and at the airport he was given a hug by Chuck

Connors, *The Rifleman*, of all people. Connors lifted Brezhnev right up off the ground.

I find it difficult to understand the political clout *The Rifleman* has in U.S./U.S.S.R. relations, unless as he picked up Brezhnev, Connors said, "You're right, President Nixon, this guy is all hot air. He doesn't weigh much at all."

Wouldn't Brezhnev have responded better to a hug from, say, Goldie Hawn, who is a babe? Maybe she could be America's Political Sex Symbol. I cannot envision Brezhnev calling Nixon on the "Hot-Line" and requesting a conference with Chuck Connors over our Mid-East policy. For that matter, I cannot envision Goldie Hawn, either.

Only one movie has won all four Academy Awards for Best Actor, Best Actress, Best Director, and Best Picture: *It Happened One Night*, starring Clark Gable, Claudette Colbert, and Frank Capra. 1935 must have been a lousy year for movies. Several movies have won three of four Academy Awards, but not all four. That little tidbit was just announced during a commercial break on WJTN.

After reading this evening, I watched *The Visit* with Ingrid Bergman and Anthony Quinn. It was okay, but I liked the play much better when I saw it in the tenth grade in Atlanta.

I had a headache this afternoon, so I came home early (not long after Brooke was angry with Roy). I began reading *The Woman's Bible* and *The Earthsea Trilogy*, but then stopped to watch *The Mike Douglas Show* because I wanted to see the New Seekers sing. They were good, but it was difficult sitting through Marty Allen, Robert Conrad, and Fabian. Neil Armstrong was cool.

Commentary: I like the song "I'd Like to Teach the World to Sing," but the New Seekers, although pretty good, were lacking without Judith Durham. She simply has the best voice. "Georgy Girl" is one of my favorite songs, especially when J.D. sings "You're always window shopping but never stopping to buy." I wonder what kind of music Annie likes.

Tuesday, June 26

I lost at chess to Roy again.

§

Will Croon and I visited his uncle Leman, the moonshiner and father of Buddy Lee and Ralston, after Thanksgiving when we were in the ninth grade. We'd been shooting rifles at tin cans at Will's grandfather's farm when the old man ran out of whiskey.

"Get over to Leman's and bring me back sump'n to drink."

That, of course, meant moonshine. He gave us two dollars and said, "Go find Leman and bring back two gallons."

"Gramps, I ain't sure if I can find my way back there," Will said standing on the porch.

"It ain't even nighttime. Git your ass up there and if you get lost dur'n the day, don't come back," the old man told us.

"I've only been there once before," Will complained.

"Once ain't as good as twice, but it's a heap better than never. I don't suspect the way you're complaining you could find your ass in the dark. Now git. Take your rifles," he said.

After dredging through the briars and wooded thickets, we found the road leading to Leman's shack. Most of the time, I thought we were lost and kept anticipating being shot by hillbillies or attacked by wild boars. As luck would have it, Leman was out of moonshine at his shack, so he shoved us into the truck. The stench of garbage on the truck floor burnt the inside of my nose like ammonia.

"Will," he said, "I know yo' kin, but I don't know yo' friend from Adam's house cat. You ev'a tell anyone ya was up here and I'ma cut yo' dick off and feed it to da hogs. Ya understan', boy?" He spat tobacco juice out the window, then wiped the side of his face with his bare arm. He rolled down the window and, as he did, the spit lumped together and sludged down the door.

"Yes sir," we said.

"You're Goddamned right you better yes-sir me."

The man rested his left arm down the edge of the window and snarled snot out of his nostrils and into the back of his throat. He hacked it into his mouth before spitting a huge lugie out the window. The sounds the man made disgusted me.

"Here's some advice. If you gotta spit, roll down the winder first. That goes for throwing up, too. That's the smell in here."

We rode down a dirt road with potholes the size of Iowa, and through gully ditches five feet deep on both sides of the road to drain the rain wash into the creek. The ground leveled off near a small bridge and Leman jerked the truck right into a creek that ran under the bridge. As he drove down the center of the creek, water jutted up underneath the wheel wells. It was a shallow creek, no more than six inches deep. We bounced and jerked as the tires twisted against the rocks and water splashed up like the Red Sea parting. The steering wheel yanked back and forth, and Leman held on like he had a bull by both horns at the rodeo.

When we arrived, I knew I would never drink moonshine unless a gun was held to my head. Flush with the ground was a blue plastic barrel cut in half, longways. It looked like a horse trough buried to the lip of the ground. Floating in the middle of the barrel bobbed a raccoon that had stumbled into the camp and drank so much whiskey that he fell in and drowned. The raccoon looked like an expanded log, bloated and puffy, his tail like a furry stick. Will and I stood watching, as Leman pulled the raccoon out by the hind legs and swung him like a gunny sack into a pile of pine straw.

He said, "Let's bottle it up, boys."

"You're not going to drink that, are you?" I asked.

"Who asked you, boy?"

"No one, but-"

Leman stepped right up close to my face and stared me in the eyes.

"But nuttin', my ass, boy," he said. "I make this stuff to sell, not to drink. Now let's bottle it up and maybe I'll give ya a pint to take home to your old man."

Wednesday, June 27

Annie asked me to go see *Live and Let Die*. I'm glad she called, because I thought all sorts of things, like she's too busy to see me or she doesn't really like me.

I used to think Bond movies were good, but I was a kid then. Now, they're corny. I had a nice time only because I was with Annie. She and I like Sean Connery more than Roger Moore. The music was good: Paul McCartney. Annie likes The Beatles and so do I, so it was a good night.

Thursday, June 28

I finally got in touch with the mechanic, after trying several times this week. Each time I was in the library, I felt like someone was watching me use the long-distance in a covert spy operation. Free long-distance is really stealing from the university. Someone should invent a credit card for telephones. Just give the operator your credit card number. I think there would be a market for something like that if someone knew how to get it off the ground. Or, let everyone call anywhere in the United States for free—that way, people would plan more trips, buy more things, and it would create more business for everyone involved. Free phone calls and free postage.

The mechanic: "My nephew cleaned all the corn and leaves off before I did anything. He's ten years old. I paid him five bucks, but once that was out of the way, I dove in. Right now, your car's sitting here in about a hundred pieces. Luckily, you did not mess up the power top. This Vette is only one of four hundred produced with a power top. You've got some damage, but it could have been worse because it's an RPO-687. You've got special front and rear shocks. You screwed up the finned brake drums, cooling fans, and the air scoops for the rear brakes. The engine is nice, but you damaged a few things, but somehow you did not kill it. It's one mighty fine two-eighty-three. The entire body needs to be repaired. You cracked the hell out of the fiberglass."

§

Downstairs, in what was our den, in the wall-cabinets, I found where Kimberly had printed her name underneath a drawer. She also drew a smiley face. The only way someone could find this is if they were on their back, looking up, as if searching for something. Who would ever do that?

I have pressed buttons, tried moving fireplace panels, and flipped light switches, all the stupid things you see on television. What would Columbo do?

This is not rocket science. Kimberly's old bedroom is locked so that's probably where the secret room is. The door, like all the doors upstairs, has old long key-locks that lock from the outside. It's the only room locked upstairs. Dr. Laighles and Emily must have a key somewhere.

A report today said that former President Johnson told the FBI to investigate Spiro Agnew because he thought Agnew tried to sabotage the 1968 negotiations in Paris. Johnson is a commie. He probably had JFK knocked off.

Friday, June 29

Roy wasn't in the office until late this afternoon, almost 3:00 p.m.

At lunch, I walked over to Annie's. I think I disturbed her. She didn't appear to want me around and didn't want to walk to Betty's Coffee Shop.

She did not allow me inside her apartment, so we sat on the steps near the driveway for ten minutes. Later, I realized I had been uninvited. Maybe she had a friend over. I don't know.

"Here's one of my secrets," I told her while sitting on the steps. "My friend, Will Croon, and I, a little more than two years ago, in January 1971, buried Linda Laura's unborn fetus in Stone Mountain Park in the Kentucky picnic area. Will got Linda Laura pregnant when we were in the tenth grade. I never knew she was pregnant until Will called me at home in a panic shortly after dinner time on a Sunday. I helped him bury the baby."

"That's horrible. I'm against abortion. I knew a girl in high school who had one."

Then Annie said she had to go back and finish her work. I think she was angry with me. She didn't ask any questions, just turned and walked up the stairs to her front door. I'm worried what I told her has upset her and she will never be my friend again. As I think about it, that was only two years ago and what we did was a crime. I never thought about it in terms of right or wrong but more along the lines of just helping him out. It's probably one of the reasons I did not have sex with Ashley, fearing she might get pregnant like Linda Laura. My subconscious probably remembered it. I feel the need to listen to Garner Ted Armstrong to find a balance in my life, because you just cannot tell a woman a story like that and expect her to fall for you. I am now beginning to understand the seriousness and implications of what we did.

§

Thank God I did not tell her the entire story.

Will and Linda Laura were in a room at the Stone Mountain Motel on Memorial Drive when he called me at home. When I got there, Linda Laura was curled up in a ball, naked on the bed, and holding a white towel between her legs. Will was in the bathroom with a pile of bloody newspapers and a fetus folded up in the middle. The room was freezing cold, as they never turned on the heat.

"I'm gonna flush it," Will said.

"Jesus Christ, Will. What's going on?"

"What's it look like? She was pregnant. This was the only thing we could do. We can't have no kid."

"Jesus. You just killed that baby."

"Bull."

"Yes, you did."

"It wasn't no baby, not yet."

"What about her?"

I wrapped Linda Laura in a sheet but it soaked all her sweat within minutes. She needed new linens and a blanket.

"She told me what I had to do, then she drank four shots of gin. She's drunker'n shit."

"Will, you can't go around killing babies. You don't know what you're doing. She could die."

"You shut up. She ain't gonna die. We used pure rubbing alcohol on everything and we didn't get any blood on anything except the newspapers and all them towels in the corner. She'll be alright."

"You got blood everywhere."

There was blood on the phone, the sink, the bathtub, toilet, on the doorknobs, and on the floor.

"It's everywhere. Look at this place. It looks like you murdered someone in here."

"You got to help me clean everything up."

"You can't flush that baby down the toilet. It'll clog up."

"What's your idea then?"

"You got to bury it somewhere."

I looked at the fetus—it was the size of a small football. I saw everything, feet, hands, eyes, ears. It was almost a baby.

"We have to get her home," I said.

"She's drunk. She can't move. I gave her some aspirin to help the pain. She can't go home until later. She can't even stand up. Plus, she's been throwing up."

"I don't know what you can give her for all her pain, but she probably needs a doctor."

"She don't need nothing. Just let her sleep it off. Look, I say we go to Stone Mountain and bury this thing somewhere. We'll go to my house and get a shovel, bury it so the rats don't dig it up, clean this place up, take her home, and forget anything ever happened."

"I can't believe you. Look at what you've done."

It was a murder scene. All I could think of was Sharon Tate and how she was murdered in California.

"Don't say another word unless it's going to help me. Did you bring the trash bags like I asked?"

"Yeah, I brought everything."

"Throw all those bloody towels in there. I'll wrap this baby up."

"See, you just called it a baby."

"Shut the hell up," Will said.

Over the next couple of hours, we cleaned all the blood out of the motel room, loaded Linda Laura in the back of Will's car, got the shovel, and drove to Stone Mountain Park, deep into the picnic areas where rarely anyone drives, except to make out. I sort of figured this is where their adventure began anyways. Will and I took turns digging a hole until our arms were tired. Then, while Linda Laura slept in the back of the car, we buried her fetus-thing, packed the ground hard, and covered it up with leaves, rocks, twigs, branches, and moss.

"Don't you think we ought to say something?"

"No."

"Come on, Will."

"I don't give a damn. I got other shit to worry about, like getting my ass out of this park before someone asks what we're doing with a garden shovel. 'Oh, nothing, officer, just burying a dead baby.'"

"I think we should say something."

"I don't. It's my problem, so I win. Let's go. I don't give a damn one way or the other. Linda Laura should never have got her ass knocked-up. I told her she damn well better be on the pill because I wasn't pulling out."

"Sometimes, man, I just want—"

"Want to what?"

"Nothing!" I yelled.

After burying the fetus in Stone Mountain, we drove around from sunset to two in the morning, while Linda Laura slept in the back seat of Will's car. We had her packed comfortably in blankets and pillows from the hotel room, which we stole. But it cushioned her ride. Finally, she woke and said she was hungry. We stopped at the Waffle House on Mountain Industrial Boulevard across from Hammermill Road, which is where Ryan Hanson's father has his firewood business.

"Are you sure you can eat?" I asked Linda Laura.

"She's fine," Will said.

"We don't need her getting sick at Waffle House. Maybe you shouldn't eat anything greasy," I told her. "Plain toast and hash browns with nothing on them. It should fill you up without making you sick."

"I'm having a burger and fries," Will said, "loaded with bacon and cheese. I'm starving."

I was also hungry but only had coffee, four orders of toast with jelly, and large hash browns, like Linda Laura. I wanted to make her feel better so I ate the same thing.

No one said too much to one another after that, but I knew Will was paying for my food. Any time you help a buddy bury a body, they are obliged to buy dinner.

Note: When I went to bed tonight, I said a prayer for Laura Linda's baby.

Saturday, June 30

Shouldn't Annie be dating men her own age? Why would she want to go to the movies with me again? I had a great time, but it felt like we were pals, especially since we brought Mike to see *American Graffiti*, with us.

Opie played this preppy guy. Annie said 1962 wasn't like that for her. It certainly wasn't my 1962.

We dropped Mike at home. When I dropped Annie off, I wanted to kiss her, but she hugged me goodnight instead. That was okay, but it left me feeling hollow inside.

I want so badly to kiss her, just once.

§

Checking the ads today, "The Thing" by Volkswagen costs $2,750. It's so ugly. A new Pontiac Catalina is $3,800. I'll never pay that much for a car. A Ventura is only $2,833, only $83 more than "The Thing," and a much better car.

During the day, I worked from home, reading so I could watch Wimbledon on TV. Nastase was beaten by an amateur in four sets. Chris Evert almost lost but held on.

Sunday, July 1

Home all day. Nothing to write about.

Monday, July 2

Today is the first of three days of the Chautauqua County Fairgrounds Festival in Fredonia, which is near S.U.N.Y., the university. Roy said he earned his undergrad degree there. He also said the fair is filled with games, rides, prizes, farm animal contests, and music. It runs through the Fourth of July. It's open to everyone, but you have to be a resident of the county to enter the competitions. Roy said The Lettermen came to do three shows last year. This year it's Glen Campbell.

There was a sign in Barone's Pharmacy:

Chautauqua County Fairgrounds Festival
GLENN CAMPBELL
July 2, 3, and 4 at 8:00 P.M.
One Show Per Evening
GLENN CAMPBELL

Annie asked me to go with her tomorrow night to see him. She has tickets to sit in front. Why is she not out with other men? I'll bet she thinks I am innocent and would never do anything with her. I hope she doesn't think I'm a queer.

My mom sent me a check for $4,752 for my tuition this fall. She saves $300 if I pay it before August 1. There is a $52 fee for student activities and athletics. Outrageous!

Each credit hour is $261. I am supposed to take eighteen hours this fall, but if I take only nine, I can pocket $2,350. I can pay for the Corvette and have money to spend on Annie. I can always make up the hours next semester or later on. I deposited the check in my bank account at the Bank of Jamestown on Chautauqua Avenue.

Tuesday, July 3

Glen Campbell was wonderful. Annie jumped and screamed when he sang "Wichita Lineman," "Dream of the Everyday Housewife," "Galveston," and "By the Time I Get to Phoenix." It was truly inspirational when, for his encore, he sang Patsy Cline's "Crazy," then a wonderful gospel classic, "Amazing Grace." Annie sang every song and when she jumped, her breasts jumped, too. I wanted to grab them to keep them from bouncing so much.

Annie didn't seem to mind that we rode in Dr. Laighles's ugly truck, which chugged along to the fairgrounds. I was embarrassed by its ugliness, but she didn't care. We tossed dimes onto glass dishes, threw softballs at metal milk bottles, and played the basketball dunking game. Annie made a shot and dunked her high school science teacher into a square plexiglass container. When he hit the water, his glasses popped off and sunk to the bottom.

"Mr. Cox, I told you I'd get you back some day for giving me a B in Biology," she yelled.

He had to swim down and retrieve them. She also won a stuffed puppy at the ring toss. We ate a bush of cotton candy and toured the exhibits of farm animals, with cows so full of milk they mooed in pain. There were two little boys who made their mother stand with them next to the cows until one of them pooped (the cows, not the boys). They thought that was the coolest thing.

I just realized that Dr. Laighles's truck is probably what Steven drove when he wasn't driving his Corvette. Annie probably did not mind riding in it because it was his.

There were hordes of fruits and vegetables lining the tables. I saw an apple the size of a soccer ball. I wasn't really sure it was an apple. There was a pumpkin weighing over 200 pounds. We had our picture taken in the Tarzan and Jane poster cutout. A Polaroid, which Annie kept. The Ferris wheel was closed, or we would have ridden it, too. A couple of men were working on something electrical and had the motor open.

Annie said that when she was a girl, her very first boyfriend took her for a ride on the Ferris wheel and paid the attendant three dollars to keep it stuck when they were at the top.

We rode the merry-go-round in a seat cut out of a swan's body. Strangers watched from the sawdust grass, and each time we passed, we waved. Strangers, they waved back. My knee touched hers and she didn't move it away. I could feel the soft warmth of her skin and every so often I pressed a little more firmly against her.

Wednesday, July 4

It's Independence Day. I'm on the front porch with the typewriter. It's warm already this morning and it feels good. Banners and flags are flapping from porches and flag poles. Some kids rode by on their bikes with red, white, and blue crepe paper woven through the spokes. I could tell how patriotic they are by the streamers in their handle grips. I once felt like that, but now, I feel deceived by my government.

Nixon, I hate to say, is becoming a disgrace, if he is not already. But, more so, I have been reading about the U.S. companies who, during World War II, helped the Nazis and essentially supported them for company profits, thus aiding and abetting the enemy. IBM, Coke, Ford, and General Electric, just like Dave Edwards said. I've mentioned this before, but if they can do it in Europe, why is Vietnam any different?

What U.S. companies are making money in Vietnam? Which CEO made enough money to buy a boat with the profits that killed Ricky Weislogel? I'm beginning to see that the U.S. is a huge corporation, and people are pawns sent to fight to keep the money rolling in.

§

Mike and I went to the parade down Summit Avenue. There was a little skirmish when some hippies tried walking in the parade. The police made them leave. Then, Mike and I cooked hot dogs on the grill and played crazy eights, all on the front porch.

There must be ten thousand sailboats on the lake. They are like handkerchiefs blowing in the wind. Mike played several games of chess against the computer, and I read a little bit, but mainly I sat in the warm and wonderful sun with the dogs and stretched out with my eyes closed, listening for the sounds of children in the park and a few cars easing by. I have this idea—if the energy in a nail that is hammered into a 2x4 remains there forever until the nail is removed, does the energy from children playing in the park remain? If not, where does it go? This is the kind of stuff I think about when I'm out here with my eyes closed.

§

It's 4:00 a.m. as I type this, and I'm exhausted. I have to be up for work in two hours and thirty minutes. I stayed out most of the night. I have a hangover—not from drinking, because I did not drink—but from no sleep.

While I was cleaning up the grill and putting stuff away, Annie rode up in an Oldsmobile convertible, which she borrowed from her dad. She and I and Mike rode to the beach at Long Point to watch fireworks. We had a blanket, a bucket of Kentucky Fried Chicken (we stopped on the way), wine, and soda. We just happened to sit next to Roy, his wife, Louise, and his daughters, Becky and Karen, who I met a week or so ago at the office. They let Annie borrow their corkscrew. She drank all the wine. I had a Coke.

After the fireworks, Annie, Mike, Karen (who by then we had managed to become friends with), and I drove around the lake in Annie's convertible. I drove because Annie could not hardly walk straight, and Karen sat scrunched next to me—between me and Annie. Mike sat in the back. Karen's mom said she had to be home by 1 a.m.

I drove everyone around while Karen and Annie navigated, telling me where to turn. I drove through Bemus Point, passed the Lenhart Hotel, and ended up at Midway Park, where we parked the car along the lake. We sat in the car eating ice cream and watched the lights across the lake. We walked around the amusement park but didn't ride anything.

"My father knows the owner, Red Walsh," Annie said.

"My dad said they're going to build a bridge connecting Bemus with Stowe because," Karen told us, "in the winter, the ferry doesn't run and people have to drive around the lake."

"It might spoil the look," Annie said.

After an hour, we drove around the other side of the lake to Dewittville and around to Mayville, before heading over to Bear Mountain. We parked on a dirt drive on Mike's property. Annie turned the heater on and we leaned the seats completely back, stared at the stars, and listened to an 8-track tape of Carole King's *Tapestry*. When the music had played through once, we drove Mike home first, then Karen.

"I might stop by the office to say hi," Karen said.

At my house, I asked Annie to have a cup of tea with me on the porch. We took the dogs outside and while we were standing in the yard, she kissed me. I did not really kiss her back because I thought it was a mistake. I thought she was going to kiss me on the cheek, but missed, and hit my lips instead. Once I realized she was really "kissing me," I sort of tried to kiss her, but then the kiss was over. It was clumsy and awkward, which was my fault.

She only kissed me once, and now I wonder if she will kiss me again, since I really didn't try to kiss her back. I feel like such an idiot. What would Sean Connery do? He'd drive over to her house, knock on her door (maybe break it down), take her in his arms and kiss her, then leave without saying more than "Excuse me, Madame, have you seen my cat?" There's something to be said for being a Scotsman.

It is 5:15 a.m.

Thursday, July 5

Everyone showed up late to work except me. I got no sleep but was at work by eight. People filtered in all day. I had a large coffee from Betty's Coffee Shop, which is a nice little restaurant.

Brooke was the first to arrive after me. We sat on the steps talking and waited for anyone with a key to arrive to open the front door. She's from Montpelier, Vermont. Her boyfriend, who is from Syracuse, works at the Prendergast Library.

When Roy arrived, he had a few boxes of candies from Betty Dixon's. My favorite were the chocolate turtles. I had three.

I caught a second wind and got a lot of work done early on, but after lunch, I nearly fell asleep reading a stack of material about headphones and stereo music and a survey from one hundred high school kids about cassettes and headphones. Once I wrote my analysis, I started to understand that there was some innovative record player in everyone's future. I went home at 3:30 p.m. and took a nap.

The news report stated that President Nixon is considering resigning because of Watergate. Even though his associates pled guilty in January, if Nixon resigns, it will look like an admission of guilt. I think resigning is a mistake, but it is looking like he was complicit. I used to think he did nothing wrong. Not any longer.

Friday, July 6

I lost at chess to Roy at lunch.

"Can I ask you a question?"

"Have at it," Roy said.

"What would you think if a woman kissed you out of the blue?" I asked Roy.

"You mean now, married and everything?"

"No. Before you were married," I said.

"If she kissed me without my having made any kind of move, I'd say she likes me. Maybe hot to trot. Some women are wild. But it's tricky. If she's younger, then she may just want to kiss, and nothing else. She might want to see if you're a good kisser. If she's older, she may want to see your reaction. If you back away, she might not try it again. If you try kissing her too much or too fast, she might throw up."

"Really?"

"Women don't like kissing a guy who doesn't know how to kiss," said Roy.

"What if you just sort of kissed her back, but not really kissed her, just in between."

"Is she older or younger?"

"Both," I said.

"Younger is hard to say. She may just think you can't kiss. That could be deadly, but if she's inexperienced she may not know the difference. If she's older, she may think it's her duty to teach you how to kiss. It's possible that you might even turn her off from men altogether and she might not want to ever kiss another guy again for as long as she lives. She might become a lesbian from that simple incident."

"You don't say? Just from bad kissing?"

"It's happened before. To a friend of mine," Roy said. "Nothing like that ever happened to me, but it did to a guy I know."

"I wasn't that bad."

"You should just kiss her and let her know who's in control," he suggested.

Control.

"Check, in case you weren't watching," I said.

"I saw that."

At lunch, Roy showed me his new license plate on his car: CHSSMAN.

§

Mike came over and we watched TV. The Indians vs. the Angels. Cleveland won 8—7 in eleven innings. In the last half inning, Annie phoned from Ithaca to say hi, and because of that, I missed the winning run. She went home to see her mother and return her father's car. Mike saw the ending but his description of what happened made me think that Nolan Ryan drove Babe Ruth in from second base. I thought maybe they might show it on the news tomorrow night.

Saturday, July 7

Veronica Lake died today. She was fifty. She was a movie star from the forties that my mother used to talk about. Her obituary said that after her career went south, she ended up working as a barmaid at the Martha Washington Hotel on East 29th Street in NYC. She was very beautiful when she was younger and called herself a sex zombie instead of a sex symbol. I think she was my mother's favorite actress, but I could be mistaken. She died of hepatitis, which I didn't think people died from, but I guess they do. She was living in Burlington, Vermont. I have been to Burlington. I feel sad for her, to have been on top, then to have fallen. I hope people remember her for a long time.

Mike and I are going camping. We are leaving in 30 minutes, so I wanted to write this. I'm taking pen and some paper with me. Writing is more out of habit now. It is 10:30 a.m.

§

Campsite: (handwritten) We loaded the truck with Mike's tent and camping gear. I'm supplying the food and the truck. And the dogs.

I heard that less than a hundred years ago, there were so many wild animals in this area, coyotes, mountain lions, and bears, that in the winter they would go right inside a house and steal a baby out of its crib if someone wasn't watching. When the forest was cleared for the Kinzua Dam, they found timber rattlers and copperheads all over the place.

§

Bear Mountain: 8:37 p.m.

It is dark now and the sun has faded beyond the trees. Silhouettes slice out from the last remaining light, dividing life into many pieces. The tree branches are being swallowed by the deep black night, while the clouds off in the far distance are brilliantly puffed out, harvest orange, and coercive blue with cotton-white shapes. They are the background for the campfire, which is slowly becoming my only source of light.

I hate mosquitoes. There are gobs of them, so I am standing up to allow the smoke to wrap around me.

Mike keeps trying to see what I'm writing. I told him to stoke the fire with the wood we collected. Eight sticks are stacked like Rebel rifles leaning together. The fire glows on to the page as I write. We cooked soup and roasted hot dogs for dinner.

We are ten feet from the creek in case the campfire should get away from us. The tent is roomy, big enough for four or five.

On the mountain, I feel so close to God. The cool wind flaps my thin jacket, as well as the tent.

I keep thinking about the Corvette. Sitting here in front of the fire, I can't even discuss it with myself—I'm so pissed off. It's all because of Caroline DeBauché.

I rolled my sleeping bag on the ground and lay upon it near the fire to keep the mosquitoes away, the smoke and heat drives them off. I'm hoping the wind picks up because that really keeps them away.

I don't know why, but I drank two Iroquois beers as quickly as I could then stared up at the spinning sky. The stars echo light that is billions of years old, and that fascinates me, to think that it is just now arriving to earth. I had to pee not long afterwards.

It's late in the evening, but there's a cool energy in the air. This year in college, I earned pretty good grades. My mother was very happy with me. My GPA was 3.7.

1st Semester		2nd Semester	
Biology I	A	Biology II	A
Lab	A	Lab	A
Algebra I	A	Algebra II	B
English I	A	English II	A
Am. History I	A	World History I	A
Art History I	A	Creative Writing	A
P.E. (tennis)	B	P.E. (bowling)	A

The fire, circled with rocks we dredged from the floor of the creek, crackles and snaps. I placed several logs on it a minute ago, and now they are ablaze. Crickets are chirping. An occasional hoot owl echoes between the trees, wondering what has entered his home. I hate mosquitoes.

Mike is moving about softly, as though to disturb as few blades of grass as possible. He is up to something. Harry is following him around, while Bess lies next to me. I cannot see what it is, but Mike is playing with the fire. I'm not paying much attention. He has been curious about my writing and I'm certain he wants me to be curious about him.

The smoky smell of the forest wood layers my world at this moment. I'm thinking about a woman. I have a fancy for Annie. Fancy is the wrong word. That's my mother's word. Desire is what I feel. Lust. I would like to do (fill in the blank) with her, but she is older and certainly not interested in me like that. She's eight years older and it will be years before I'm at her level, which I understand exists but cannot begin to perceive—

grad school and now a doctorate. She is simply more mature than me. I will not tell her my feelings, because in a fair fight, a woman always wins.

I wonder what Ashley is doing this evening. Is she still working at McDonald's, or did she ever get the job waitressing at Mary Mac's Tea Room? Is she dating someone? I wonder but make myself not care.

Mike brought over a pan of s'mores. They are crushed and a mess of goo.

"They fell apart," he said.

The chocolate is melted all over the graham crackers and the marshmallows are sticky and stringy. We forgot silverware, so I am eating them with my fingers and trying to write at the same time. I am getting goo on my papers, but this will not transfer to the typewritten page, so I am mentioning it.

Bess licked the chocolate off my fingers.

Sunday, July 8

I built a fire and silently prayed to whatever God was awake and listening. Coffee over the open fire!

I got back from the mountain to discover that after a billion days of rain in England, Billie Jean King defeated Chris Evert in the finals at Wimbledon 6—0, 7-5. I bet if Evert had won the second set, she would have won the match. Jan Kodes of Czechoslovakia won the men's final over Alex Metreveli of the Soviet Union. Who cares? Mr. Brezhnev probably called Chuck Connors on the "Hot-Line" to talk tennis for an hour or two before discussing invading Florida via Cuba.

Billie Jean King and Owen Davidson won the mixed doubles,

but the radio announcer didn't say who their opponents were, nor did they give the score. King had a great week.

Monday, July 9

Annie called me at work today. She didn't mention anything about kissing me. Maybe she forgot. She said her sister and some friends are coming up to visit her in Lakewood. She invited me over for dinner.

"If it's nice outside, this time we will have a picnic," she said.

§

Brooke and I had lunch at The White Front, which is a hot spot in town—friendly, good food, and not expensive.

There are black folks at the university, some professors and a handful of students but not like in Atlanta. Brooke is the only person around here I really know who is black. When I was at the library a few weeks ago, I looked up the demographics of Jamestown. Only 3.8% of the population is black, whereas in Atlanta it's about 40%. I bring this up only because Brooke talked about dating Charles.

"His family doesn't like me and my family doesn't like him, all because of the color of our skin. I can't live in the white neighborhoods and he can't live in the black part of town, over near Washington Street."

I've never met him and maybe she did not realize it, but from what she said, Charles is white, which causes a lot of problems for her.

"Where do you live?" I asked her.

"In Ashville off of Alexander Road. We're renting a house. It's old. I mean real old. But it's quiet and no one bothers us. Plus, there are two ponds and we like to fish. We like taking the boat out on the lake, but sometimes it's nice stepping out the back door and walking fifty feet to cast out my line."

§

Mike and I ran Harry and Bess to the park after I got home from work, then went to see *The Sting*. I have to say Paul Newman is my favorite actor. I like him best in *The Hustler* or being mentioned in *The Outsiders*, "I had only two things on my mind: Paul Newman and a ride home."

The Outsiders is one of my all-time favorite books. It was published when I was in seventh grade, and I thought it was perfect, simply the best story I've ever read. I identified with Pony Boy because I've felt alone many times, just as he did when his parents died.

Will Croon also loved the book, until he found out S.E. Hinton was a woman.

"What's a woman doing writing about a guy? She can't do that. I figured that guy was a real guy, not some dumb girl who wants to be one. She's probably a lesbo. This shit ain't even real—it's made-up," Will clamored.

"Of course, it's made-up. It's supposed to be. It's fiction," I told him.

"It's shit. If it ain't real, then it ain't worth a crap."

"What'd you think, that this guy was real?"

"I don't know what I thought, but I didn't figure it was no woman writing about being a guy. I figured he and I were pretty much the same. I already asked my momma if he could come stay the night."

"You did what? That's the dumbest thing I ever heard."

"So what? Shut up. The dumbest thing I ever heard was a woman writing about being a guy. She probably wants a dick of her own. I never heard about a guy writing about wanting to be a woman."

"I like it."

"It's stupid. Look, there are things you need to know. Women are never stronger, smarter, or faster than men. It's just the way of the world, and no woman should go 'round pretending she's a guy in a story and making people believe it's a guy. That's just dumb."

As far as I know, *The Outsiders* is the only book Will ever read. When I stepped out of the movie house, I had only two things on my mind: Paul Newman and Annie Spangler.

Tuesday, July 10

At lunch, I left the office and drove to Busti where there was a celebration, the 150th Anniversary of the town. I bought a program and a house plant from the woman who owns the Duncan Andros Nursery. It was a display of hostas.

"I'm buying this for a girl I know."

"Oh, she'll like this. Here, this one is one of the better plants. I'll tell you a secret, if you dab a paper towel in milk and rub the leaves, it'll make them shine."

She was there with her youngest daughter, who asked if I wanted my face painted.

"I'll paint a peace sign or heart for twenty-five cents," the young blonde girl said. "Both for forty cents."

"I have to go back to work so you can't paint my face."

"I'll paint your hand. A peace sign on your left and a heart on your other hand."

I paid the young girl forty cents and headed back to the office where, throughout the day, no one noticed my hands.

As I was walking back to the truck, there was a baby parade in the park. I overheard a woman say that the parade had been postponed because it had rained that morning. I didn't see any babies that were particularly cute. One woman had her baby dressed up like a bumblebee, while another looked like a sunflower. Neither baby will ever recover from the indignity. I'm sure that when Paul Busti founded the town in 1823, he never envisioned a baby parade with babies as ugly as a cow's butt.

§

Annie and her sister, Lauren, and a friend of hers, Shannon, stopped by the house to visit.

"Peace," Shannon said, holding up her fingers.

"Yeah, peace, man," Lauren said. "I like your hands." She circled her finger over the Peace symbol on the back of my hand.

We had dinner, (a picnic) at the 100-Acre Park. Annie cooked all the food at her apartment, packed it up, and kept it warm. All I had to do was ride along in her dad's convertible. She drove. I was in the front, scrunched between Annie and Shannon, while Lauren rode shotgun. All four of us were jammed in the front seat. I was so close to Annie, I could smell her perfume.

Lauren and Shannon are twenty-three. They both quit their jobs yesterday at Ruth's Department Store in Ithaca, where they worked in the shoe department.

"We were in the breakroom and I said, 'Let's quit.' So we did," Shannon said.

"I hated working there," Lauren told us. "Our boss's such a jerk. He would schedule us one day for eight hours and then the next day for four hours, but if it was slow, he made us go home, so we never made any money."

"Yeah, last week, it was slow," Shannon said. "He called me at home and said not to come in. Two hours later he called me in when it picked up. I worked three hours and then he sent me home again."

"He pinched Shannon's ass," said Lauren.

"Yeah, I've got a bruise. I'll show you."

"We weren't on break or anything when we quit. We were back there getting some napkins and paper towels because a woman had spilled her can of pop on the showroom floor. We were really busy, but then as we hurried to get the towels and clean up everything, Stan—that's our boss—got irritated with us and said we had to stay late, but he wouldn't pay us overtime. Lauren and I cleaned up the mess and then decided we were tired of Stan the Man," said Shannon.

"Oh, hell, it was funny as fuck," Lauren said. "We grabbed our purses and told Stan we'd be right back. He must've had ten people to wait on."

"You walked out?" I asked.

"We wrote a note and put it on his desk, 'Hey, asshole, we quit.' And that was that." Shannon and Lauren started laughing and hugged each other. Annie shook her head in disbelief.

"If I had worked in another department, I'd probably have stayed," Shannon said.

"Yeah, we liked everyone else," Lauren said. "They were nice, but Stan was the owners' son-in-law, which is the only reason he has a job, so their daughter and grandkids don't starve."

I could never do what they did, but then, Lauren and Shannon are kind of hippie-ish anyway. As I said, Annie cooked dinner, a bunch of stuff I wouldn't normally eat. No meat, because Lauren and Shannon are vegetarians. She spread everything on the picnic table.

"Here's what I have planned out for dinner," Annie said. "We have assorted fresh nuts to nibble on before dinner. And raw veggies too, all fresh from the store this morning: yellow peppers, green beans, thin slices of beets, and cucumbers. We have stuffed mushroom appetizers. They're stuffed with diced kale, broccoli, cauliflower, and sprouts, and mixed all together with yeast flakes and a little almond milk, which we also have as our drink. It took an hour to dice all that stuff."

"Almond milk?" I asked.

"Yes, you'll love it," Lauren said. "It'll make your dick hard," she laughed.

"Lauren," Annie warned.

That embarrassed me. I didn't know what to say so I shook my head, but then they laughed again.

"We also have salad."

"What's in it?" I asked Annie.

"Healthy stuff. Peas, corn, pinto beans, lima beans, kidney beans, black beans, both black and green olives, chickpeas, lettuce, and carrots strings, all topped off with avocado green goddess salad dressing, which I made from scratch. I've never made it before so I hope you like it. We have corn soufflé and then the main course is Meatless Macaroni Masterpiece."

"Good, because you know I don't eat meat," Shannon said.

"I know, which is why I found that recipe," Annie told her.

"I don't eat milk or eggs, either."

"I know that and that brings me to dessert. Wacky Cake. No eggs or milk."

"You know what goes good with almond milk?" I asked. "Pizza from Mike and Sam's."

"Yeah!" Lauren screamed.

"Just toss out the almond milk and grab a cold beer."

"Come on," Annie said. "You need to give it a chance."

Annie went to a lot of trouble preparing all the food, so I told her I liked it, even though I thought it was terrible. I liked the salad and filled up on the raw vegetables because the meatless macaroni tasted like soggy newspaper, and the Wacky Cake was as dry as a mouthful of Hershey's Cocoa Powder. All I had to wash it down with was almond milk, which had a faint taste of almonds but was more like watered-down powdered milk. None of it filled me up.

Afterwards, we walked around the park, then sat at the picnic table and played *Aggravation* until it was too dark. I tried knocking Annie's marbles off the board. Once, when Shannon dropped a marble in the grass and she bent down to get it, I looked down her blouse. She wasn't wearing a bra. She has tiny breasts, but big, big nipples. That was the best thing about dinner.

I like Lauren and Shannon, not the way I like Annie, but they are a lot of fun, too. And because I don't have the same feelings for them as I do for Annie, I seem to have more fun around them. That is odd. I don't feel as if I need to try. Unlike Annie, Lauren has dark brown hair, real dark, and gorgeous brown eyes. Shannon has black hair. Lauren is a tad chubby, but a cute chubby. Shannon is just skinny. Too skinny for me. I like a little meat.

With the convertible top down, Annie drove us all over Kingdom Come, for hours. With the radio on, we sang all the songs that WJTN broadcast over the valley.

"Annie doesn't have an extra bed," Lauren said, "just a sofa, which sleeps only one. Shannon can't sleep on the floor so can we stay at your house?"

Annie drove everyone back to Dr. Laighles's house and dropped us off. She didn't stay.

"Let's get ice cream first," Shannon said in the kitchen.

"Nothing's open at this time of night," I reminded her.

"I'm still hungry. You've got food, don't you?"

"I have food, but it's not vegetarian or anything, except for the vegetables."

"That's okay, I'm too hungry to care."

While Lauren and I took Harry and Bess outside, Shannon started breakfast: scrambled eggs, toast, bacon, and sautéed mushrooms and peppers.

"I love eating breakfast late at night," Lauren said.

"I'd like a cup of coffee, but if I drink it now, I'll never get to sleep," I told her.

"Here, try this," Lauren said.

She had a handful of herbal tea packets in her purse, so we made a pot of tea. It was okay but left my mouth with a dry feeling. I don't get it—tea, which is made with water, leaves my mouth dry. Isn't that the pinnacle of all things odd and weird in the universe?

"Right now," Shannon said, "I could go for a pizza."

"Yeah, from Mike and Sam's," I said, but they were long closed for the night.

I wish Annie had stayed the night, too. She could have slept in the other bedroom, but I would've liked her to sleep in my room with me, keeping me warm. The three of us ate our "2 a.m. breakfast" and talked about Watergate and Nixon. They hate him. Shannon and I drank a bottle of Dr. Laighles' wine.

"This looks like it goes with breakfast," Shannon said.

"Yes, I believe it's the perfect after-breakfast wine," I retorted.

I drank too much and got drunk, but I did not do anything stupid. I just laughed a lot.

Wednesday, July 11

I had to be at work by nine (I was more than an hour late).

I put Lauren and Shannon in separate rooms last night, but when I woke them up at seven, they were in the same bed.

I made certain the girls were up early, which they didn't like. I wanted them out of the house before I left for work. I don't think either brought a change of clothes or pajamas or a toothbrush, because they both asked to borrow mine. I let them, but I will buy a new toothbrush.

"I don't like getting up before nine o'clock," Shannon said. "That's one reason we quit Ruth's."

I made coffee and when I brought a cup to Lauren, she was still under the sheets, and I saw that she didn't have her undies on. Shannon was already in the shower. I didn't see her naked or anything. I made tea for her.

When I dropped them off at Annie's, I was hoping Annie would be outside, but she wasn't. The girls each gave me a hug. Shannon is too skinny, but Lauren's boobs pushed right into my chest. I wonder if she would hit me if I grabbed them. I don't mean grab them hard, but soft like I was massaging them. A girl might like that.

§

"This is what really pisses me off," Roy said at work. "People do a lousy job and no one gets fired. Rule number one—the world is incompetent."

I stayed clear of him the entire day to be on the safe side. He was not angry about anything that happened at work—he was irritated at his bank for messing up some transactions. I figured he was going to yell at me for being late. I can't afford to be fired. Roy would go an hour or so and then start complaining about the world, about the local government.

"Do you want to play chess before you leave for the day?" he asked me. I couldn't say no, but I was eager to see Annie again. At 5:45, Roy leaned his head into my cubicle.

"Hey boy, are you going to work all day or what?"

"I'm almost done. Did you read this story about the two guys from Erie who were caught having sex with a cow?" I asked Roy.

"Can't say that I saw that one."

§

We played two quick games that I lost, even though the second game was close, all because I wasn't concentrating. Instead, I told him about these idiots from some town outside of Erie: Larry Van Atter (24) and Scottie Twitchell (25). They are from Harbor Creek, which I had never heard of before.

"These two guys drove from Erie to Findley Lake to go fishing but then ended up breaking into a barn. The sheriff caught them having sex with a small cow, at the same time. One guy from the front, while the other guy was in the back. When the sheriff confronted the two perverts, he startled the cow. She bit down and took off the first guy's dick with one bite."

"It's your move."

"I know but isn't that the strangest thing you've ever heard."

"Not by a long shot. Just wait. Give it a year and you'll understand that those guys are nothing."

"They had to rush Van Atter to Saint Vincent's Hospital. The article didn't say what happened after that."

'Well, I doubt they were able to sew his pecker back on," Roy said.

Roy had a wooden chess clock, so we timed the games. It was cool. It was French, I think, made by Garde. He set it for thirty minutes each, meaning the longest a game could last no longer than one hour.

I was beating him, but I ran out of time. He knew I was about to win, too. I could sense it. When my time ran out, he had two minutes and seven seconds remaining. Next time, I'll be the victor.

I told Lauren and Shannon about the secret room. They thought it was "super cool" and said they'd help me find it if they stayed in town. I wish I had seen both of them naked this morning. That would be a good way to start the day.

§

Dr. Laighles called today from Paris. He and Mrs. Laighles were out all night. He sounded a bit drunk.

"How's Emily?" I asked.

"Drunker than a skunk."

They're going to Germany next week then back to Paris for a few days then London, Scotland, and Liverpool. His research is going well, he said.

"I found a note about the secret room Steven found. Do you know what Steven meant?"

His voice steadied. "Yes, well, I'm not sure about that. Emily and I have talked about it, but we think Steven made it up and was playing a joke on us, which is something he did all the time. He was a real prankster."

"I found an entry note in your card catalog."

"I started that after Steven died. We had so many books and he always said that I should catalog our books."

"Do you think the secret room is real?"

"I don't think so. I've never bothered looking for it. Emily is sending you a care package of foreign delicacies from places we've visited. It should arrive next week."

Thursday, July 12

I took half the day off from work today and waited for Jerry Scott to deliver the Corvette to the house. He arrived at ten-thirty with the car in an enclosed trailer. When he rolled it down the ramp, it looked like a wild animal preparing to pounce and take off into the wilderness.

"Listen to this," he said as he started it.

He revved the engine. There's no other way to describe it—Steven's car growled like a lion with a deep, throaty, thunderous howl. It screamed POWER.

"Want to drive it?"

"No, maybe later. I just want to park it in the garage for now."

"Suit yourself. It's all back together and better than factory. If you ever want to sell it, let me know. You've got three hundred and fifteen horses in there so when you drive it, watch out. If you're not ready, she'll get away from you. That Four-Speed Synchro-Mesh transmission is nothing to screw around with, not until you know what you're doing. Along with the Speedlite Flywheel, you should easily hit sixty in under four seconds."

I walked around the car several times, then sat in the driver's seat and revved the engine. It scared the hell out of me.

"If you race it on the street, I suggest wider rear tires, just to grip the road better. Me and a buddy took it out yesterday, drove it on I-20 toward Rochester to test drive it. I got it up to one hundred and fifty-seven for about a mile. It was scary fast, but no vibrations. Like I said, better than factory."

Sitting in the driver's seat, it was like being in a showroom. It was immaculate, virginal clean, and tight. Mr. Scott opened the garage door for me, I eased off the clutch, and she purred herself right into the open bay and next to Emily's Volvo.

"We rode the quarter in twelve seconds," he said, "but it was nothing official. Just our best estimate. One thing, we had a bitch of a time starting it. It starts fine when cold, but after she ran for a while, it was a pain in the ass getting it started again. We finally made the correct adjustments so that issue should be gone. Just thought I'd mention that."

The last thing he said to me was, "If you can't get pussy with this Corvette, there's no hope for you."

I wrote him a check for the full amount, the entire time knowing it was next semester's tuition. I was at work before noon.

I'm broke. Financially, and as a man.

It cost $3,711.78.

§

It is currently 11 p.m. I took the Corvette out for a spin earlier this evening and stopped at Annie's to take her for a ride.

"That's Steven's car. What the hell are you doing driving his car?"

She refused to go for a ride when I asked her. In fact, she was so pissed off, I ended up leaving. It was too late in the evening to knock on her door because she was already in her PJs. I should have exercised better judgment.

"Take that back home and park it where it belongs."

I drove around town for about thirty minutes but did not open it up to let it growl. Then I started feeling guilty because Annie was angry at me, so here I am back home.

§

The other day at Annie's, when she, Lauren, and Shannon weren't in the room with me, I stole a nude picture of Annie. It's an 8x10 and is sitting beside me as I type. It is a frontal shot of her leaning against the wall in an archway, with her arm curving back around the top of her head. She's blonde, but her pubic hair is light brown. Her picture's like a loaded gun sitting on the coffee table—you can't stop thinking about it.

If Annie knew I stole her picture, I bet she'd think I'm a pervert. I believe she's worth worshiping. I stared at her picture for about an hour.

The New York Stock Exchange was up 1.26 to end at 1,784 today. The volume was 18,730,000. I can see a day when the index Industrial Average will top the 2,000 mark, but economists say that will never happen. I bet it will go beyond 3,000 because I plan to live in a time of prosperity.

Friday, July 13

Work, work, work, work. Today I went to work and stayed all day! I brought my lunch, so I never left my desk.

I walked around the garage this evening to see if the Corvette was still there in its restored condition. I ran my hand over the fiberglass. It was smooth and looked brand new.

§

"What the hell, Robert," Roy yelled when I told him the cost over a game of chess. "You paid that guy?"

"Yeah."

"I think he ripped you off."

"No. You need to see it. It looks better than showroom. Plus, he explained all the damage underneath, all the stuff he had to fix. It could have been worse."

After chess, Roy and I drove over to Dr. Laighles's place, and I showed him the car and the itemized list of repairs. He started it and sat in the driver's seat revving the engine.

"It purrs like untamed pussy."

"I told you."

He settled down about the price, saying that he just didn't want to see me get ripped off. But now he agrees. Jerry Scott did a remarkable job.

§

There was an article in today's paper about a Ripley man who died in the shower. He was renovating a 110-year-old house that was in ragged shape. The authorities listed the cause of death as an accident because he apparently slipped in the shower, but when he tried to brace himself against a rotted wall, it caved in and he busted out of the second story. The neighbors found him draped over the barbecue pit in the backyard. He had hit his head and broke his neck.

It's Friday the 13th, and according to the Channel 4 newscast, a Dallas woman gave birth to her 13th child, and her doctor was a 13th child himself. In San Francisco, when a man went out to his car to start it, the motor ran, but the wheels didn't turn because someone had stolen the drive shaft. And, in North Carolina, a man has a license plate, 13-13-13. He says it brings him luck.

"I've never had a speeding ticket."

His wife said, "Yeah, but he's had four accidents."

"They weren't my fault."

§

To write this, I fear the world will conspire against me. Maybe that means I'm a fatalist. I have fallen in love with Annie. She and Mike came over after he talked her into looking at the garden, which isn't much yet, just nubs of the future poking through the soil.

We walked the rows of the garden and pulled any weeds. Some of the veggies have been chewed down by either raccoons or rabbits. The arugula was large enough to pull up and add to our salad. Mike calls it "rocket" lettuce. I'm not sure where that comes from, unless it grows so fast it "takes off." The broccoli's doing pretty good but is not ready to be picked yet. Same with the radishes.

Annie and I sat on the porch, while Mike was in the house playing the computer chess. There was no wind this evening and while we talked and looked out over the lake, the mosquitoes attacked.

"Hold on. I have something," Annie said. She ran to her car and then went inside the house. She returned with an ashtray, a pack of matches, and eucalyptus incense.

"I bought it this morning at Linwood's after I went running at Allen Park. I bought this and some rose sticks to help me relax and focus."

Annie lit the eucalyptus, which smelled pretty good, and it kept away the mosquitoes. We both stretched out in Adirondack chairs—she in one, me in another—but bumped against each other every so often.

"Can I ask you something?"

"Fire away," she said.

"Do you have a boyfriend?" I asked Annie.

"Not currently."

"Have you ever had a boyfriend?" I asked.

"What do you think?" she asked with a smirk.

"Just curious."

"No duh!"

"Why did you kiss me the other night?" I asked.

It took a lot of courage for me to ask this.

"It just seemed right. You looked handsome standing on the porch. I couldn't resist the temptation of kissing you, but you didn't kiss me back. Did you know a kiss holds the world's emotions together?"

"I didn't know that."

"It does. But you didn't kiss me back, so maybe you don't have any emotions," she said.

"I have emotions."

"I couldn't tell."

"Kissing is very personal," I explained.

"Kissing's the most intimate action. It reveals a person's emotions, but they have to be shared. Think about it. You can't kiss yourself and enjoy it. It's not the worst thing in the world to want to kiss someone," she said.

Later when Annie was leaving, she said she would drive Mike home.

"Mike, will you wait in the car for a few minutes?" Annie asked.

Her car was parked on the side of the house near the garage and out of our view, which meant that we were out of Mike's view. As we stood on the porch, Annie kissed me, and I kissed her back. It was a short one, but then she kissed me again, and this time it was a real long kiss that gave me a boner. I hope she did not notice.

"Your perfume smells wonderful."

"It's Chanel No. 5. It's the only thing Marilyn Monroe wore to bed."

She kissed me one more time. I kissed Annie Spangler and I loved it.

§

I am up typing right now, and it is nearly 2 a.m., but I haven't been able to sleep. I tried, but all I can think about is Annie.

Saturday, July 14

I worked today to earn time and a half. The only people in the office were me and Harry Hirschberger, a guy in charge of quality control. I'm not sure what he does exactly because he and I never really see each other or talk, but I think he reviews all the reports. He's never had a problem with anything I've written, except a few times his secretary Sheryl has asked me to explain something in more detail or more clearly.

I still like George Harrison's "Give Me Love" but now my favorite song on Casey Kasem's Top 40 is The Carpenter's "Yesterday Once More." If asked, I'd deny that. "Smoke On the Water" is a good song, too. And "Bad Bad Leroy Brown." I like Karen Carpenter's voice. I might be able to confess that to Annie but no one else.

The Bucket of Blood has been open for two weeks, and today was the first time I stopped in. I walked over at lunch, by myself, and shot three games of pool and had a BTL, along with a plate of Swanson's Potato Chips. I was the only person there besides the waitress and cook.

"It's slow today," she said, "but you should have seen it last night. It'll pick up in the afternoon."

"I like what you did in here to renovate it."

"Mr. Card, who lives down the street, and his son, Bob, did all the work. They worked real hard at night and on the weekend to make this place spiffy."

After work, I returned with Mike, and we played several games of pool. I won them all. He doesn't seem to be able to focus on the balls, and as a result, we counted anything he hit that went in. The hard crack of the break sent the balls scattering in an atomic explosion, and the plunk of a ball in the pocket made me feel like Paul Newman in *The Hustler*, except I have no pool skills.

There were about a dozen people inside at 6:00 p.m. when we arrived. When we left at eight, the place was jumping. There were even three boys standing at the shuffleboard game carefully sliding the steel pucks with a deft touch as they tried to knock the other pucks off. The younger boy was all power and random luck as he fired the puck in an effort to knock all the pucks off the board. I think the three boys were there with their grandfather, because when they were leaving, I heard the old man say, "Don't tell Ellen I brought you in here."

We both ate six hotdogs and drank as many Cokes. I did not drink beer because I am trying to live a better life.

Sunday, July 15

Quiet. Nothing to write. Except I have had diarrhea. I'm on the porch and looking out over the lake but keep running to the bathroom every ten minutes. I probably ate too many hotdogs last night. I've been reading all day, which is okay. No complaints except for the bathroom troubles.

Annie called to ask if I would like to go roller skating. I said yes but not today. "I don't feel well so I'm staying around the house." I did not elaborate.

§

Wait. The game was on TV. I just watched Nolan Ryan of the Angels pitch his second no-hitter of the year against the Detroit Tigers. The other no-hitter was against Kansas City. It was in color, too, because Dr. Laighles' TV is out of this world.

"Ladies and gentlemen," the announcer said as his voice crackled over the speaker, "only two other pitchers have thrown two no-hitters in a season: Johnny Vander Meer in 1938 for the Cincinnati Reds, and Allie Reynolds in 1951 for the Yankees. Vander Meer pitched them back to back."

This Ryan is good. The Mets should have never traded him. Management lacks vision.

Monday, July 16

Roy invited me to his house for dinner tomorrow night. I accepted. Today, I almost won at chess. The chess clock ran out of time again. But, when the game ended, Roy was nearly out of time, as well. He had forty-six seconds remaining. Toward the end, I checked him six times in a row, but he escaped like a greased monkey. I knocked him out of position and had his pieces scattered, but I couldn't draw it to a close. Soon. Soon.

I rode my motorcycle to the countryside after work. I don't know where I was, just somewhere among the trees. It will be my last ride, because Wayne McArthur, one of the mechanics at Waite's Keystone on Fluvanna Avenue, said he'd give me two hundred bucks for my motorcycle. I need the money. I bounced a small check at the pharmacy. The bank charged me three dollars. Outrageous!

I went into the pharmacy and apologized to Mr. Barone then I settled up with him for three bucks. I paid cash. He was nice about it.

Tuesday, July 17

The Getty boy, J. Paul Getty III, was kidnapped ten days ago, and now his kidnappers say they are going to cut his finger off to prove they are serious. Mr. Big Bucks himself, J. Paul Getty, said he's against paying any ransom because it encourages kidnappers. I bet not paying it encourages kidnappers to become murderers.

§

When I arrived at the Patersons' for dinner, Roy had not returned from the office. His wife, Louise, met me at the door. Their youngest daughter, Becky, immediately vied for my attention away from Karen.

When Becky and her mother went upstairs to pick out a different shirt to go with Becky's pink hip-huggers, Karen said, "I just turned sixteen two months ago. My sister's only eleven. Can't you tell? I swear, at times, she's so boy-crazy it just about drives me up the wall. I've smoked pot. Have you?"

"A few times," I whispered.

"I love the buzz. My father'd kill me if he ever found out. Sometimes I sneak beer out of the house and ride my bike over to Allen Park to drink with my friends. They have these huge cement drainage pipes—they're so big you can stand up in them. We go in there to get high. My friend, Donna, she gets the best pot. She calls Lakewood, Lakeweed."

When Louise hurried back into the kitchen to stir something on the stove, Becky sat down next to me.

"I got on perfume," she said.

"Good for you," Karen said.

"Smell." She bent her wrist back and twisted it under my nose. "Mom, Karen kicked me."

"I did not. It was an accident. I was stretching my legs."

"You two, behave," Louise said. She stirred the mashed potatoes as Roy opened the kitchen door. He gave Louise a kiss.

For dinner, we ate fried chicken with mashed potatoes and gravy.

Also, green beans and peas. They had something I've never seen before, Stovetop Stuffing.

"I helped make the stuffing," Becky said.

"Oh, like that was hard. It came out of a box. Our retarded dog can make that," Karen snipped.

Becky was sitting to my left while Karen was across from me. Roy and Louise sat at opposite ends of the table.

"I love drinking wine," Karen said.

"When do you ever drink wine?" Louise asked.

"We don't get to drink wine with dinner, ever," Becky said.

"Well, it's a special night," Roy said, raising his wine glass. "We have a distinguished guest."

"I'm not so sure about that," I rebuked.

"We never drink at dinner," Louise said.

"This is a California Zinfandel from a vineyard in the valley that has been making wine since before the gold rush," Roy said. He turned his glass around as if he was examining it.

Everyone had a goblet of water and a small wine glass. I'd never tasted a Zinfandel, but it was fine with the chicken. When I took a bite then a drink, the wine absorbed into the chicken, which was needed because Louise overcooked it. That was okay with me because I like my chicken crispy-dry. The stuffing was really good.

"It's Shake 'n Bake and I helped," Becky blurted out, which made everyone laugh, except Karen.

"It's Shake 'n Bake and I helped," Karen mimicked. "For the love of God, can't you shut up?"

"Hey, hey, hey," Roy calmly said.

"How do you like college?" Louise asked.

"Chautauqua's great. I was pre-med, but I've switched my major to history. I really like my professors, but it was a tough year. I made good grades but all I had time for was studying. I don't feel as if I had a good time, if you know what I mean."

"I'm going to Syracuse or Sarah Lawrence," Karen said. "Chautauqua's right in my backyard, but I want to go away and have an adventure."

"You can have an adventure right here," Roy said.

"Oh, yeah, that sounds like fun, Mr. Where-Are-You-Going-All-the-Time. You need to know every little thing I'm doing," Karen retorted.

"Yes, I do," Roy laughed.

"He'll probably want to know regardless of where you attend college," Louise said.

"Great."

"Very few people know my middle name is Wilbur," Roy said, "so named after my great-grandfather on my mother's side of the family."

"Daddy," Becky asked, "who am I named after?"

"Can't you shut up for one minute?" Karen nipped again.

"Karen, be nice," her mother said.

"You weren't named after anyone at all," Karen said. "You were illegitimate."

"Hey, hey, hey," Roy said. "Be nice. You were named after my great aunt Rebecca who lives in Cork, Ireland."

"Who was Karen named after?" Becky asked.

"No one cares," Karen replied, with her mouth full of chicken.

After dinner, as they were washing and drying the dishes, I saw

Roy kiss Louise with a soft, warm peck on the lips. When he didn't think anyone was spying, he pinched her butt.

Everyone played *Crazy Eights* after the kitchen was cleaned up, and I made a conscious effort to keep Karen from winning. I could tell that she tried keeping me from going out, too, even at the expense of losing. I tried to help Becky win.

"Let's play Old Maid," Karen said.

"You are an old maid," Becky replied.

Wednesday, July 18

Work was quiet today. I mainly filled out reports from what I read on Monday and Tuesday. Roy invited me for dinner again sometime, which I accepted.

Mike came over to watch TV tonight. He brought some apples. I've eaten so many, I'm about appled out. We played baseball pinball. It was the best of twenty-one games. I bought a case of Genesee Cream Ale on the way home from work from Newhouse's on Clifton Avenue. By the time we'd finished the marathon World Series, I'd drunk eight beers. Mike had three. Yet, I still won.

We both wrote down our starting lineups. At first, we had decided to be the National and the American Leagues against each other, but then both of us wanted other players on our team.

	Mike's Team	Robert's Team
1st Base	Hank Aaron	Willie Stargell
2nd Base	Rod Carew	Joe Morgan
3rd Base	Ron Santo	Brooks Robinson

Shortstop	Murray Wills	Gene Alley
Catcher	Carlton Fisk	Johnny Bench
Leftfield	Pete Rose	Roy White
Centerfield	Lou Brock	Frank Robinson
Rightfield	Mickey Mantle	Roberto Clemente
Starting Pitchers	Catfish Hunter	Nolan Ryan
	Mickey Lolich	Jim Palmer
	Steve Carlton	Fergie Jenkins
	Tom Seaver	Bob Gibson
	Ken Holtzman	Tug McGraw
	Don Drysdale	Sandy Kofax
	Juan Marichal	Holt Wilhelm
	Burt Blyleven	Warren Spahn
Relief Pitchers	None	None
Utility Players	None	Willie Mays
		(I insisted)

When one of us grabbed a player, we complained to one another because we both really wanted him. For instance, when I chose Sandy Kofax, Mike railed about how unfair that was, but then he chose Don Drysdale. The same happened when he took Hank Aaron first. That was my mistake. I didn't think Mike would pick Aaron in the first round. I took Clemente, but he took Hammerin' Hank because he knew Aaron is one of my favorite players. In the end, he had a better fielding and hitting team, but I smoked him with pitching.

All Mike wanted to talk about was Hank Aaron hitting his 700th home run last week. He brought over all his Hank Aaron baseball cards. Aaron needs only fourteen homers to tie the Babe, so it should happen before the end of August, at least before the season's end. I'm looking forward to watching him break the record.

I read a story last month at work about how Aaron keeps getting phone calls and mail from people who hate his guts for trying to break Ruth's record. What if he does? It's not going to change Babe Ruth's greatness. He's still the best baseball player in the game. Aaron is great, but he's no Babe Ruth. He's Hank Aaron. Be who you are. Some people have threatened his life. I don't understand that. Let the man be who he is and do what he does. If he's the best, then he's the best. His color should have nothing to do with it. Aaron is in my top three favorite players: #1 Roy White, #2 Roberto Clemente, #3 Hank Aaron.

I ended up beating Mike 16—5. I was up 9—1 early on and was on a roll.

After Mike left, the phone rang.

"Dr. Laighles?" I assumed.

No. Annie's sister, Lauren.

We talked for about ten minutes before she asked, "Can I come up again."

"Sure," I said, thinking how odd she sounded.

Thursday, July 19

Karen came by this evening while I was mowing the lawn. She rode her bicycle to the house. She didn't say much, just giggled a lot while sitting on the front porch. Strange days indeed. She's pretty though.

"I don't have a light on my bike, and if Buck Cline catches me again, he'll give me a ticket."

"Who's that?" I asked.

"Officer Cline. He's the deputy around here. He's a nice guy, but he'll write you up if he's warned you before. He stopped me last week for no light."

"I'll drive you home. I'll put your bike in the back of the truck."

"We don't have to go home immediately. We can drive around or go get ice cream or do something."

"Let's go to the Hotel Lenhart and sit on the porch and watch the boats come in."

"Yuck. That's where my parents always go. How about Mayville. There's a bar in the Hotel St. Elmo."

I did not want to go to a bar and get a drink, not after eight beers last night. We drove over to the Tastee Freez on Foote Avenue, got our ice cream then went to Allen Park and sat at a picnic table.

"I want some action," she said. "Let's go to Mayville."

§

Tired. I'll write later.

Friday, July 20

Nothing happened last night with Karen. I wanted to sit on the porch at the Hotel Lenhart and have ice cream, but she had wilder ideas. Allen Park and ice cream cones just wasn't enough excitement for her. She convinced me that the Hotel St. Elmo in

Mayville was the happening place. I had only one beer. She had three drinks—a Cosmopolitan, a glass of red wine, and a 16-oz Schlitz. It was a slow night. There were only three other people in the bar and the bartender didn't ask Karen for her I.D.

While driving around the lake, she said, "Let's go to Midway. I got to pee."

So, I drove to Midway Amusement Park. Mostly, we played Skee-Ball but then she wanted to ride the Twirl-A-Whirl. We did, and about two minutes after, she said, "I don't feel good."

And, about thirty seconds later, Karen threw up in the bushes. She barfed two more times before I had her in the truck.

We drove around with the windows down, but she did not barf anymore.

"Can I go back to your house to clean up before I go home?"

She was cleaning up and I was sitting outside the bathroom talking to her when she turned and threw up in the toilet. She cleaned up again and I took her home.

I hope that was enough excitement for her because it was for me: mowing the yard, Tastee Freez, Allen Park, St. Elmo Hotel, Midway Park, driving around a drunk girl. By the time I took her home, she was no longer sick. She might have still been drunk, but Roy can't get angry with me. I offered her a quiet evening, but she chose the Twirl-A-Whirl.

§

I played double-solitaire with Mike for an hour. He brought over a new baseball lineup that he had scrutinized to the nth-degree, as if

that was the reason he lost the other night. I am supposed to pick
my team but cannot use any of his players.

Mike's New & Improved Lineup

1st Base	Hank Aaron
2nd Base	Rod Carew
3rd Base	Brooks Robinson
Shortstop	Murray Wills
Catcher	Johnny Bench
Leftfield	Pete Rose
Centerfield	Lou Brock
Rightfield	Roberto Clemente
Starting Pitchers	Nolan Ryan
	Catfish Hunter
	Bob Gibson
	Sandy Kofax
	Jim Palmer
	Warren Spahn
	Steve Carlton
	Tom Seaver
	Fergie Jenkins
	Don Drysdale
	Juan Marichal
Relief Pitchers	Mickey Lolich
	Ken Holtzman

Tug McGraw

Holt Wilhelm

Burt Blyleven

Utility Players   Willie Mays

Mickey Mantle

Willie Stargell

Joe Morgan

Frank Robinson

What the hell!!! Who is left for me? He cherry-picked the best!

Since there is little to write, I will note the MLB scoreboard leaders:

National League East -- St. Louis	58—49
National League West -- Los Angeles	67—41
American League East -- Baltimore	56—46
American League West -- Kansas City	62—48

It's difficult for a team to finish .500 or better, and currently, of the twenty-four MLB teams, only thirteen have winning records. I note this because the announcer the other night said that from year to year, usually less than half the teams finish above .500. The Braves are playing a dismal .438, while San Diego is an embarrassment at .340.

It will be interesting to see which teams make it to the playoffs and whether or not the teams in the running as I type this will still be contenders come October. The Oakland Athletics, last year's World Series winners, are only a half-game behind Kansas City. I predict they will not repeat as champs this season. My prediction: Pittsburgh over Baltimore, just like in 1971. My hope is that the Pirates will make a late run at it.

Saturday, July 21

I was playing with Harry and Bess in the backyard when Karen stopped by the house late this afternoon on her bicycle.

"Wasn't that wild last night?" she said.

She asked to use the bathroom, and when she walked out afterwards, I could tell she was no longer wearing a bra. I didn't say anything, but it was obvious that she had taken it off because when she chased the dogs and jumped around, her boobs bounced everywhere. She must have put it in her purse. I could almost see through her t-shirt. Her nipples poked out like strawberries.

I took her on a tour of the house and told her about the secret room.

Harry and Bess did tricks for her, and she fed them dog treats. Before she left, she used the bathroom again, and when she came out, I noticed she had put her bra back on.

Karen had only been gone for forty-five minutes when Annie called to ask if she could come over. I quickly washed my face, brushed my hair, and threw on a few drops of cologne. Not too much.

I hit the bottom of the stairs just as she rang the doorbell. Her silhouette was a foggy figure, angel-like, behind the milky cuts in the glass door. She wore a light shade of red lipstick the color of raspberries.

We sat on the front porch and shared a Coke.

"Do you know what this thing is for?" I pointed to a metal plate that looked like a doorstop. It's screwed into the wood planks on the porch.

"That's a boot scraper. The French call it a décrottoir. People keep them near the front door so you can scrape the mud off before entering the house. That's probably been there since the house was built. It's really old."

Will Croon would die if he saw how beautiful Annie is.

I want to tell her that I love her, but she would probably run for the hills and hide. She has never said anything remotely like that to me, so I kept my trap shut. I certainly am in love with the idea of how lovely Annie is.

Without much forethought, we took in a double feature movie at the Lakewood Drive-In, *Cahill U.S. Marshall*. Annie loves John Wayne. Me too. The second picture was *Dillinger*, which was pretty awesome. We took her car and rode with the top down, but it began to sprinkle, so we stopped on the side of the road to raise the top back up.

Odd . . . we have the entire house to ourselves, and yet, we go to the drive-in to make out. I felt Annie's breasts, and my Lord in Heaven, she is a goddess.

Sunday, July 22

Annie drove home today, to her house in Ithaca, which bummed me out.

I ate lunch at Perkins Pancake House and sat in a booth. Behind me, having a cup of coffee, sat a man and woman who are married.

From what I overheard, his mother is a real piece of work. I could not help but eavesdrop on them.

"How did she talk you into this?" the woman asked. "Here we are, barely making ends meet, and she talks you into buying her a television on credit. Then I get the payment book in the mail today with my name on it. You put the loan in my name without me being there. Why did you let her sign my name? And then she leaves this morning to drive back to Texas. Well, we're not paying for this. Tell her to bring the TV back or make the payments herself."

§

This evening, Mike and I went to the movies. He wanted to see Bruce Lee in *The Chinese Connection*, but it was sold out, so we saw *Billy Jack* instead. I actually wanted to see *Scarecrow* with Gene Hackman and Al Pacino. Afterwards, Mike kept trying to karate chop me like Billy Jack.

I cannot stop thinking about Annie. When will she return? The mail came, but not Emily's care package.

Monday, July 23

President Nixon said today that he will not turn over evidence related to Watergate, and that he would not turn over tape recordings and documents sought by both the Senate Watergate committee and prosecutor Archibald Cox. Part of me doesn't believe Nixon did anything wrong. I believe the Democrats are embarrassed because Nixon did not start the Vietnam War, yet he's ending it, when LBJ did nothing. My parents are Democrats and I have always been a Democrat. I'm in Nixon's corner a little more than I am comfortable being, and it's probably because he's ending the war.

Annie and I went skating at Ivey's Skating Rink in Celeron. I'm okay, but not great at skating. It didn't matter because I got to hold Annie's hand all night. It was moderately crowded, but I didn't get in anyone's way or embarrass myself. Annie's a good skater and kept me balanced most of the time. I only fell down twice.

"How'd you get so good at skating?"

"I grew up skating here," she said. "I took lessons. Plus, Mr. Ivey's the owner, and I went to school with his daughter. She had a beautiful Corvette, a convertible. I don't remember the year, but one day she and I washed it in her front yard and all the kids next door came over—that would be on Hallock Street—and they helped. Afterwards, we took it for a ride in the country with the top down, two blonde girls with their hair twisting around in the wind."

After skating, I took her out for pizza at Mike and Sam's. It may be the best pizza in the world. It's square—not round—but on each square they've cut, there is a huge thick piece of pepperoni. I ate too much, but I couldn't control myself.

"This is where my mother and father met each other," I told Annie.

"Is that so?"

"They were in the same high school but didn't know each other even though they had a lot of mutual friends. One night, after a bunch of kids were bowling and hanging out, my father came here and that's when he met my mom. They started dating in high school."

Tuesday, July 24

Annie asked me over for dinner this evening, just the two of us. I wonder if she knows I write about her in my journal.

When I came home from Annie's this evening, Mike was sitting on the front porch drinking a cup of hot chocolate.

"It's a little muggy for hot chocolate, isn't it?" I asked. I stretched out in a lawn chair, sliding in between the dogs who did not want to move. I snuggled up with them and scratched their ears.

"Tastes good," he said.

"How'd you get into the house?"

"Floyd has a key in the garage."

Mike did not want to go home. He had an argument with his father, so I let him sleep in the second guest room. He wouldn't tell me what had happened, so I left it at that.

I asked if he would like to play a joke on several people at the same time. He agreed to bring all his pink flamingos over to the house. He didn't even question how I knew he had them.

The dogs are restless. They are wrestling at the foot of my bed, which jiggles the typewriter. I have called them to stop, but they start back up a moment later. Children!

§

Tonight, dinner at Annie's place was black like a cave until she struck a match and lit two white candles. The dancing flames twisted and turned. She toasted our friendship, sipping a terrible-tasting wine that I drank regardless. A Chardonnay? A Chardon-garbage.

When she toasted our friendship, I was worried I was in the friend column, which Dave Edwards warned me about last year.

"If you're not in her pants, you are her good friend and that means no touchdown. And once you are her special friend, you are screwed. You can never escape."

I don't think I am in the special friend category because the other night at the drive-in she let me play with her boobs. I'm hovering in the in-between place.

§

During dinner, Annie told me, "When I was a little girl, I wanted to be famous. I thought being a movie star would be the greatest thing in the world, so I always loved pretending I was Marilyn Monroe. I wanted to be Miss America, like every girl. But, when I was a sophomore in high school, my mom took me to the Miss Jamestown Pageant and I was cheering for Rae Larson, who was stunning. She lost. Well, she came in second in the evening gown, but she wasn't even in the five finalists. I knew right then it was fixed. She was the most beautiful of the contestants and she was as talented as can be. I'm not saying the girl who won wasn't deserving of it, but she couldn't carry Rae Larson's makeup bag. The other four finalists absolutely did not deserve to be a finalist ahead of her. After that, I never cared one way or the other. My mom still watches Miss America.

"My mom watches it, too. I never watch it," I said.

"I don't watch anymore, but when I was younger, my mom used to put lipstick on me and curl my hair. I'd stand in front of the mirror for hours pretending to be Miss America and being kissed by Cary Grant. I remember standing in front of the mirror dressed like a Go-Go dancer, listening to Elvis and just shaking my whole body and bouncing on the bed.

Annie and I played three games of *Scrabble* by candlelight, which in no way influenced my ability to lose. Annie clobbered me the first game but only won by three points in the second. The third game was another whipping. I wasn't happy about losing. I will seek a rematch.

"When was the first time you were ever kissed?" I asked as I played my word, kiss.

"That's not going to be enough to beat me," she laughed. "I was nine years old and it was a little boy up the street. He and his parents were from Brazil. His father was a math professor. I still remember his name, Paulo Macedo, but everyone called him Pauly. We used to play make-believe in my basement, and one day, I told him he would have to kiss me if he wanted to play. He took over an hour to make up his mind, but finally he said he would, if I didn't tell anyone."

Annie played her word, svelte.

"I told my mother. She was so funny. She asked me if I liked it. I told her I wasn't sure. She said I shouldn't kiss and tell. Girls that kiss and tell don't get kissed again. So, after that I didn't tell. He lived in Lakewood for only two years before they moved back to Brazil."

My next word was *valid*, which played off of her word. She immediately played *dybbuks*, which I made her use in a sentence. I didn't even know what it meant. She looked it up in the dictionary to prove it was real. After that, I had no chance. She is simply smarter than I am.

"Paulo and I always played together, but then we started writing plays, just little scenes where a boy and a girl fell in love, and by the end of the scene, they had to kiss. That was our excuse for kissing. Because it was in the play, we had to do it. I mean, that's what the writer and the director required of us. Before he moved, he said he'd write me, but he never did."

Annie kissed me tonight, and I kissed her. It was a wonderful evening.

Wednesday, July 25

It's a little after 7:00 p.m., and I am just now getting home from work. Roy and I have been playing chess since 1:30 p.m. He wanted to play the best of seven, with each game being thirty minutes for each side. I won the first two games, then he tied it up. I should have won game four, but I made a mistake. In the end, I won 4–3.

"Shouldn't I be working?" I asked during one game. "I mean, won't I get in trouble for goofing off?"

"Hey, Bobby Fischer, I'm concentrating. Let me concentrate. Considering I run this place, no. Just shut up and play."

§

Annie and Mike stopped by.

"You wanna go to the movies?" Mike asked. "We're gonna see *Scream, Blacula, Scream!*"

"It's playing at Dipson's Palace," Annie said.

I was exhausted from playing chess, but agreed, nonetheless. We went to the 9:30 show, but when we got there, the manager said, "All the movies have been canceled. The sprinklers accidentally went off this afternoon and we're still cleaning up water. All the seats are wet."

§

"I'm hungry," Mike said, as we walked around the block trying to figure out what to do next.

"Let's go to The White Front for a sandwich," Annie suggested.

"Is it open?" I asked.

"Probably not," she remembered.

"I'm a member of the Rod and Gun Club," Mike said. "Let's eat there."

We didn't believe him, so he showed us his membership card.

"My grandfather was a founding member."

When we were in the lobby, he showed us his grandfather's picture with all the other founding members.

After eating, Annie and I dropped Mike off at home then drove back to Dr. Laighles's house. We sat in the car with the top down and looked out through the windshield at the lake. There was a slight breeze coming off the water, which brought a chill to us, so we snuggled together with the heat on. The breeze lifted strands of Annie's hair, but I molded them back into place like a sculptor. Across the lake, the lights flickered, and when I looked up, the stars flickered, too. Annie's hair glowed in the moonlight, her soft lips were like rose petals, and her eyes were sapphires, filaments of fire.

She bought the new *Janis Joplin Greatest Hits* 8-Track and we listened to it. With the seats reclined back a tad bit, it was nice having Annie leaning into my body while the music played. I ran my fingers through her hair and massaged her temples and forehead. She closed her eyes and lay across the large front seat. I wanted to take off my tennis shoes, but I knew my sweaty feet would stink and that would gross her out.

"My favorite song is 'Me and Bobby McGee,'" I told her.

"I love that one, too," she replied.

"Not long ago, I read where Kris Kristofferson had been a helicopter pilot in the Army and completed Ranger School."

"No kidding," she replied.

"Yeah, I'm not sure if he was in Vietnam."

§

The dogs are in bed with me. Bess is lying alongside me and Harry is at my feet as I type this. I cannot move in any direction, or I'll disturb them. Bess's chest moves up and down, filling up her lungs in relaxing sighs. She is happy. I want to tickle her feet but won't. A cool breeze is ruffling the oak tree outside my open window, and it is lifting the curtains into the room.

It's very late and very quiet. It was a special night. We did not manage to do everything we wanted to do today but being together was wonderful. It's all I needed.

Thursday, July 26

Today was Roy's birthday. He's forty-four. That's more than twice my age. There was cake and soda in the office this afternoon, and funny gifts like a magnifying glass, and a pair of glasses with a big rubber nose attached. I bought him a subscription to *Chess Life* and a membership card to play tournaments where he can compete at his level.

He received a book, *Jonathan Livingston Seagull*, which I saw him reading later on in his office.

Before the end of the day, he made everyone in the office change their password.

I must discipline myself. I'm staying out much too late and drinking far too much. I was tired at work, which is not good. I don't know why I cannot control myself and behave. I tell myself and I write that I am going to live a better and more honorable life, yet the clock turns the day over and I seemingly have forgotten all that I request of myself.

Annie's sister, Lauren, called this evening. She's driving up tomorrow and is going to stop by the house. She asked me not to tell Annie she was in town. I promised, but that was weird. I wonder if she is trying to surprise Annie.

My plans for tonight: Nothing. I'm staying home, taking the dogs for a walk, eating healthy, and looking forward to an early bedtime.

Friday, July 27

I've been up since before yesterday.

I made a mistake last night around 8:00. I decided to read a novel from Dr. Laighles's bookshelf, and I chose *The Exorcist*, which scared the hell out of me. This may be the scariest thing I have ever read. On top of that, to relax I made a pot of coffee. Duh! I didn't even think about the caffeine. It kept me up all night. I didn't even get thirty minutes of sleep. Behind my eyelids, it's a yellow and blue electrical storm of activity. I just could not fall asleep.

So much for my proclaimed discipline. I was pretty useless at work today. Again! At one point, I fell asleep at my desk. I am absolutely worthless! If I were the boss, I'd fire anyone like me.

§

Lauren arrived at the house around 6:30 p.m., and when I opened the door, I saw in her eyes that something was wrong.

"I'm pregnant. You cannot tell Annie."

"I won't say a word."

"Promise?"

"Yeah, I promise."

"Will you drive me to Canada to get an abortion? There's a woman there."

"No way!" I told her.

"You're the only one who knows. I really need your help."

"Lauren, you don't need my help. You need to tell your mom, or at least, Annie."

"Absolutely not. I can never tell them. They think I'm a virgin, just like Annie."

"Why are you coming to me with this? You don't even know me. We met a few weeks ago for a few hours. How can you even trust me?"

"I know you. Annie's told me. She talks about you all the time. She said you're a nice guy, the kind of guy who's dependable and will do anything for his friends. I need you to drive me to St. Catherine's and drive me back. There's a woman who'll do it for a hundred and fifty bucks."

"Nice guys don't take girls to Canada for an abortion."

"All you have to do is drive me."

"I don't have any money."

"I've got the money. I just need you to drive me and let me stay here a few days."

"Right! Like I can hide your car and you from Annie, or worse, Mike. He knows everything that goes on around here. Heck, he's got twenty ways to get in the house."

"Park the car in the garage, and I'll stay upstairs until I leave. I won't even come down. All you have to do for the weekend is keep everyone out."

"How pregnant are you?"

"Pregnant, pregnant."

"You know what I mean."

"I'm twenty-one weeks, which means I'm very pregnant and I've got to have it now. I can no longer hide it. Just look at my boobs. They're huge."

"That's five months."

"I know that!"

"You don't look like you're pregnant, at least not that much."

"Well, I am. Annie asked me why I've gained so much weight and I told her it's because I'm eating so much junk food and not exercising. I'm a vegetarian and I never eat junk food. She didn't put it all together, but she's not stupid."

"Isn't there a clinic or hospital you can go to?"

"No one in New York or Pennsylvania will give me a legal abortion when I'm this far along. A friend of mine gave me the name of this woman in Canada. She doesn't care how far along I am."

"She's a doctor, isn't she?"

"I think so. She knows what she's doing and she won't tell anyone. I went to her about three years ago."

"Jesus Christ, this is your second abortion? What the hell! Didn't you learn any lesson the first time?"

"Look, yelling at me won't help."

"I'm sorry. I'm not trying to be upsetting. You're nothing like your sister."

"No, I'm not. Annie's perfect. She's so perfect, she's a saint."

"I don't want anything to do with having to bury this fetus in the woods."

"What the hell are you talking about? You don't have to bury the fetus. They take care of that. God, that's gross."

"Look, Lauren, I'm just the driver. I drive the car—that's all. I drive the car up, and I drive the car back. Understand?"

"Yes, but don't pass judgment on me. I'm not a bad person. I've been on the pill, you know. Shit happens. I'm not proud of it, but what can I do, have a baby? I'm not even finished with college."

"I'm not here to tell you what to do, but you need to get it together, finish school, and think about what you're doing."

"Thanks. I'll get on the straight and narrow as soon as we get back. Maybe after this is all finished, I'll come back up here and have sex with you, as payment for driving me."

"No way. You're so fertile, if your undies hit the floor, you'll get knocked up."

That made her laugh.

"I thought you were really nice."

"I am nice. I just got pregnant. Don't be such an asshole."

§

When we were sitting on the porch having a cup of tea, she asked, "Can I ask you another favor?"

"Yeah, but it depends."

"I don't like sleeping alone. Can I sleep in the bed with you? I promise nothing will happen. I just like being in the bed with someone."

"Fine, but you have to wear pajamas. You cannot sleep naked."

"How about my underwear and a t-shirt?"

"Fine. However, here's my secret that you cannot tell anyone. I've never slept in a bed with a woman before, and, well, there's the maxim, 'Boys wake up, up.'"

"You're a virgin?"

What could I say? I didn't want to lie to her, but I was embarrassed.

"Yes, and boys wake up, up."

"I know. I won't touch it."

"That's my fear, being in bed with a beautiful woman and having a massive hard-on, and she has no interest in me."

That made her laugh, too.

"I'm worried that if we're in bed and bumping and cuddling, I'm going to bump you, if you know what I mean. It isn't me trying to do anything," I assured her.

"That's my greatest fear, being in bed with a guy who has a massive boner, and he doesn't want to do it with me."

That made both of us laugh.

Lauren is pretty, but very pregnant, and knowing this now, I can tell.

"Let's make a deal. We can cuddle and be close while sleeping, and I might even feel your big boner poking me—that's okay. I'm not going to grab it and you're not going to pull my panties down. But, during the night, it's possible that we will hug and intertwine our bodies, simply because of being in the bed together. Just to let you know, it'll be okay if you cuddle into my back. You can even wrap your arms around me. My boobs are sore, but that doesn't mean you need to rub them."

When we went to bed, Lauren turned toward me and gave me a kiss goodnight on my cheek, then she turned around and scooted her back into my front. She grabbed my arm and swung it around her waist.

I tried to go to sleep but found it difficult.

It's currently 3:14 a.m. I am downstairs typing. Lauren is sleeping in the bed with me in the guest room even though there are other rooms. That sounds a lot more salacious than it is. Of course, I'm not there right this moment. I like having her in the bed because she's warm, but I keep touching her accidently because the bed is a twin, and when I do, I feel awkward because she is sound asleep. She likes holding on, which makes it difficult for me to turn over. Each time I bump her, or my hand brushes her butt or boobs, I feel as if I am doing something wrong.

I'm not an asshole. I just don't want the responsibility of this. Abortion has been legal since 1971, but I guess not for what Lauren needs. I have no idea if abortion is legal or not in Canada, and I'm not going to jail for Annie's sister. I'd go to jail for Annie, but not

Lauren. I went through this with Will Croon, and I do not want the burden of burying a fetus like before.

Saturday, July 28

Lauren and I are back from Canada. I didn't say anything to her on the way home. Not one word. She slept in the back of her Beetle. I pulled the back seat down, which allowed her to spread out with a pillow and a sheet. I played soft music for her, but the grumble of the VW's engine was directly underneath her head, so I don't know how she slept. On the way back, I took the back roads to steer clear of the toll booths and people. It took three and a half hours.

I helped her up the back steps and then upstairs. I parked her car in the third bay of the garage and covered it up with blankets. As I type, she's sleeping, and from time to time, I bring her a hot water bottle.

On the front page of *The Columbia Union* today was Mildred Wren and a picture of her front yard with a flock of pink flamingos. The headline read, "75 Flock to Front Yard; Owner Not Tickled Pink." Somehow, it's not as funny as it probably should be. Mildred Wren looked like a mosquito.

§

Mid-afternoon: I am sitting on the front porch, and it is so quiet I can hear the kids' screams and laughs echoing up from the lake and the nearby playground. I remember the cool, moist grass and flocks of other children jumping around, swinging, and running alongside the miniature merry-go-round when I was a child. Every day during the summer, my mother walked Kimberly and me to the playground. She talked with the other mothers and did crafts that the park commission had organized for that week.

At the end of the summer, there was always an arts and crafts show, and a winner was named. There was a contest for the parents, too (mainly mothers). My mother never won. Kimberly and I never won, either. We weren't very good at crafts. Mom liked books. She read a part of a book to us every night. Sometimes our choices for books would last several weeks before we'd finish one, occasionally a month. She always read poetry on Sunday. Her favorite was Theodore Roethke's "Elegy for Jane."

One night she read us that poem and began crying before she could finish it. In the seventh grade (this was in Atlanta), I memorized "Elegy for Jane" for a recital that our language club did for the parents, the only ones who could appreciate our efforts.

"Hey, Yankee," Will said, "You read the best even if your poem didn't rhyme."

I keep checking on Lauren in her deep sleep, about every fifteen to twenty minutes. The woman who performed the abortion gave her some pain pills. I do not like this business at all, but I don't want her to be in pain, either. She is completely out. I have been rubbing her forehead with a wet washcloth. She is a nice girl.

Sunday, July 29

There was a story today in *The New York Times* about a woman who lived in eight different states in the last twenty years, and each time she moved, she had her mother's body exhumed and buried wherever she went. There isn't a law against the number of times you can have a body moved, but it's a major undertaking to transport it across state lines. Wouldn't it be less expensive to simply visit her grave a few times per year?

Monday, July 30

Roy told me today about Galileo, a spacecraft that's going to be launched in 1977 with the express purpose of going to Jupiter. It's supposed to get there in the 1990s, probably 1995 or 1996. That's over twenty years from now, but people are making plans. I cannot imagine what I'll be doing in 1995. Maybe Ashley and I will be back together.

When I came home at lunch to check on Lauren, she was gone. On the kitchen counter, there was a note.

"Keep a secret. Thanks. I'll call soon. Love Ya, L."

That's more than a secret!

§

Tonight, Karen came over. We sat in the dark, listening to an old-timey mystery radio show. I kissed her in the hall before she left to go home. After kissing Annie, it's easy to kiss a younger girl. Nothing scares me now.

Tuesday, July 31

Annie called me at work to say hi. She was in the library all weekend doing research for a paper she wants to write for some professor next semester. That worked out well for Lauren.

§

Mike came over and wanted to know what I was typing, but I would not let him see. I showed him the book I bought today instead, *The Pigman* by Paul Zindel. The cover looks good.

I handed him my baseball list, which he took into the pinball room and studied. He pulled his own list from his pocket. After marking up his list and making the comparisons, he said, "I'm ready to play ball. You know, on paper, there is no way your team can beat my team."

"True, but like the game itself, nothing on paper matters. You have to play the game."

Robert's More Awesome Lineup than Mike's

1st Base	Harmon Killebrew
2nd Base	Davey Johnson
3rd Base	Tony Perez
Shortstop	Bert Campaneris
Catcher	Manny Sanguillen
Leftfield	Roy White
Centerfield	Curt Flood
Rightfield	Tommy Agee
Starting Pitchers	Blue Moon Odom
	Denny McClain
	Phil Niekro
	Gaylord Perry

Dock Ellis

Jim Kaat

Claude Osteen

Luis Tiant

Vida Blue

Sam McDowell

Sparky Lyle

Relief Pitchers   Rich Gossage

Steve Blass

Don Sutton

Wilbur Wood

Rollie Fingers

Utility Players   Willie McCovey

Rusty Staub

Frank Howard

Dusty Baker

Darrell Evans

"Best of seven, just like in the World Series," I said.

It took two hours, but I defeated Mike's team, 4—2.

"My starting pitchers will be better tomorrow," he proclaimed.

§

While playing W.S. pinball, Mike gave me an idea. I'm going to have
a party and cook hot dogs and corn on the cob over an open fire in

the backyard, and everyone can eat all of the veggies I grew in my garden. I'll invite Roy and his family, Annie, Mike, and his father. Everyone. We can have picnic tables set up in the backyard with all the food and drinks on them. Dr. Laighles already has a brick pit for cooking. At night, we'll roast marshmallows.

Wednesday, August 1

Roy said he'd bring the beer, and when I called Annie, we decided on the weekend of the 18th and 19th, when the garden is ripe. Not all of the vegetables will be ready to pick, but we'll eat what we can.

Thursday, August 2

I did not write this yesterday, but when I was sitting on the back step watching Harry and Bess running around in their pen in the backyard, I could have sworn I saw Kimberly step out from behind the garage. She was wearing a white church dress. When I looked back, she was not there. I swear I saw her, which made me shiver. I got scared and went inside the house.

I've heard about things like this happening. That is to say, occasions when people see someone who is dead watching over them. At work, I've read a series of stories about this exact occurrence.

There was a man in his thirties from Arizona who had an experience and was interviewed by a sci-fi magazine out of California.

"When I was twelve, I was swimming in my grandmother's pool in Farmers Branch, Texas, and out beyond the red wooden fence I saw my grandmother looking into the backyard at me and my cousins, her grandchildren. I was the only one who saw her. And then she was gone, as if she had needed only a moment to see her grandchildren safe and at home."

I did not go into the garage or walk around it. I was scared I might actually see Kimberly again. Part of me wants to see her. The other part of me is a coward.

§

Yesterday, Roy said that my vegetables won't be ready for the picnic.

"There's a reason the harvest is in the fall. It takes the summer for everything to grow. They won't be ready until September."

I didn't know this, so I guess I'll be buying everything for the party from the Quality Market.

§

God has been disturbed and He is cleaning out his freezer with a torrential hailstorm. A gray sheet of rain is smashing the sidewalk with marble-sized hail. I'm inside, looking out the porch window while I type. The storm was predicted by the National Weather Bureau and arrived like a brush fire across a prairie. It's hitting everything on this side of Lake Erie.

Mike showed up at the house soaking wet. He got caught in the rain while riding his bicycle. I didn't have any clothes that would fit him, so I gave him Dr. Laighles's bathrobe to wear while his clothes were in the dryer. At one point, the lights flickered on and off like a strobe, then the electricity went off.

It's still off, which is why I am next to the window. It's not so dark outside that I cannot type.

§

I found a large candle in the kitchen. Mike and I sat playing checkers for a while. He told me he was frightened.

I started writing a letter to Ashley, but I have not finished it. I stuck it in my shoebox with her letters.

Annie called to see if we lost our power, too. On her end of the line, she sat in darkness with only birthday candles to light. Each lasted only a few minutes before sputtering out. We were like the two people on the Grecian Urn, unable to touch, communicating by voice and around a curve. Maybe we would see each other's fingers reaching out, but we'd have only our voices and intellect to fall in love with.

How much does a Grecian Urn? About minimum wage. That was Dr. Leibrandt's joke from English class.

Friday, August 3

Mike and I are going camping again. I asked Annie to come along. When I mentioned it to Roy, he casually said that he and Louise are taking their daughters to a doll show in Toronto tomorrow morning. As a result, I will not ask Karen.

§

I skipped out of work a little early today. Currently, it's 4:30 p.m., and Mike will be over soon. I have everything ready and I'm just waiting. Mike owns a *Pocket Instamatic 60* and is bringing it to take pictures.

Saturday, August 4

It is 5:17 a.m. and dark outside. I am the only one up and I have the fire burning—just large enough to cast heat toward me and keep the mosquitoes away. I am writing on a yellow tablet, scratching out my thoughts. I hear a squirrel in the trees.

6:30 and the crickets call for love as the sun begins to rise far in the distance. Mike is still sound asleep, snoring like some brand of animal. Annie is also sleeping, curled up in our sleeping bag. I have been up for more than two hours. When I first awoke, I lay next to her and listened to her sleep. She's warm and smells nice. I smelled her hair several times. She and I shared a sleeping bag in one tent because Mike forgot to bring an extra one. It was tight and a little uncomfortable, until we settled our arms and faces.

Mike acted funny when he found out we only had two sleeping bags. He insisted Annie use his.

"Bob and I can share in my tent."

Harry and Bess slept with Mike.

While getting comfortable, Annie said it was okay if, to do this, we intertwined our limbs. It was a necessity, and as difficult as it was, I endured this torture. I did not say a word about my intertwining experiences with Lauren.

§

The smell of coffee has Annie stepping out of the tent. She's in her underwear and a t-shirt.

"What are you doing?" she asks.

"I'm writing."

"What?"

"I have an idea for a novel, but I can't get beyond the characters' names and the big picture of the plot. I don't know how to get started."

Annie thinks I am writing a novel, but I'm watching her bend toward the fire, cautious as she pours a cup of coffee.

"Good morning," she says, kissing me on the cheek, and I turn my pages away from her. She is sitting down next to me in the lawn chair, and I am helping to wrap her up in the other blanket. I turn my pages even further away so she can't see what I'm writing. Annie is respectful and allows me some privacy. The dew on her feet reflects the morning sun. Bits of grass lie across her toes.

Annie is holding her cup with both hands, sipping it as the steam rises up around her face then disappears.

"What are their names?"

"Isabella and Vincenzo."

"Isabella is a beautiful name. If I ever have a daughter, I might name her Isabella."

§

I am back. What a declaration! Shouldn't this be everyone's motto?

I had to stop writing for a spell when Mike woke. Annie convinced him not to eat s'mores for breakfast.

§

Down at the creek, Mike is standing knee-deep in the water, trying to catch fish with his hands. This is in real time.

Earlier, before they were awake, I read up to page eighty-seven in *All the King's Men*. Jack Burden and I are both narrators. He is probably a better man than I am. I gawked at Annie in her underwear this morning. In my defense, no mortal can resist.

I have Mike's camera and periodically take pictures of him and Annie. I have one of him falling forward into the water when he grabbed for a fish and Harry jumped on him. Annie is sunning herself in the lawn chair at the moment, reading *The Stepford Wives*. I've taken a few pictures of her doing nothing but lying in a chair.

§

It's later in the afternoon. We have just returned from a walk along the creek and in the woods. We looked for flat rocks for Annie's newest passion, flat rock collecting. We walked the entire length of the creek from where it comes out of the northern end of the woods, where the thickets are a massive collection of interwoven twine, to the southwest end, where the creek drops down an eight-foot falls and cascades over the elephant rocks to a round pool at the bottom. It sounds huge, but it isn't. It's like minnow-sized Niagara, something small enough to build in your backyard.

The pool of water at the bottom of the waterfall is four feet deep and a great place for swimming. The dogs jumped in before we had made our way down the grassy hill, which has a small but overgrown path. Annie and I swam, but the water was chilly. Under the waterfall, it was cold.

§

I have dried off and am sitting in Annie's chair. The creek is about twenty feet from our campsite. As quickly as it opens wide, it closes, narrowing its width to about three feet. It's like a snake swollen with a rat.

Mike and I carried the rocks for Annie, and she carried milkweed and cattails that she snipped with Mike's pocketknife. I took a picture of them standing on the edge of the bank, as well as a few pictures of Harry and Bess soaking wet and shaking off the water.

§

Night has fallen and the wind is full. Branches slap. The fire crackles with life as the wood burns into charred embers. Annie and Mike have gone to bed. I am left to lament perpetual motion. Annie went to bed after asking me if I would turn in for the evening, but I wouldn't. I am not certain if I need to watch the fire or if I need to write. Regardless, here I am, keeping watch over all things important in the world.

Tonight, we sat around the fire, on a blanket, and sang songs. We played a game similar to "Name That Tune" where one person sings the lyric, but not the chorus, and the others have to guess the title of the song. That was fun. I tried singing a Glen Campbell song, and even though I messed up the words, Annie got it.

Sunday, August 5

My mood has changed. I am angry with myself at this moment. The day almost passed without my remembrance of the date. Kimberly died on this date eleven years ago. My parents, I know, are in pain. The past does not forgive.

§

I was the last one up this morning. Annie finally woke me. She and Mike cooked breakfast. Mike was running with the dogs in the field while Annie had spread Mike's crumpled sleeping bag in the lawn chair where she was comfortably relaxed. I was in my underwear and made her turn away while I put my pants on.

§

Annie has twisted her ankle on a divot in the ground, and though it didn't swell up too much, I tended to it. I unlaced her tennis shoe and massaged her foot and calf for a long time, telling her it would help ease the pain. I cut my socks into strips and dipped them in the cool creek water, then wrapped her ankle with them. As the socks dried, they acted like a coolant. I dipped them in the creek and changed them every thirty minutes and it seemed to help. I wonder if I could fool her into believing that rubbing her breasts will ease the pain in her ankle?

Will Croon might have approved of Annie coming along on this adventure. He was right: girls don't like to pee in the woods.

§

I have tried to stay away from the house today, but I know I must return. Nothing else has caused so much pain in my life and the lives of my parents. A day does not pass that I don't think of Kimberly. I've walked in on my parents sitting together, and at times, alone, and I could tell they were crying.

The angst and loneliness I have endured follows me with each step I take. Had I been there with Kimberly, maybe she wouldn't have fallen out of the treehouse. If I hadn't gone back in the house for my sneakers, things would be different. What if I had still been there when she leaned over to pull up the rope and the basket with her books in it?

It was an accident. No one was to blame. Yet, I blame myself each day. My mother blames herself for relaxing in the other room with a book and not supervising us more closely, and my father blames himself for having the treehouse built. He blames himself because he's a man and a man protects all that he loves with all that he has in his body and mind.

§

11:00 p.m.

Obviously, I'm home and typing my written notes. Karen has just left. She wanted me to show her the house again, so I did. She talked about her jaunt to Toronto and what they did there. She also talked about all her favorite rock stars, as well as a new band I haven't heard of, KISS. All caps, she told me.

"They don't have an album, yet, but I saw them at a club back in May in Palisades. That's not far from New York City. Me and Jenny used our fake IDs to get in. We told her mom we were going to the movies but went to the show instead."

"Did you drive all the way from here?"

"No, me and Jenny drove down with her mom to her grandmother's house for a few days."

Karen also likes Elton John, Paul McCartney, Vicki Lawrence, Sweet, Cher (but not Sonny), Deep Purple, Seals & Crofts, Carly Simon, Roberta Flack, Chicago, and a whole lot more. It was a long list, and I cannot remember all of them. She said if she doesn't go to Syracuse or Sarah Lawrence, she wants to move to Chicago and go to school there.

When we got to my bedroom, she wandered in to see what it looked like.

"It's just a guest room. None of this stuff is mine."

"I heard that the kid who used to live here died."

She bounced on my bed—not like jumping up and down, just bounced her butt on it.

I coaxed her through the rest of the house and downstairs to the kitchen, where I made some spiced tea, and she shuffled a deck of cards. She knew how to play Casino, so we played a few games.

"Was that picture of Annie, the one on the dresser?"

"Oh, yeah. No one's supposed to see that."

"I won't tell."

"She doesn't know I have it. I stole it from her."

"Really? That's so cool."

"It's not trashy."

"I didn't think it was. I mean, I'd do that too if I was as pretty as Annie. Nudity doesn't bother me at all. When no one's home, I like to walk around naked. Once, Jenny and I painted our faces like Flower Children then ran around her house naked. I want to do that in Allen Park, down by the bandstand."

Monday, August 6

Roy was in a pissy mood all day. Both Brooke and I stayed clear of him and went to lunch together at Lisciandro's.

"Charles, that's my boyfriend, we're thinking about selling everything and moving to Colorado to work at a resort. Just check out of the business world. He can tend bar, and I can be the cart girl at the golf course. We don't have kids, so there's nothing holding us back. Plus, I want a Jeep and a cowboy hat and Charles loves John Denver."

"Try this blackberry pie," I told Brooke.

"My god, that's delicious."

"Isn't it?"

I watched Johnny Carson tonight. John Davidson was the host, and Sally Struthers was a guest, but she was so damn stupid that it lowered my I.Q. David Frye, who I had never heard of, redeemed my intellect. He was so funny.

Tuesday, August 7

Annie came over and stayed late. We sat on the carpet and leaned against the sofa as we watched Johnny Carson. Fernando Lamas was the big name, and was good, but Diana Rigg was as sexy as ever. Dorothy Uhnak is a writer, but I had never heard of her before.

I made popcorn and when I handed the bowl to Annie, she jumped on me and tickled my ribs. She pinned me and I became embarrassed when she lay spread-eagled over me with her knees holding down my arms.

"You didn't think I was this strong, did you?" she asked. "I've had to fight off stronger guys than you."

Wednesday, August 8

"Art is I; science is we," so said Claude Bernard sometime between 1813 and 1878. I just read this in an almanac.

At lunch, I met Annie at the park and sat on a bench. Afterwards, we walked to the Lakewood Quality Market for ice cream sandwiches. Mike was working in the parking lot, carrying groceries out to a woman's car. He tried saying hello to us while loading the groceries into the woman's Ford Galaxie.

As we were looking for ice cream, he found us in the store.

"That lady only gave me fifteen cents. That's not worth pushing the air out of her way."

This didn't sound like Mike, but more like something the other kids might say.

§

Tonight, Annie dragged me to a poetry reading at Jamestown Community College, which is the first community college in the country. I only went because she asked. I would not do this for any other woman—not a shot in hell. However, I actually had a good time. Annie and I sat with a woman named Marlene, who was older and, years ago, was Annie's fourth grade teacher. Annie hadn't seen her in more than ten years. Marlene was there because the poet, Stephen Corey, was her student many years ago, sometime in the late '50s, I think.

"I'm sitting way back here," Marlene said, "because I don't want Stevie to see me. I don't want him getting nervous. I'm nervous for him. He was always one of my best students, and now look at him, he's a poet, too."

This was a first for me, and I enjoyed some of what this guy had to say. At one point, I grabbed a napkin and wrote down a few lines that were particularly poignant. He read a poem that worried me, "For My First Lover and Her Mother." I think I understood it, which is what was unnerving. It was about going to the hospital with his lover to visit her mother who is dying of cancer.

Even though Annie and I are not lovers, I am in love with her, and sort of think I could love her for the rest of my life. I imagined myself and Annie in a similar situation like the poem. I understand that there would be so much pain for her if she had to visit her mother in the hospital. I would never want that for her. I remember one line from this poem, "Growing undoes what we are." Somehow, that also made me sad because maybe we grow up and stop being kids, or fun, or curious. It made me want to hold Annie and tell her that I will always be here for her.

I wonder if the lover he talked about is his wife now.

I wrote down on my napkin, as best I could remember, a phrase from a few of his poems, but I only remembered one other title:

> You thought it was breeze through the window—it was her hair grazing your face.

> Once again I am the poet of emptiness

> Ropes can pull us to places different from those we have known

> From "Divorce"—I don't know how to leave, which woman to clutch as I turn, which wrong choice to make once more.

I don't know how to write poetry, but I always enjoyed when my mother read it to me and Kimberly. I enjoyed this guy's stuff, and he was somewhat funny.

There was another poet who read, a guy from some town near Chicago. I cracked a joke to Annie about his black turtleneck and beatnik mustache and goatee. She laughed but then told me to be quiet.

"Be serious."

"I am serious. I'm serious that he really loves his car way too much. All his poems are about cars and telephones. I don't get what he's all about. Do you?"

"No, but we're here for the experience."

Well, here's my opinion: Mr. Goatee-wearing beatnik was too full of himself. I swear, the greatest admiration came from his own love of himself. This Corey guy was pretty good. He even dedicated a poem to his wife, who I think was sitting in the front row. That was nice of him, and it made me think I could dedicate a painting to Annie. I liked Marlene, too. She was super nice, and for being older, she was beautiful.

This night reminded me of a movie where everyone at the art gallery is hip and then ends up drinking gallons of wine, talking about intellectual ideas from Proust and Sartre to Joseph Campbell, and then everyone sleeps with someone they didn't know before they arrived, or even after they left. None of that happened, of course.

Before heading home, Annie and I stopped for ice cream cones at the Tastee Freeze on Foote Avenue. She had strawberry. I had a vanilla dip. I'm not sure what everyone else did after the poetry reading, but I kissed Annie. On the way home, she had eaten a cherry flavored Jolly Rancher then she kissed me at her front door. Her lips and tongue tasted like cherry. Quite incredible.

Thursday, August 9

Roy invited everyone in the office to dinner tonight at Caprino's Pizza Palace on Fairmont Avenue for pizza. I sat next to Brooke, whose perfume smelled wonderful. Charles joined us, and he's a lot older than she is. He works at the library as a research assistant but he's also a computer programmer.

When I got home, I took the dogs for a run, then I painted until midnight: two watercolors and one acrylic painting on a very small canvas. I went to bed smelly. I forgot to shower after my run. Yuck! No woman would ever want to sleep in these sheets.

Friday, August 10

Next Sunday is the day we've decided to host the backyard picnic.

Annie made a list. I'm in charge of the corn on the cob, the other vegetables, and the firewood for the grill. Roy is bringing the beer. Mike said he and his father will bring the soda and iced tea. Annie's buying the hot dogs and buns. We'll have to ask a few people to bring hamburger meat and buns.

"I want to make the dessert, too. We can roast apples," Mike stated while playing pinball.

With the money from selling my motorcycle, the cash from Dr. Laighles, my secret $50 emergency money, and with what I am making from working for Roy at Chautauqua Indoor Advertising ($935), I have $1,362.52. I have spent some money, but I'm being frugal. I have it all in cash in a Mason jar. I need to deposit it. Of course, this does not take into account the financial mess I made with the Corvette and my tuition. I will work it all out somehow.

I would like to take Annie away for a weekend. I don't know where we would go or how much it would cost.

Maybe I can keep working for Roy. Or, get a better job doing something else, just so long as I'm near Annie. A smart, strong woman like her expects a lot from the guy in her life, which is fine with me.

Saturday, August 11

The corn in the garden is about as tall as Mike, and when the wind blows, the golden tassels snap back and forth, whistling through the stalks. We planted Early Sweet Corn but for some reason, the corn is stunted, no bigger than my thumb.

"When does corn really grow?" I asked Roy.

"I'm no farmer, but usually it's not big enough to eat until September or October. My grandfather always had a garden, and we ate a lot of corn in the fall."

For two dollars, I bought a beat-up copper tub at Heldeman Brothers' Salvage Store to boil the corn in over the open fire. I'll buy corn for the picnic at the grocery store.

I drove to Annie's apartment to pick up the flat rocks we collected when camping, to line the pit with them to absorb the heat and keep the fire hotter.

Mike asked if he could bring someone to the party.

"I'm gonna bring a girl."

"Heck yeah, man! You can bring anyone you want. You don't have to ask me for permission," I said.

"I asked because you have Annie, and she's beautiful. My girl's okay."

I guess Annie is my girl. I hadn't thought about her like that yet, but we are always together and we kiss a lot. I want her to be my girl. I wonder if I'm her guy?

Sunday, August 12

Karen rode her bicycle over to the house tonight to see about helping with the picnic. We played Crazy Eights at the kitchen table, and she kept bumping into me accidentally on purpose, kicking my foot under the table. Whatever that means.

Monday, August 13

It feels like Christmas with all the excitement surrounding the picnic. It started out small, but now there are a lot of people I don't know who are showing up. Roy asked Dean Stanton and his wife to the party. He's the president of the college. I've never met him before.

"He and Sally are good friends of Louise's, plus they live next door to us."

I feel as if everything is out of my control. All I wanted was to have a few friends over for a cookout. The list is more than thirty people.

§

I did not read anything at work today, but instead, Roy and I moved old equipment from the second and third floor to the basement. We did that all day and now I am too tired to eat dinner.

Let the record be straight—I did most of the heavy lifting. Roy didn't do squat except boss me around and tell me where to put stuff. He helped some, but I did the bulk of the lifting.

Tuesday, August 14

Annie came over this evening to talk about the picnic. We played *Risk*, then watched Johnny Carson. James Garner and Roger Miller were good. Bret Maverick is one of my favorite TV characters.

"Have you ever kissed a married man?" I asked her.

"I plead the Fifth. I don't think I should answer that."

Annie was quiet for several minutes with an afghan wrapped over her bare legs, though it was warm this evening.

She said the ceiling fan was chilling her.

"Yes," she slowly said.

"Yes, what?" I asked.

"Yes, I have kissed a married man."

"I kind of figured you might have."

"Thank you. Oddly, it's almost as if it never happened. I rarely think about it. Of course, no one ever asks."

Wednesday, August 15

School starts back on September 14. I received a postcard from Dr. Laighles and Emily. They're in Dublin. They'll be back in the states on September 1st. I still have not received her care package.

Mike came over, and I showed him the card.

"I got one the other day. Did Steven go with them?" he asked.

I did not answer.

We played some solitaire, and he went up against the computer in chess for a few hours while I read my books for work.

The other day, Annie told me that Mike can read and write a little bit but that it takes him hours.

"All that happened after the accident," she said. "He cannot add or subtract so he is terrible with money. He knows what change and dollars look like, but he can't make change very well."

Thursday, August 16

At work:

"The mayor is a good friend of Dean Stanton. He's coming. Sheriff

Milner's wife, Shauna, is bringing the potato salad. His children are coming, too."

Each guest is bringing one dish. Potluck. Heck if I can keep this stuff straight.

Annie has the list. Each one is bringing a dish of their choice, plates, or other things. I'm nervous about this whole damn orchestra. The whole situation has seriously gotten out of hand.

"Don't worry about it," Annie said. "What can go wrong? People show up, they bring food and drinks. Everyone will pitch in to help, and we'll all have a good time. No one expects you to do everything. It'll all work out."

§

Annie graduated college with a degree in English and a minor in Psychology.

"I almost took a job as a waitress because it paid more than anything else. I didn't have too many choices. I took a year off and worked for an actuarial company in Ithaca. I worked in their library. They were very nice people to work for, and I liked everyone, but I knew it wasn't right for me. My professor, Dr. Maffett, suggested I get a master's degree or go to law school. I thought about being a lawyer once but gravitated toward being a psychologist."

§

Annie and I watched Johnny Carson tonight. She ate an entire bowl of walnuts. Rich Little was funny. He did an impersonation of President Nixon.

"The house is really a mess. You'd better clean this place before Floyd and Emily come home," she said.

She and I have slept in the same bed four times now, not counting the sleeping bag on the campout. We haven't done anything.

"We can sleep and cuddle," she said, "but no hanky-panky."

We kiss a lot. Before we fall asleep, Annie lets me play with her breasts. I massage them for her and that helps her fall asleep.

Friday, August 17

What fatalism has surrounded my life? Do I attract Machiavellian characters into a maelstrom of trouble?

The evidence in my corner says yes. I have tried to look within myself for guidance, to choose the right path and eschew trouble as much as possible, but once again a devilish villain has found me. Caroline DeBauché is back in town. That snake. Medusa.

§

At lunchtime, I grabbed a few items at Loblaw's grocery store and filled up the gas tank at the Minute Man. When I was about to pull the truck onto Fairmont Avenue, Caroline and her brother, Allen, pulled their car up beside Dr. Laighles's truck. I locked my doors. Allen walked like an armored tank up to the car and tugged on the door. I cracked the window enough to put a finger through.

"That's him," Caroline said, standing outside their car.

"Get out of the car and I'll knock your head off," he said.

"You'll have to offer more incentive than that."

He drew his arm back and punched his fist into the hard metal of the truck. What an idiot.

"It's me you want to hurt, not the truck," I said as he jumped around in a circle, clutching his hurt hand.

"I'll find you." he said. He shoved his hand under his arm pit. "I know where you live."

"Come on over," I yelled. "I've got a couple of guard dogs who'd love to chew you up."

He looked at Caroline, who nodded her head to confirm my rebuttal. I knew Harry and Bess would do nothing more than bark, howl, and wag their tails.

"Doesn't matter. I'll find you somewhere, and when I do, you'll wish to God you never raped my sister."

"Hey, I never touched her."

"She said you raped her."

"I never touched her."

"You're as good as dead."

"If I raped her, then why doesn't she call the police?"

"We take care of our own," he yelled, pulling at the door handle with his unhurt hand. "When I catch you, I'm gonna kill you."

"I never touched your sister."

"Get out and fight."

"Educated men don't fight, haven't you heard?" I yelled back. "They pay someone to fight for them."

"You're bogus, man."

I squealed the tires away from them, turned around, and made a U-turn in the middle of the road. I drove around the lake to settle my nerves.

I'm tired of people believing they can control the world. Caroline and her brother don't belong here. This is my world.

§

After work, Roy and I loaded six picnic tables from the Rod and Gun Club, where he is a member, and we arranged them in the backyard. The corn from the garden is still very puny and wormy (a major disappointment), so we made a run to the Super Duper. The entire time, I was on the lookout for the death squad. I wasn't too scared with Roy around, but I didn't need an embarrassing situation.

We bought fifty ears of corn but couldn't put all of it in the copper boiler, so we washed out Harry and Bess's big aluminum bathtub and soaked the corn in saltwater over night. I washed it out twice just to make certain it was clean.

"Don't mention to anyone that this is the dog's bathtub," Roy said.

"Yeah, no one will eat the corn if they know."

§

I did not mention to Roy the situation with the DeBauché clan.

It's late and I keep thinking about what trouble may lie ahead with Caroline.

Annie and Mike have been here all day and are too tired to make the trek home, so they're spending the night. Mike is already in bed.

Annie has fallen asleep on the couch. I will wake her in a few minutes and put her to bed. Roy went home hours ago. I cannot enjoy this time of my life for what is beyond the walls of the house. I double-checked the locks and the windows before going to bed.

Saturday, August 18

I woke to screams this morning.

I ran out of my bedroom and down the hall to find Annie wrapped in a towel in the bathroom. Mike was leaning against the wall. He walked in on her by accident while she was in the shower.

§

"Hey man, you're winning," I said, pointing to the chess game.

Mike didn't say a word. He sat at the kitchen table and stared at the chessboard. The dogs were out in their pen, wrestling and kicking up pebbles. Bess started barking, which meant Harry had jumped on top of the doghouse and wouldn't come down. She can't jump as high as he can. He jumps up there and walks around until she turns her back, then he leaps down and chases her, and jumps up on the doghouse again.

"I should have knocked on the door," Mike said.

"It's okay. You couldn't have known," I said sipping my coffee.

"Are you mad at me?"

"No. I'm not mad. It's no big deal."

"Is Annie mad?" he asked.

"A little embarrassed, but she's not mad."

"She's beautiful, isn't she?" he asked.

"Yeah," I agreed.

"My girl's all right, too" he said.

"When do I get to meet this mystery woman?" I asked.

"Tomorrow. Her name's Gloria. Just like the song," he said. "G-L-O-R-I-A."

§

Annie helped Mike peel a half bushel of apples this morning. They cut the core out of the center of each apple and sprinkled cinnamon in the middle with a dab of butter and a large piece of freshly cut pineapple. Each apple was wrapped in tin foil.

"All we do now is place them on the hot coals. They'll cook up nice and juicy, sweet and hot," Annie said.

"Not now," Mike said.

"Right. We'll cook them later on," she replied.

"Bob, don't let Annie cook the apples now," Mike called out.

Annie cut up several stalks of celery and spread peanut butter and Philadelphia Cream Cheese on them. I tried snitching some food but Annie grabbed a big wooden spoon off the kitchen counter and chased me around the house, smacking me in the butt until I promised to stop.

We listened to Jim Roselle on WJTN's "Times of Your Life."

"My dad went to college with him at St. Lawrence," Annie told us.

I helped slice squash, cucumbers, zucchini, and carrots. I had never eaten raw squash. Planting squash was Mike's idea. It's not bad, especially with French Onion Dip.

Sunday, August 19

It's 1:30 p.m. I've been reading the newspaper to keep my mind off the picnic and Caroline. People will be here in 30 minutes or a half an hour, whichever is fastest. Louise and Annie are already here, in the backyard, setting the tables.

Hank Aaron passed Stan Musial yesterday for extra bases with 1,378. Musial is my dad's favorite player. Hank is mine.

Monday, August 20 (My BIRTHDAY, as well as Kimberly's)

I AM IN THE HOSPITAL.

WCA Hospital to be exact. Since yesterday. I have a headache and my left arm is broken. My head feels like it is encapsulated in a hollow drum, and someone is pounding on it with a golf club. People become cranky in the hospital, and I am no different. I'm not a terrible patient—I just want to be left alone. I also want some reasonable clothes. I'm nice to everyone, respectful, but I don't like being in a hospital gown with my butt hanging out. The cloth is like onion paper. Earlier, the nurse gave me some Tylenol for my headache, which helps.

I'm being kept for observation until later this afternoon. It is 10:10 a.m. I have a concussion.

I have purloined a pad of paper and a pencil from the nurse, who has been very nice. I am writing with my right hand, and it is nearly illegible. I'll type this in later when I am home. I write for a little while then sleep. Wake up, write, back to sleep.

§

The picnic was a success, at least until a certain point. Mike counted forty-two people. He, Gloria, and Becky walked around with a notepad for everyone to write down their name, just like at a family reunion. They were the official record keepers. Several members of the fire department stopped by. Gloria, Mike's date, was a cute redheaded girl who lives down the street from him.

Annie made a cassette tape of Credence Clearwater Revival, Glen Campbell, The Beatles, Patsy Cline, Dionne Warwick, Elvis Presley, Ray Charles, The Bee Gees, The Supremes, John Denver, and The Beach Boys. I wrapped the ears of corn in aluminum foil and cooked them in the hot coals, turning them over every few minutes. Roy was in charge of cooking hamburgers and hot dogs. Louise took charge of the games— badminton, croquet, and Jarts.

§

My left arm is in a cast from just under my armpit to my wrist and around my thumb. I can write with my left hand, but my tendency is to move my entire arm because of the cast. Doing that hurts considerably. When I write normally, with just my fingers, the pain is less so.

Around seven o'clock, after everyone had eaten, Jack Milner and I stacked six logs in the fire pit. It was a glorious fire dancing several feet high and teetered on the brink of getting away from the fire master, which, of course, was Jack.

"Once, when I was a kid, we built a fire at the Long Point Beach—

this was before there were any rules around this place—we had wood piled ten-feet high. When we lit it, the flames rose twenty-five to thirty feet in the air and illuminated the other side of the lake."

"You can't do that nowadays," I replied.

"You certainly cannot. I'll have to arrest someone. This will be nice and roaring for roasting marshmallows," Jack said.

"That's the one thing I forgot to buy. Let me run over to the Super Duper," I volunteered.

"I'll go with," Karen said.

As she and I walked out of the Super Duper with marshmallows and a few other items, the oily smell of black asphalt rose up, and there in the parking lot was Caroline, her brother, and some other guy. They were sitting on the hood of a Dodge Duster.

"That's the guy," Caroline said, pointing to me, holding a brown sack.

"Get in the truck and lock the doors," I told Karen.

She ran to the truck.

"What do you want?" I asked.

"I'm going to teach you a lesson. You raped my sister," Allen DeBauché said. "If you can walk away after we're finished, you'll be lucky."

"I didn't touch your sister."

"She said you did."

"Listen, I don't have time to play your game. You got a problem, spit it out, or go home," I said, as he stepped closer.

Allen was bigger than me by at least thirty or forty pounds and five inches. Plus, he was muscular. I knew there was going to be a fight. I also knew I wouldn't get more than two shots at him.

The last fight I was in was in the eighth grade with Will Croon, when we were playing basketball and he purposefully hit me in the face, twice, with the ball. I went after him. I lost, but he didn't do that again.

Before Allen swung at me, I threw the bag of marshmallows at him, then kicked him on the side of the knee, buckling his leg. He went down, bending over to grab his knee. I folded my hands together in a tight ball and uppercut him in the jaw, which sent him flying backwards against the side of his car. He rolled off and hit the ground hard, and as I turned to run to the truck, like a skittish gazelle running from the lions (I'm not afraid to admit), the other guy came at me with a baseball bat.

He hit me in the thigh, which slammed me to the ground. Karen jumped out of the car, screaming. He pushed her away against the truck. Allen got up and kicked me in the ribs several times. As I curled up into the fetal position, I saw the long fluorescent tubes from underneath the store front canopy. Bugs flew like dusty angels around the strobes of light between the two men as they spun like dizzy children with airplane propeller arms. Then, the pain hit. And then there wasn't any.

That's all I remember.

§

The hospital restricted my visitors until after twelve o'clock, because I keep falling asleep and waking up. That, according to the nurse, is from the pain killers they gave me still in my system. There is no TV in my room so the only thing to occupy my time is my chicken-scratch writing on this yellow tablet.

"You need to drink water," the nurse said. She handed me a large paper cup. "Here, finish all of this. It'll flush out when you pee."

"Can I have some Gatorade?"

"All I have is water and orange juice, but if you drink OJ, you might get sick. Just drink water and rest. The doctor wants to keep you until seven just to make sure you're fine. Is there anyone who can drive you home?"

From 1 p.m. until just a few minutes ago—and it is now 3:37 p.m.—everyone has shown up to say hi: Roy, Annie, Mike, Karen, Becky, Louise, Jack Milner and his wife. Dean Stanton and his wife stopped by, as well. They've filtered in at different times. Everyone joked with me, all trying to make me forget the pain and to ask what prompted the attack. My left arm throbs. My right is fine, so I am still writing with a pen.

Roy brought me three novels. "Here, you have to read these by tomorrow and have the reports ready."

They all brought balloons and cards.

"What about the mess in Dr. Laighles's backyard?" I asked.

Dean Stanton said, "No need to worry. I asked the Boy Scouts to help out a fellow Eagle. They cleaned up everything, extinguished the fire, returned the picnic tables, ate the rest of the food, and policed the area. They even cleaned out the fire pit. It looks like Donald Card's Landscape Company was hard at work."

The nurse came in and made everyone leave, but I insisted Annie stay.

"This is my ride home," I said, pointing at Annie.

"How's your pain level?" the nurse asked.

"About the same. The side of my head is tender and my thigh hurts, too, but not like my arm."

"You have deep bruising under the scalp and whiplash from the blunt force of the baseball bat. I don't want to give you anything more for a few hours but let me know if the pain worsens. You can stay another night."

Once the nurse left, I moved over and Annie scooted onto the small bed so she could sit on the edge. She tried to lean on me, but that hurt too much.

"Robert, I was so scared when the call came over Jack Milner's radio that you'd been taken to the hospital in an ambulance. Buck Cline called it in to him. I thought you'd been in a car accident. I'm ashamed of myself," she said, as tears slowly lined her cheeks.

"I was so scared riding with Jack on the way to the hospital. They said you were bleeding from the head after being beaten."

I said nothing. I stared at the chrome bar at the end of the bed. It had a dull shine like the rest of the room.

"I tried calling your parents last night. The school didn't have their number, and long-distance service didn't have a listing for anyone named English in Stone Mountain. Jack even tried, but there's no listing."

"It's unlisted, and not under our last name. It's under my mother's maiden name, Connelly."

"Give me their telephone number, because I'm calling to tell them what's happened."

"Annie, if you call them, they'll be here in the morning, and I don't want my parents coming up. Not yet. Not this summer."

I was reluctant, but I eventually gave her the number.

"Promise me that you will give my parental units a clear understanding that I am perfectly fine, and that they don't have to rush up here."

"I will, but I have no control over their actions."

"But make it sound like I fell off a bicycle or something."

"Do you realize that you might be dead if it hadn't been for Mike? He was the hero yesterday. Minutes after you and Karen left for the store, he and Gloria drove in her car to catch up to you to buy graham crackers and chocolate bars for s'mores. I wasn't there, but Gloria and Buck Cline told me this, so it's secondhand. Even so, you can believe it's the truth. Mike and Gloria drove up in her car and arrived as Allen DeBauché and Guy Byrd were attacking you. Mike jumped out of Gloria's car and grabbed the bat when Guy Byrd swung it at him. Mike yanked the bat out of his hands and tossed it to the side, then began swinging punches at him. He knocked Byrd out cold. Caroline's brother then jumped on Mike's back from behind, but Mike uppercut him in the jaw, knocking him out flat on the pavement like a limp sack of wheat. It was as if Mike had undergone a metamorphosis, reaching beyond his own physical and mental power to unleash a wrath of fury."

Buck Cline told Annie that Mike looked like he did in high school when he played defensive tackle.

"But, you know, I'd forgotten that Mike wrestled in high school. They never laid a hand on him. He ripped right through them, and when Buck Cline pulled up in his police car, squealing into the Super Duper parking lot, Mike had Allen over his shoulders like a wrestler on TV."

"Mike, put him down," Buck Cline said.

For several seconds, Mike stood, staring at him.

"Come on Mike, please put him down. He's hurt."

Mike turned around and arched his back, but instead of throwing Allen DeBauché on the hood of the car or through the store window, he gently set him on the pavement next to Guy Byrd.

§

I am home now, and it is very late. I cannot sleep so I am typing all the aforementioned details with one hand from my hospital notes, which is faster than I thought it would be. I can use my left pinky or index finger to hit the shift key, so typing isn't too bad. My right hand is pretty fast. I have painkillers so it could be worse. Plus, I'm drinking a Genesee Cream Ale, which I know is not a good idea with the painkillers, but I think the experts mean not to drink whiskey with prescriptions. Beer is probably fine. I'll have to ask Mr. Barone for the skinny on that.

There is some irony in this whole situation: Caroline is in jail for premeditated assault and conspiracy to commit a criminal act. Allen is on the second floor of the WCA Hospital with seven stitches in his forehead, two broken ribs, some torn cartilage in his knee (that was my doing), and a broken finger. Once he's released, he'll be charged with conspiracy, assault, and assault with a deadly weapon. Jack Milner will then take him to the county jail in Mayville.

"He and Byrd are one floor up from here, on opposite ends of the wing from each other," Annie told me in the hospital. "Jack said they are handcuffed to the bed."

Caroline's boyfriend, Guy Byrd, has several cracked ribs and a broken jaw. He has stitches above one eye and he cracked his front tooth off.

There's only one cell in the Lakewood jail, and Caroline currently lives there.

§

Before I was released, the nurse and doctor paid me a visit. He checked my arm, looked into my eyes and ear. He listened to my heart.

"You broke your ulna, that's this bone running down the pinky finger side."

"I know. I'm pre-med at Chautauqua," I responded.

"Ah, good for you. Study hard, kiddo. It only gets tougher," the doctor said, opening and closing the fingers on my other hand.

"You'll experience a throbbing pain for several days, but it will subside. They busted your arm pretty good. The muscle is very tender. It was bruised internally and quite deep—the same as your thigh. You'll have a nice bruise for a while," he explained.

He kneaded my leg like bread dough, flexing it back and forth at the knee.

"Tell me if this hurts."

He rotated my ankle in a circular motion, then up and down. "You have a pretty good friend, the guy who helped you."

"He's my best friend," I said.

"He's outside in the waiting room," the doctor said, working on the other leg. "He's been there most of the day, waiting, along with a woman. He keeps asking all the nurses and other doctors when you're getting out. Is that your girlfriend?"

"No. That's my fiancée," I lied.

"Really, I didn't see a ring," he said, which made me realize that he had checked her out and was interested. I felt immediately inferior to him and knew there was no way a guy like me could compete with a guy who's a doctor. I'm just a kid. He's a man with a profession. He saves people. I only read books. He has money for a vacation.

He lifted the Ace bandage circling around my chest and poked up under my ribs with two fingers.

"Ow! That hurt."

"It's supposed to. Nothing's broken. It's bruised. I think you can go home so it looks like I'll have to let you go. Just a couple things," he said, leaning on the silver support bar on the bed. "No swimming. No showers. You can't get the cast wet or moist. When you take a bath, get someone to help you. The throbbing will go away in three to four days. If it doesn't, stop by. I'll want to take a look at it. If you have any problems, come see me. Regardless, I want you back here in two weeks. You broke your arm, but that's because you blocked the baseball bat—that's how it broke. Otherwise, your head injuries would be severe, perhaps fatal."

When he pushed away from the bed, his stethoscope stuck straight out and suspended for a brief second, then fell to his chest. He wrote a prescription and gave it to the nurse.

"Your black eye should go away in a few weeks," he said.

The nurse set a plastic basket on the foot of the bed that contained my clothes. It was awkward trying to balance myself to dress. She put my socks over my feet. They were on crooked and felt like the way my underwear does when it's twisted, but I didn't say anything to her.

§

At home, Annie fixed soup and sandwiches. She has been very quiet today. Mike took the dogs out for me.

"I've been over here three times today to take Harry and Bess out. Do you want me to run them?" he asked.

"No, that's good. Thanks for your help. How did the apples taste?"

"We didn't eat them. We forgot and they got burned up. The Boy Scouts ate some." Mike responded.

It was too late to call my parents, but I promised Annie we could in the morning since she had not called them yet. She drove Mike home and then returned. She stayed the night. Nothing happened, but we slept in the same bed again, which was nice. She cuddled up, but it was cuddle-lite, not too much pressure on my body. It hurt to turn in any direction.

Tuesday, August 21

The doctor told me "no work," but I don't care. I'm bored. I'm supposed to rest in a dark room. I need to make some money, and I need to get out of the house.

Because I had promised Annie, and because she insisted, I called my parents this morning while Annie and I sat at the kitchen table and stretched the cord across the room. It was my agreement with her that she could talk to them after I was done.

"Mom, it's me. Is Dad there?"

"Yes, what's wrong?"

"Nothing. I just need to ask him something."

I waited until she put him on the phone.

"Dad, I don't want Mom getting worried or flying up here, so I wanted to tell you first."

"What's going on?"

"I got beat up by two guys the other day."

"Were you smarting off?"

"No, it was mistaken identity. I didn't even know these guys. They're from out of town and got me mixed up with someone else. I'm fine, really. I'm bruised up and went to the hospital, but the doctor said I'll be perfectly fine. I promised Annie I'd call and tell you."

"Who's Annie?"

"She's right here. She's my girlfriend."

When I said that, I looked at her and saw her smile.

"She's really nice, and you're going to like her a lot. She's helping out and taking care of me."

"Where are you now?"

"In Lakewood."

"Be more specific than that," he said.

"I'm sitting here in the kitchen with Annie and she just made me lunch. She wants to talk to you, but especially Mom."

I handed the phone to Annie, but I did not want to be in the room when she talked to them. I let the dogs outside in their pen. They're too large for me to handle with one arm, so I sat on the steps and watched as they ran around in their pen, which I realized takes up over half the backyard. I have cheap sunglasses to help with the glare and brightness. The nurse said to wear them for a few days, but they look stupid.

When I lived here, we did not have any pets. I know that back in the 1800s, the land behind the fence was farmland. I've seen old photographs at the library.

Annie talked to my parents for about twenty minutes, then came outside to sit on the cool steps.

"Why haven't you ever told me about your sister?"

"See that tree stump?" I pointed. "Kimberly died right there eleven years ago."

Annie had a few questions for me, and I answered them—no secrets—but I guess she could tell that I wasn't comfortable talking about it. People have secrets. Kimberly isn't a secret, it's just something I like for myself.

"Your parents are not coming up here. I explained everything to your mom, but she started crying, especially when she realized you were living in your old house."

§

Around 1:30 this afternoon, Sheriff Jack Milner dropped by the house to see how I was feeling. He asked me to come down to the police station to answer some questions.

"It's just to fill out a few preliminary reports," he said.

"Thank God, Jack," Annie said. "Robert's about to jump out of his skin. He needs to get out of the house."

He drove Annie and me to the station in his police car. I had not thought much about the seriousness of the assault by the DeBauché clan. Sure, Caroline was held in jail overnight, and rightly deserved it, but the district attorney is serious about prosecuting her. I'd just as soon let them go back to Boston and forget the whole mess.

"The district attorney is trying to up Allen DeBauché's charge to attempted murder," Milner said in the squad car as he drove down Summit Avenue. "In her statement, the Paterson girl told us that DeBauché said he was going to kill you. He won't be charged until he's out of the hospital, then he'll be bound over. That'll be tomorrow, I suspect. Of course, it depends on you."

In the police station parking lot, Jack asked how my mom and dad were doing.

"Tell them I said hello."

"You know my parents?"

"Sure, we grew up together as kids. I've known your father since I was born. We lived four houses away our entire childhood. He's only six days older than me."

Jack sat in the sheriff's thick, padded chair, swiveling back and forth as he talked and asked me questions. I'm amazed that he knows my folks. I just realized that he probably responded to our house when Kimberly fell from the tree. He probably knows all the details, even things I haven't been told. What I thought was a secret is not. I thought I knew the world, but the world, in all its dark alleys, knows me.

"Judge Wilkins hasn't set bail for Caroline DeBauché. He's in court in Dunkirk today, but we sent someone after him. He's just going to love that girl. She's a pistol," Jack said.

"What do you mean it depends on Robert?" Annie asked.

"We're holding the Gang of Three until Judge Wilkins is back, but we can't hold them if you don't press charges. You haven't filed the papers yet, and you'll have to file them by tomorrow for me to hold them."

"You mean I don't have to press charges?" I asked.

"Not really, but it depends. Certain crimes warrant us to press charges, but not every crime. I'd like to see these punks busted. You don't have to press charges, but I'm going to be pissed as hell if I have to do all this paperwork for nothing. I've given this kid three speeding tickets in the last year alone in that yellow Duster of his, and his old man just pays the fine. Fine. I get it, but he isn't learning any kind of lesson."

"No, I'm going to press charges," I said.

"Just remember who broke your arm. You didn't fall on that baseball bat," Jack cautioned me.

"Can I see Caroline? I want to talk to her."

"Sure, but that girl wrote the book on being a bitch."

"I sort of already know that. I just want to talk to her. Is that okay?" I asked.

"Fine with me. She's right there in the back."

Jack Milner escorted me from his office to her cell, which was through a door and twenty feet away from Deputy Cline's desk, but he wasn't there, as he was out on patrol.

The jail cell looked brand new, as if no one had ever stayed in it before. Caroline was lying down, facing away from me. The leather soles of her shoes were new, and I could read the words "Walter Steiger" imprinted on them. The walls were a pale yellow. There was a gold-framed picture of Jesus on the wall and a toilet with a shower curtain that wrapped around for privacy, hovering six inches above the floor so your feet showed. Brown wall-to-wall shag carpet lined the floor. Although clean-looking, it was cheap, like a throw rug used to cover up a blood stain. The bed frame was a metal skeleton, low to the floor, and had only a brown blanket over the thin foam mattress.

"Hey sweetheart, you've got a visitor," Jack said.

Caroline quickly sat up.

"You have to stay outside the cell. When you're done, you'll need to sign the papers," Jack told me before he returned to Annie.

I leaned against the cold black bars.

"Hey, Ma Barker, wanna break out of this joint?" I asked her.

"That's not at all funny," she said.

"It's funnier than the twenty years your brother can get for attempted murder. He'll probably be out in half of that. How much time will you spend in prison? Maybe you can tour the country speaking to juveniles or start a company that caters to the rehabilitation crowd."

"We happen to own a publishing house, among other things," she said.

"That's right. Discounts on all books for the inmates," I said, putting my cast between the metal bars to rest it. "And your boyfriend, Guy Byrd. What a loser."

"He's not my boyfriend," Caroline said.

"He looks like Eddie Munster. You could have done better than him. I hope you're not sleeping with that jerk. I hate to think what might happen if you go to prison," I said.

Her eyes lit up like caramel marbles reflecting the sun.

"I wouldn't worry, you'll get probation."

"Did you come here to terrify me? 'Cause if you did, you can stop," she said.

"I'm not here to terrify you. You'll get enough of that in prison. I came to make up. I'll say this, you look natural behind bars."

"Is that so? Well, you're a natural jerk." she yelled.

"Is that all you can say? At least throw something at me. Can't you apologize?"

"You can leave any time you like," she said motioning to the door."

"You know damn well I never touched you."

"So what?"

"Caroline, not everyone has money and power, but somewhere down the line, we get a chance to even the score with people like you. How we do it tells a lot about our character."

"What makes you think I care?" she asked, sitting down on the squeaky bed.

"Look, I can drop the charges, but I haven't made up my mind. Be nice. I could ask for a favor to help me forget the entire incident."

"What kind of favor?" she asked.

"How about an arm for an arm?"

"Sure, here. Break my arm," she said, holding her arm out towards me.

"I don't want to break your arm, but I never raped you, and you know that's the truth.

"BFD. You already said that, so who cares?"

"I care."

"What do you want me to do about it now?"

"Your brother and Guy Byrd are going to prison. That's a given. You might get off with probation, but you're not going to law school. Let's finish what we started before you went off the deep end."

"I'm not sleeping with you. I'd rather die than let you touch me."
I think I disgusted her at this point.

"Don't think of it as having sex with me. Think of it as the final act of loyalty towards your family. Stand up for something. Well, actually, lie down," I said.

"You're an asshole. That's blackmail, in case you didn't know."

"I find it quite noble. You've never loved anyone but yourself. You've never suffered. You've never gone hungry."

"Get out of here before I scream."

"Go ahead. Cry rape?"

"My father will have me out of here before you know it," she said.

"That's true. In fact, I'm anticipating it, but I guarantee Allen's going to prison."

"I'll say you raped me," she growled.

"I'm leaving, but before I do, here's how this will work. You'll be let out when your parents and lawyers show up some time today. A preliminary meeting has just been arranged for Thursday at the courthouse, the day after tomorrow. Come to my house tomorrow night, by yourself, nine o'clock. That's Wednesday night, and before you get angry and start yelling, be nice to me because I can simply walk out that door and then you and Allen are screwed. I'm simply going to slip your clothes off, and we can do it in the hallway. I'll let you keep your sneakers and socks on. If you show up, I think we can work out our differences. If not, we'll see how the judge handles it."

"I'd rather be dead than have you touch me."

Wednesday, August 22

Karen came over early in the evening, almost right after I got home from work. We talked some and she signed my cast. A lot of people at work signed it, too. Roy drew Mickey Mouse on it. Brooke drew a caricature of me. I did not know she could draw so well.

I made certain Karen was gone by eight o'clock so that I was sitting on the front porch if Caroline showed up.

"You're late," I said.

"I forgot how to get here."

"Have a seat."

"Let's just get this over with."

"Have a seat in the chair."

She sat down on the flat end of the Adirondack chair a few feet away. The cushion compressed and squeaked.

"It's dark and I can hardly see you, just your silhouette. You're creepy just sitting there."

"I figured you wouldn't want anyone seeing you, so I turned off the porch lights."

"Let's just go inside and take care of this. I'm ready for it to be over."

"It's already over."

"What's that supposed to mean?"

"Caroline, I'm not pressing charges."

"Are we still going inside?"

"Does that matter?"

"Wait, I thought you wanted to coerce me into having sex."

"No. I only wanted to see if you would go through with it to help your brother and that pimp friend of his."

"I don't get it. You don't want to do it?"

"No. I don't like you. I certainly don't want you on my list of women. Not at all. See, I'm a man of honor, but you are not a woman of honor. I only wanted to see if you could give yourself to save another person. You have proven me wrong."

"Wait, I'm confused. That's it?"

"Yeah, you can leave."

"Every guy on campus wants to get in my pants, except you."

"At one time I was on that list, but not now. By giving you a free pass, I will always own you. You owe me and you always will."

"I owe you nothing."

"If that's how you see it."

"It's the only way to see it. If you don't want to fuck me, then fuck you."

"In time, you will understand that I am giving something to you that cannot be purchased. I'm allowing you to free yourself from all that binds you to the way you are. You are free to go, but you will always owe me."

"I'd rather do it right now on the porch than owe you anything for the rest of my life."

"But you have no say in the matter."

"What if I said I want to do it right now?"

"I'd say no."

"What if I started screaming and the police came?"

"I don't care. Scream all you like. They're just going to wonder why you showed up at my house."

"Just for the record, you don't want to do it, and you're still going to drop the charges?"

"Yeah, pretty amazing, isn't it?"

"You are so weird."

"Remember, you'll owe me for the rest of your life, and that's how I'll always have power over you."

And that was the end of Caroline DeBauché. She did not say another word to me. She simply stood up, walked down the porch steps then down the long sidewalk to the street, turned left, and headed toward the university.

§

It is four-thirty in the morning, and I can do nothing except type like the world is about to end. I must get everything on paper. I have typed a considerable amount but feel like I started only twenty minutes ago.

Thursday, August 23

My arm is not throbbing as much today except when I move it in the wrong direction or lift something heavy, which is anything more than a pencil. I have been taking a few more painkillers than were prescribed, and that makes me lightheaded, so I'm lying down a bunch to rest and read. Annie said to eat a big breakfast.

I type a lot for a while, but then take fifteen-minute power naps whenever I start losing concentration. They seem to help.

I took a bath and did as best I could to keep my cast from getting wet by wrapping my arm in a garbage bag then tying it off with rubber bands, but that procedure is a pain in the butt.

§

Court is today.

I dressed in jeans and tennis shoes—that's all I had that was clean. Annie and Roy accompanied me to court. Annie wore a pink flowered dress with a belt in the middle, and Roy wore a suit. Everything was so formal, which made me nervous.

The preliminary meeting took less than ten minutes. Judge Wilkins, a stern, lengthy-framed man, sat talking with Annie, Roy, and me in his office, which was engulfed with legal books and fine leather chairs.

"The accused are ready," Jack Milner said, stepping into the judge's office.

He and Deputy Cline accompanied the judge out.

We walked in together to another room, where at the far end of a long, handsome, wooden table sat Caroline, Allen, Mr. and Mrs. DeBauché, two lawyers, and a stenographer. On the opposite side of them sat Guy Byrd, his father, and his lawyer, a big fat man named Osmond.

The room was a long, narrow chamber with tall windows with wooden blinds that allowed the sun to streak across the table.

"This is cut and dry, gentlemen," the judge said. "We've got several witnesses who have testified that Allen DeBauché and Guy Byrd assaulted Mr. English on the afternoon of August 19, 1973. As well, Ms. DeBauché was a conspirator."

"I object," Osmond said. His stomach sloped over the chair like rising dough in a pan.

"Object to what?" Judge Wilkins asked.

"It's not been proven that my client was involved in these so-called actions perpetrated against Mr. English."

Judge Wilkins lowered his head slightly to look over his glasses.

"I want to make it clear, set the record straight," Osmond said.

"Jennifer, this is off the record," the judge said.

The stenographer stopped typing.

§

Long story cut short:

I dropped the charges. Everything took about forty-five minutes because Osmond objected over and over until the other lawyers told him to be quiet.

The judge said, "Mr. English is doing everyone a huge favor. We're going to settle this the old-fashioned way, through compromise. Mr. English feels that these young people do not need their records tarnished, not when the rest of their productive lives are ahead of them. Take a minute and discuss it with your client to see what each would like to do. If your client would like his day in court, I'm certain we can reinstate the charges. It's up to you."

It took the Boston Gang less than a minute to conclude.

The judge spoke up: "You have until four o'clock this afternoon. If payment has not been made for the damages, I'll issue the warrants for their arrest. Do not leave the county before paying."

I had expected Osmond or Caroline's attorney to say something, but neither did. They all stood up and walked out. In the hall, Mr. DeBauché smacked Allen in the back of the head with his open palm. His head snapped forward like JFK in Dealey Plaza.

Man's motivations are as crooked as a corkscrew.

§

After the proceedings were over, Roy went back to the office, and Annie drove me around the lake for a while. We had the top down, which felt nice as the sun baked on me. We stopped in Mayville at The Lakeview Restaurant for beef-on-weck sandwiches. The little old lady who waited on us must have been over ninety. Her name is May and was such a sweet person, so helpful with everything on the menu. She really piled on the beef.

"The horseradish is the best around," May said. "My sister makes it, but I'll warn you, it's hot."

Annie and I spoke very little at lunch. Less so on the ride back.

Friday, August 24

A mirror does three things: it presents a true picture of how things are, it reveals a picture of how things ought to be, and it reflects a false picture.

I found the secret room.

I mowed the yard this afternoon, using one hand. It was tough turning the mower, but then Annie showed up and finished for me. I don't feel as though I have kept up my end of the agreement with Emily and Floyd because I have not been a good steward housesitting my childhood home.

Saturday, August 25

I worked all day today, typing reports with one hand. It is easier to type on the computer than Dr. Laighles's typewriter. I have considerably less pain today. Since last week, I have done nothing at work. If I do any less, Roy ought to fire me.

As the sun fell this evening, the sky turned orange, silhouetting the clouds behind purple hues. Shadows whispered faint and long, as the lights flickered across the lake. I cannot see across the lake to the details of life at each house, but I know in each yard, on each sleepy street, bands of children are playing hide and seek or kickball, trying to get in one final inning before dusk swims over them.

Karen, Annie, and I went for a walk down by the lake. They had the dogs on their leashes. I had a sling for my arm.

The boats were heading in off the lake, lights on, trying to make their way to the canals to tie up to their dock slips. We walked through the park, passing parents and children packing up to go home. There was a policeman walking casually along the sidewalk as if he were off duty. He nodded towards us when we passed. The big glow of the sun reflected off the water, like an orange flare skating miles down the lake.

I never wanted Caroline to go to prison, and yet, a tidal wave of guilt sits heavy in my heart, as if I still did something wrong.

Sunday, August 26

No matter our age or the condition of the mind, each of us needs reinforcement, to feel we have the ability to succeed.

Mike has been playing Roy's computer chess game all summer

and he has not won a single game. What I take for granted as a simple pleasure, he sees as a preeminent task.

Annie and I were sitting at the kitchen table this morning after breakfast, maybe around 10:30, my face half buried in *Time Magazine* with Nixon and Agnew on the cover ("Can Trust be Restored?"). I have my doubts. Things look bleak. Annie was reviewing some material the university sent her about the new school year when Mike walked under the arch of the doorway, holding the computer. Its lights were blinking in defeat, like a checkered runway, on and off to signify man's superiority over machine. He just stopped in the kitchen doorway looking at the computer board, staring.

"Mike," Annie said, looking up, "is something wrong, honey?"

"I'm okay."

"Have a seat. We're just hanging out." She motioned for him to sit.

I glanced over the top of the magazine to see the computer lights flashing.

"Mike? Is there anything wrong?" Annie questioned again.

"No."

"You look upset."

"I won," he said. "I beat the computer."

"You don't have to cry, dear," Annie said. "It's just a game."

Annie rose and hugged Mike.

It wasn't just a game though. I am just now realizing this. The boulder each of us must push up the hill is tremendous in its own personal way. Each journey is momentous.

I scrutinized the computer. The entire time I thought Mike had it set to Level 1, the easiest. It was set to Level 5, which Roy said a human cannot defeat, that it is too difficult.

Monday, August 27

The house is quiet this evening. Mike left hours ago. The dogs are curled up on the carpet near the fireplace. Annie and I watched The Tonight Show with Joey Bishop as the guest host. Dr. Joyce Brothers was a guest and I think this inspired Annie because she said that she has read her articles in *Good Housekeeping*. She might be Annie's hero.

11:23 . . . Annie just asked if I'm coming to bed. I am.

Tuesday, August 28

Annie is warm and smells like talc. When I came to bed last night, she helped lift my shirt over my arm. It is a careful exercise because the wrong movement sends shooting pains through me.

She gave me a little kiss, but then she gave me a real kiss. When she got up to close the bedroom door, I thought she was leaving, but she locked it. Her t-shirt flowed like gossamer. She turned on her 8-Track tape player and pushed in *Tapestry* by Carole King. Afterwards, when "Will You Still Love Me Tomorrow" played, all I wanted to do was tell Annie, "Yes, I will love you tomorrow and forever."

I feel uncouth as I type this material, like a voyeur. I don't want to diminish what happened last night by writing about it, yet I made a promise to myself to write about everything this summer. I have all but stopped thinking about Isabella and Vincenzo, and I have written almost nothing about them. That is not the real world, and I am only interested in realism.

Writing about Annie making love to me, I feel as though I'm cheapening it by chronicling the details. I have not registered the specifics as pornography would. I have, for instance, not said,

"Annie's breasts filled the palms of my hands like grapefruits, and her nipples tasted like dry walnuts." This would jeopardize our confidentiality.

Love is confidential. I like how that sounds. Love is confidential.

Perhaps I should say, "Annie and I made love last night for the first time. We were both virgins. She lifted her t-shirt over her head and pulled me into her. I felt her warmth and smelled Chanel No. 5 in many places, and we were out of breath and dizzy from all the kissing. I just wanted to hold her closely and talk and sleep and be with her. Most of all, I never wanted to leave her arms."

Wednesday, August 29

This morning, Annie and I were giddy. We couldn't stop smiling at each other. She wrapped my arm in a plastic trash bag then we took a shower together, then made love, then took another shower.

Because of my arm, everything was awkward, and I tired quickly from holding myself above her stretched out body. We improvised and that is all I will say.

I had to work, and she had a full day scheduled with administrators to discuss an internship she had applied for. We agreed to meet for dinner.

§

1:30 p.m.

I left work early. I told Roy I was not feeling well. It was a lie. I feel perfectly fine.

I made a pot of coffee and sat at the bottom of the steps, petting the dogs and enjoying one cup.

All summer I have wondered about the secret room Steven found. This wasn't rocket science. The secret room was there as I had expected it would be. It was all very simple: a house, a little girl, a secret room. Logically, where would Kimberly hide? Steven's bedroom was her room. Duh! I just could not find the key. All the bedrooms have old hotel locks with long skeleton keys, which is what my dad called them. They are like house keys for inside doors.

I had looked for a key, but I did not want to rifle through Emily and Floyd's personal belongings. It would have been dishonest. I don't like snooping around, not when they have entrusted me. Still, in the back of their closet I found a wooden box with personal belongings and there were a handful of keys. One key had a thin blue ribbon on it.

§

I was nervous about opening the bedroom door, but after a minute, I turned the knob. The door creaked and the room smelled of stale dust. I doubt anyone has been in there for a few years. It was gloomy. I turned on the lights. The window had a shade pulled down and red curtains drawn shut to keep out the sun.

On the mahogany bookshelves, lonely and layered in dust, stood three baseball trophies, two football trophies, and a small, tarnished gold lightbulb for a science fair project. On his desk was a picture frame with several photos of Steven and Annie when they were teenagers, laughing, kissing, in their high school graduation gowns, and one of him in a football jersey and one of Annie in her cheerleader skirt. There was a Beatles poster behind the headboard of the bed, a photo of Petula Clark in a black vinyl mini-skirt, and a grungy shot of the Rolling Stones. Behind the bedroom door, a poster of the 1963 World Champion Cincinnati Reds was pinned with thumb tacks. A small roll-top desk sat neatly open with a pencil and a tablet of paper in the middle.

I opened the closet door and looked at myself in the full-length mirror on the back of the door. Steven's clothes hung from the closet rack. His shoes were lined in long rows, each one accompanied with its twin.

In the back and at the bottom left-hand corner of the closet, waiting all these years to be discovered like the Lost Dutchman's Mine, there was a small wooden doorknob the shape of a chestnut. It was small enough to be overlooked for an eternity and blended in like a lion in high grass. The wallpaper was old, with a style that looked like it was from the 1920s or earlier. Perhaps it was Art Deco, with green, gold, and black stripes and crisscrossing patterns so that the small door panels blended in.

I measured it, and the wooden door was 18x24 inches, easy for a child to crawl through, but uncomfortable, yet possible, for a teen. It looks absolutely impossible for a full-grown adult. If this was a hotel during Prohibition, this would be the perfect place to hide their illegal spirits. There were no hinges on the outside. If a person ran their hand down the wall, they might feel a ripple in the wallpaper, but no hinges to give the room away. The hinges were in-laid on the inside of the small room. Whoever built the room did so to make it as inconspicuous as possible. When was this room built?

I cast a cane of light into the room with my flashlight, then laid down on my back, crossed my broken arm over my chest, and slid the flashlight handle into the front of my jeans. I reached my right hand up into the hole, closed my eyes, pushed against the floor with my tennis shoes, and slowly scooted into the room. I opened my eyes to see black.

I turned and twisted and inched into the room.

The air was thick and dry. I felt as if I might be breathing in old germs. I turned on the flashlight and found a light switch with a one-inch string above me. The room was no more than four feet high and five feet wide and nine feet long. My first thought—bootleggers could hide a lot of whiskey in here. There was enough room to sit up but not stand.

Here's what I found in the secret room:

* A small, oblong mirror with a pink handle—a girl's make up mirror, a vanity.
* Kimberly's toys: A small rubber ball I bought her for Christmas years ago. It was pink, but now it had faded to a dull grey with some patches still glimmering in its original color. The rubber coating had flaked and peeled. I remember when I bought that ball. My mom, dad, Kimberly, and I went shopping at Bigelow's.
* A red Corvette for her Barbie doll, which Kimberly received for Christmas the same year she received some Barbie outfits I gave her.

* Her Barbie doll, sitting motionless in the driver's seat of the plastic car with her arms bent at her elbows, unable to grab hold of the steering wheel.
* A little ball of lace.
* Some school notebook paper with drawings.
* Her Teddy Bear and Baby-J doll. They are the avatars of time, so I didn't touch them.
* One roll of Art Deco wallpaper. It must be old as dirt. It has twine tied around it.

I sat in the room for a lengthy stretch, taking Barbie out of the car, exercising her legs, arms, and other joints. I pushed her around the small room, going forwards, backing up, popping wheelies, driving on two tires, pretending that she was a model on her way to star in a movie.

I set the Barbie doll back in the car, placed her arms down by her side, adjusted her beach hat, and parked the car in the corner where I found it. I set the rubber ball in the passenger's seat. It was oversized and stuck out above the windshield.

I picked up the papers and brought them downstairs, where they are now sitting in front of me on the kitchen table. I am looking at them as I type on Dr. Laighles's typewriter. I have chicken noodle soup simmering on the stove and I just made eight pieces of toast with butter and jam.

When I crawled out through the opening, I scooted out feet first, and as I looked up, I saw a board on the ceiling that was a smooth, pale color, without a wood knot to blemish its texture. There was a crayon drawing of a smiling sun and a little girl stick figure, and a date June 5, 1962, written in a determined, carefully executed, classroom print.

§

I have been sitting in front of the window in Dr. Laighles's office, my feet stretched out and propped up, leaning back, letting the wind sift through the open curtains. Next to me are twenty-four crayon and pencil drawings, and three poems from Kimberly. Part of me wants to take them home to my mom and dad.

The drawings are stick figures of a little girl with a dog and horse in a pasture. The most detailed one is a pastoral scene with the sun smiling through the sky, a full, glowing circle with rays sticking out of it, winking with one eye fully open and the other closed in secrecy. There are birds flying above three mounds of grass. On the first hill, there is a knight holding a lance and riding a horse. On the third hill, there's a similar knight and horse posed identically, except the knight is holding a spear, a shield, and a sword. The horse's left leg is bent inward in an advancing position. The hill in the middle, the most labored-over part, has a girl standing with her left arm at her side. In her left hand, she is holding a rag doll with bright red hair, while her right hand is held up with her palm open, as if waving good bye. The girl's hair is blowing backwards.

I'm conflicted. Should I tell my parents? Would they like to see Kimberly's drawings and poems? What pain would that resurrect?

It's almost midnight, and I have read my dead sister's poems over and over. I have been sitting in the Florida room, doing nothing, for the past few hours. I finished off a bottle of

Chardonnay that was left over from the picnic and has been chilling in the refrigerator. It was partly stale, if that is such a thing. I don't drink much, but this is how I had to do it. The phone has rung numerous times. It's probably Annie. I cannot see her tonight.

These are the three poems Kimberly left in the secret room. They are all in pencil and printed in her careful handwriting.

Poem #1

Yesterday my brother called me
a bad name. Today
he gave me half his candy bar.
Mother baked a cake
and asked where I play

In my room I told her
I play games
but she couldn't find me
I am invisible
I said so are my friends

Father came home early
from work, first time this week
mixed a drink
with his big finger
kissed Mommy on the cheek.

Poem #2

Bobby came home from baseball practice
carrying his mitt and bat
I gave him for Christmas
He had dirt all over his pants
and on his good shirt
mother told him not to wear

He got mud all over
the kitchen floor
and Mother got angry
and started to swear
It took him a half hour
to mop the floor
Gracious the mud wouldn't go away

I watched while playing Go Fish
with Teddy Bear and Baby-J
They laughed at Bobby
which made him angry
We were clean
and smelling sweet
Mother made him take another bath

The water splashed
and Teddy Bear and Baby-J
ate cookies and sipped tea
that Father brought home from Canada

We didn't understand why Bobby sang
in the bath, even my invisible friends,
who are wise, didn't understand

They said he'd stop singing someday
We agreed today would be fine enough

Poem #3

Our fort is in a tree
and high enough
to hang Christmas lights
Baby-J says our tree is oak
it will never grow peaches

Watch your head under its branches
Teddy Bear doesn't like riding in the basket
I use to lift him up
He says bears are tough
like little boys
but tough guys
still get hurt

Father built my house last year
and I bring my guests
their favorite food

Mommy is a pretty lady
I look a lot like her
My kitchen is the living room

When we get tired
we sleep in the bedroom
like Goldie Locks

The neighbor kids come to my house to play
I say my games are real, go away
but sometimes I let them
climb the ladder

Most of the time
they want to pretend my friends
have parachutes and drop them
from my tree

In my tree
I am free

Thursday, August 30

Annie came over after work. She was testy all evening.

"I made you a sandwich, but you haven't touched it," I said.

"I'm sorry. Your mother told me something the other day that I should have told you. She asked me to tell you, since you won't listen to her."

"What's so important in the land of Dixie?"

"Sometime around the end of May, you received an invitation from Stone Mountain."

"Yeah, Ashley's graduation notice. She's a year behind me, Class of 1973. I didn't open it."

"Why not?"

"'Cause, I'm not going."

"That wasn't her graduation notice. Ashley dropped out of high school. She never finished. She went to school for a few months, then quit."

"How's that my problem?"

"You used to love that girl."

"Yes, I did. But then she broke my heart when she slept with my best friend, Will Croon. Once that happened, I stopped caring about her."

"Your mother didn't know any of this until a few weeks ago. Ashley's been working at Waffle House."

"Waffle House! No way. She'd never work there."

"Well, she is. And that wasn't Ashley's graduation notice. It's her wedding invitation. She's getting married on September first. That's in two days."

"What do I care?"

"You might not care now, but you will later on."

"How do you know?"

"God, Robert. Don't you think other people have lived their life too, and made decisions and mistakes they wish they could change? I've got seven years of life experiences on you. Your mother and father have twenty-something. Don't you figure we know a little more about some things than you do?"

"So, you've made mistakes in your life. Name one."

"I can name fifty."

"Name one."

"I have deeply loved and cared for several men in my life, but I let them slip away for no apparent reason. I've always found it difficult to tell them how much I love them. Don't roll your eyes like this is insignificant. I've hurt many people, and myself. When I was twenty-three, I dated a guy from Joplin, Missouri. He was in grad school. He was three years older than me, and we had been dating for almost a year when he wanted to get married. I told him I couldn't, and we stopped dating. There was no huge fight, no nothing. We simply stopped seeing each other. I still wasn't over my old boyfriend, but I loved this man, and it was extremely difficult not seeing him. I'm not sure I loved him enough to get married. He wasn't the only man I could not commit to or tell him how much I loved him. About five months after breaking up, I called him out of the blue, and the second he answered the telephone, I knew he was engaged. I could tell by his voice. He told me he had met a woman after breaking up with me, and they were going to get married. He wanted to start a family."

"Is that all?"

"You can be the biggest jerk sometimes," Annie yelled.

"What you're really telling me, and let's be honest, is that you're unable to have a meaningful relationship because you cannot move beyond something that happened in your life."

"What we did the other night, you're telling me that wasn't meaningful? I've never had sex with anyone. I saved myself for someone I really love, someone I want to be with, someone I could marry. I've only felt that way one other time in my life."

Friday, August 31

I did not sleep well. I woke up early and walked the dogs to Packard Field around 7:30. It was difficult holding two leashes in one hand. I was worried they might knock me down on my arm. I walked over toward the Yacht Club and the Red Door Apartments. I wanted to apologize to Annie. She did not stay last night because she was irritated with me, and rightfully so.

Mr. and Mrs. Lenna (Reg and Betty) were walking their dog, Ralph, when I came upon them.

"I named him after my brother," she said laughing.

I knew who Mr. and Mrs. Lenna were because their picture is in the paper once in a while because of the philanthropic work they do. Mr. Lenna owns Blackstone.

Ralph and Harry and Bess liked each other, but I couldn't talk to the Lennas long because the dogs wanted to wrestle, and I couldn't hold them still with one arm. Mr. Lenna had to help me settle them down.

§

I took the dogs home but returned to Annie's apartment. She was not home when I knocked on her door.

I typed for a while, then took a shower. I felt better and ended up making it to work by nine-thirty.

I did not call Annie and she did not call me today.

I have not been entirely honest with her.

§

Tonight, after dark pulled the bed covers over on the day, Karen stopped by the house. I had the lights turned off and was sitting on the porch when she rode her bicycle up to the edge of the stairs. She stood the bicycle on the kickstand, and I watched her take each step slowly and thoughtfully up the stairs. When she reached the porch and tip toed towards the door, I said, "Hello, Karen."

She gasped and placed her hand over her heart.

"You scared the shit out of me. I wasn't sure if anyone was home. The house is so dark. How's your arm?"

"Fine. I've been taking my medicine and I've had a few beers tonight, so I'm feeling pretty good right now."

"Can I have a beer?" she asked.

"Sure, they're on ice right here. It's Genesee. Is that okay?"

"That's what my dad drinks, that and the cream ale."

She grabbed a cold beer and pulled the top off.

"Where do you want me to put this?" she said sitting in a lawn chair.

I held out my hand and she placed the ring pull in my palm.

"It's a chilly night for shorts."

"My sweatshirt keeps me warm. Are you going with us to Long Point on Labor Day?"

"I'm looking forward to it."

"I bought a new bathing suit yesterday at Bigelow's. It was on sale. My dad said I'm not allowed to wear a bikini, but my mother said I could."

"What time am I supposed to be at Long Point?"

"We're going to have breakfast around eight-thirty or nine. You'll love it. This is sort of a family tradition. We've eaten Labor Day breakfast at Long Point since I can remember. Eggs, bacon, coffee, breakfast rolls. It's a lot of fun."

"Emily and Dr. Laighles are coming back soon. I won't have the house much longer. Plus, Mike and his dad are in Canada for a few more days so there won't be any interruptions."

"I go back to school in a few weeks. I'll be a junior this year. Jenny gave me a joint the other day and I'm hiding it in my room. Maybe we can smoke it in Allen Park?"

"Sure, we can do that."

"She said it's Acapulco Gold."

"Is that the good stuff?"

"I don't really know. It'll get the job done."

"We'll find out," I said, which made her laugh.

"I don't have to be home until eleven o'clock tonight."

§

It is 10:46 p.m. and Karen just left on her bicycle. She had a new light, so she won't get a ticket. I wonder how difficult it is, or scary, to lie there and let some boy make love to you for the first time?

We were both very nervous, and a bit drunk. Her whole body was so soft and warm. This did not happen with Annie, but Karen screamed and pounded on the mattress with her fists. Most of the time, we held each other and talked. She had a beautiful smell to her body. She liked rolling on top of me and placing her chin on my chest as she talked. She had to be careful not to hit my arm, because when she was lying on top of me, it hurt to breathe. My ribs are still sore.

I did not have a condom when Annie and I made love. I didn't even think to use one. In fact, I have never bought one in my life. I think you have to ask the pharmacist because they are locked in a vault, but there's no way I'm asking Mr. Barone. Annie is older and I expected her to take care of it, but I would not have made love to Ashley under the same circumstances. Karen and I did not use a condom or have anything, but I pulled out.

Whatever happened to Lauren? I thought she was going to call. I bet she's embarrassed, and I bet I never see her again.

Saturday, September 1

At work today, I found an empty office, and from there I called Annie. I apologized for my behavior, but I told her that I could do nothing about Ashley getting married.

"Why are you whispering?" she asked.

"I'm at the office and the walls are thin."

§

How could Ashley have dropped out of high school? That is all we discussed: graduation, college, studying together, lifting herself out of the grips of physical labor that suffocated her parents, breaking free of the average, reconstituted, hum drum complacency of middle-class life. In her case, lower middle-class. I guess any idea of her becoming a doctor is shot to hell.

Have I destroyed her life? Did I twist it like clay and gouge chunks out of the mold with a dull chisel? No. She made her decisions. Why did I not at least answer her letters from home? The world is rhetorical.

I do not know the guy she will marry. Clarence J. Lawrence, the invitation says. What an awful name. Ashley Lawrence. Mrs. Clarence Lawrence. Yuck! He had better treat her right.

I have fought too often with words, and now, war is the color of my lover's eyes.

§

It's 6:00 p.m., and Ashley is married by now. My world is not my world.

I'm asking myself: should I have rushed to Atlanta, stormed the church, and in the angst-filled style of Dustin Hoffman in *The Graduate*, swept Ashley off her feet and into my arms? Should I have pounded on the church windows, screaming, "Ashley! Ashley!"

Who gets married on the opening day of football season at five o'clock in the afternoon?

Sunday, September 2

My mood is shadowy. I realized something: Primal desires usurp logic. If you do not fall in love with a person, if that love does not last, if it burrows deep in your heart even when you walk away and abandon the person you love, they will, as you will, most inevitably, find another person. This is the cruel trick nature plays upon people. You feel as if you cannot be replaced. The awful truth is— everyone can be replaced. Someone else is always waiting in the shadows to take over and do the job you will not do or abandoned. The world will always procreate.

Monday, September 3 (Labor Day)

Tuesday, September 4

It's actually Wednesday, September 5th at 3:04 a.m. I have not written in a few days. I cannot sleep, because Mike has died.

Tomorrow at 11 a.m., they will bury him.

§

Ashley got married on the 1st, and I was in pain. On the 3rd, my best friend died, and I have been dying on the inside.

§

I have sifted a pot of coffee past my lips, fending off sleep. The words I am looking for have not arrived and I am overdosing on caffeine. My stomach grinds from the acidic coating.

The greatest men of our time cannot help me in this hour even as I search their volumes for clarity, truth, and understanding about the invisible hand that drives the world. I cannot write of death.

I had to call Annie at her mom and dad's house to tell her about Mike. It figures, Lauren answered the phone. When I told Annie the news, she burst into tears.

§

8:00 a.m.

Why was I asked to give the eulogy? I know nothing.

8:47 a.m.

Louise, Roy, and Karen are sitting at the kitchen table, waiting for me. They are not allowing Becky to come to the funeral. I guess she's too young. Roy helped me put on my shirt. He tied my tie for me. We will pick up Annie and ride together to the funeral home. I am in the other room typing this, but they think I'm working on the eulogy.

§

As a society, we are in the grips of decay. Alice Cooper is the prevalent entertainer of my time, with ghoulish make-up and macabre stage shows, and, yes, I like some of his music, but not the look. *Pretties for You* is one of my favorite albums because it is like Dave Brubeck of rock, with weird syncopations. I also like "I'm Eighteen" and "School's Out." I do not want censorship, but perhaps self-control. Not limits on where we can expand, but whether or not we want to go there. What are the consequences of all of our expanding efforts? What is next after Alice Cooper? Can we surpass ourselves and maintain our humanity? Karen said last week that she heard how Alice Cooper was challenged to a gross-out contest, and to win, fifty people spit into a bucket for him to drink. I know this isn't true. But what difference does it make? Karen felt it was true enough.

I'm sure Dr. Leibrandt would ask: how will we look back on this exact day (September 5, 1973) and remember what contributions each of us has given to the world? Alice Cooper will flicker, then extinguish. Will he leave the world a little better? Perhaps, but I have strong doubts. He may only be paving the way for the next expanding generation to offer more in the way of social exhaustion. Will Grand Funk Railroad be the prophets of our generation, the cornerstone by which we judge ourselves and how far we have matured? Again, I have doubt. Will television be all game shows, like *Match Game, Celebrity Sweepstakes, Let's Make a Deal*, and *The Price is Right*, and will they provide us with life's answers? Or will we shop at home using our TV? My favorite television shows, for what it is worth, are:

* Laugh-In
* Johnny Carson
* Kung Fu
* Room 222

But, really, does anyone give a damn? No. And they should not. This is frivolous information.

I am angry. I am hurt. I am ready for the funeral.

§

10:42 p.m.

I'm in the house and it is too quiet for me to stay here much longer. The World Series pinball machine will forever be silent.

I gave the eulogy today in the only manner I know. I did not preach of goodness and values, or one's thirst for life cut short. I had no oration of originality.

I told a few stories about Mike that made people laugh. I told everyone that Mike was the Pink Flamingo Desperado. That really made them laugh. I recited the following poem by Eduardo del Masso, published sometime in the 1950s.

Homage, My Friend

The market will not open this morning
and the birds will not fly.
Squeeze all the baseballs into their gloves

and rest them in the closet before grief subsides,
let the beggars beg in the quiet park
where no one walks by, place all the books

upon the shelf to collect an inch of dust.
The bicycle gears will not shift, and the cars will not start,
nor will the man on the weathervane twirl his arms.

All the horses will freeze mid-gallop
like bronze statues in a parched field
and tonight, the wolves will stop their hunt

so the elk may sleep without concern.
Turn off the television, the water spigot, yield
to all the mind's traffic, disconnect the radio, tell the children

playing in the street to go home. Quiet
the newscaster's microphone, hush
your lovemaking, please ask the rain not to fall.

I've locked the doors, nailed the windows shut,
snapped the Tupperware closed, and sealed the hearth
of all that is unresolved. We know only by unknowing,

we know beyond what there is to say,
whom now will I ask about the world?
The days will continue, and coffee pots will perk

in silence as old ladies stand alone in their kitchens
cooking casseroles and making Jello with oranges
for today and forever more each bright star

born deep in the universe will have darkness
trailing behind like a boy trying to catch up
to his father on a crowded city sidewalk.

As I stood to the left of the casket, quoting Eduardo del Masso, I
looked over Lind's Funeral Home filled beyond capacity. People
stood along the walls and in the doorway. Neighbors, schoolteachers,
and friends attended. I kind of counted people for a while. It was

between 300 and 400 in attendance. It was only a guess. Though I noticed them, I did not see them individually. I don't remember looking at any one person for too long. del Masso's words allowed me to vocalize what is difficult. I spoke the poem I memorized as a child. The simplicity of del Masso moved me in tribute. I told everyone how Mike and I played pinball and had our own baseball lineups and how he just wanted to hang out. I told them about Roy's computer chess game and how Mike defeated it. That made a lot of people smile and laugh, as well.

Each of us has our own private recollections, personal thoughts, or anecdotes that make us glide retrospectively down the corridors of our life. I do not know what I am doing as I tap letters out this evening on this manual typewriter. I want what I say to be more than myself. I am doing only what I know how to do, and it is never going to be enough.

§

From the funeral home, Roy drove us to Sunset Cemetery across the road from Southwestern High School, with its copper trellis on top, long since painted over in flat white. The sun on our backs heated our bodies and the only salvation was a breeze from the west. Annie held my hand much of the time. Karen sat by her mother and was pretty in her Sunday dress. Roy was quiet in his dark suit. He didn't say much of anything and was extraordinarily polite, opening the car door for all the women.

I saw one woman and knew from the picture on Mike's dresser that it was his high school girlfriend. She was with her husband. She was a beautiful woman, but the pain of Mike's death stretched across her face.

The cemetery was plush and peppered with flower gardens. There were no tombstones. The markers are flat bronze plates. The Methodist minister wore a black robe with red trim along the sleeves, but I could not wear my only sport jacket because of the cast on my arm. I felt grossly underdressed.

I wondered how each person was related to Mike, and what memories I could ask them for, for my journal, but I did not intrude upon their past. With all the world has to offer, a funeral is the only time the city and country come together.

Before Annie and I went back to the car, I asked her to walk with me.

"Take your time. We'll wait in the car," Roy said.

She and I walked up the narrow lane to a brick sidewalk jetting out to a path of black maple trees. I looked back to see Roy's car in the distance.

We walked to the end of the sidewalk and stopped not far from the peacocks that the cemetery keeps in a large wire cage. These birds, when they squawk, sound as if they are saying "help." Maybe it is a cry for help or for love. Between the cracks in the cobblestone bricks, moss grew.

"Why are we stopping?" Annie asked.

I did not answer.

"You okay?"

"Yeah."

I took a breath and guided Annie to a marble bench, where the copper plates gleamed in the sun and shined upward to blind our eyes. I knew where I was going. I had been here before. Eleven years ago. I stopped, and Annie stopped.

"Kimberly Anne English," she read.

"My sister."

"Robert."

"You know," I said. "I've been going to school here almost a year and this is the first time I've been able to visit. I've driven by, but I've never stopped."

The end of life is what comes after death. We sat on the marble bench, and I thought how the living must keep living after death.

"It was an accident," I said to Annie. "In the backyard, where the stump is, there used to be a tire swing hanging down, a ladder, and a treehouse. One day we were playing in the backyard and Kimberly climbed the ladder, then tried to hoist her basket of toys into the treehouse, but she had too many things in the basket. I told her to wait and I'd help, and then I ran into the house for my sneakers. It was only fifteen feet high, but I didn't want to climb the ladder with bare feet. I was only gone two minutes. When I returned, Kimberly was lying on the ground and her toys and dolls were scattered on the lawn. I ran for my mother, who was reading a book. She came rushing out, then went back inside to call the ambulance. She was hysterical, crying, screaming, gasping for air. I can still hear her voice. Sometimes, I still try to decipher her words. To this day, I hear something new in what she was saying and piece it together with everything else."

I didn't realize this at the time, but I have come to understand the details of the day more so as time moves on. Annie and I sat on the marble bench for about ten minutes, and I told her that before the ambulance arrived, my mother knew Kimberly was dead. She grabbed me by the arm, pulled me into the house, and made me go to my room to stay. I ran to the attic window and watched through the porthole—the ambulance driving up, the police car soon after, which as I typed some time ago, must have been Sheriff Milner or Deputy Cline. Our neighbor Mrs. Peterson came inside the house looking for me. My mother made me stay with her until they came back. I bolted from room to room, hiding. I ran down the spiral stairs to keep away from her. Mrs. Peterson couldn't find me, and I remember, still, how she called out my name throughout the house.

Not a day goes by that I don't remember Kimberly's face when I turned her over. I knew she wasn't coming home.

§

"I didn't know how much time passed from when Kimberly fell to when I found her. It was no more than a minute. I swear I felt her soul leave her body. I felt this presence touching me all over and kissing me, then floating away."

§

While sitting with Annie, I heard the tires of Roy's car softly crunch the gravel behind Annie and me, a sign to move on. Annie took my hand and she led me to the car.

Roy dropped me off at the curb of my house.

"Do you want me to come with?" Annie asked.

"I'm going for a walk. I'll catch up with you soon," I said. "I'll be over later on."

Karen got out of the car to let me out and offered to walk with me. I did not say anything. She looked into the car and shrugged her shoulders at everyone. I walked on without saying a word, but she caught up to me. Louise, Annie, and Roy drove back to the Lakewood Methodist Church for the reception.

I don't even remember where Karen and I walked, just up and down small streets and around town until we stopped and sat on a bench that looked like it was for kids waiting for the school bus.

I had told everyone that I would stop by the church for the reception and to pay my respects to Mike's family, but I never did. Once I was back at the house, I just could not leave. I closed up all the doors and shut the windows.

I do not want to write about Mike's death, but there is much that can be said. Perhaps one day. I will say that he was having fun when he died. Mike, Becky, Karen, and I were tossing and kicking a football around, though I could not do much with my arm. I could kick the ball, but that was about it. Mike could really throw the ball through the air, although half the time, it wobbled through the sky like a wounded duck.

I am feeling guilty now that it is late in the evening. I should have attended the reception at the church. All the TV stations are off the air and Harry and Bess are downstairs curled up on the carpet not far from the baseball pinball machine. They are sleeping back-to-back. I am too tired to walk up the stairs so I will sleep on the sofa tonight.

Thursday, September 6

At 7:30, Annie was on the front porch ringing the bell and knocking on the window. That did not wake me but Harry and Bess howling did. I went to sleep at 5:45, so I have had less than two hours of sleep. I feel like I have a hangover.

"Come on in and make yourself at home. I'm going back to sleep." Which I did.

Annie hung around while I slept. I'm not sure what she did for three hours, but she did clean the kitchen up. Things have been a huge mess since the backyard picnic.

While I was asleep, my mom called the house, #8431, the same number as when we lived there except now there are three numbers in front of it. She and Annie talked. I only know this because Annie told me. I never heard the phone ring.

§

"You have greatly upset your parents."

"Are they flying or driving up?"

"No, I talked them out of coming up here, but they're angry with you for housesitting your old house."

§

It's two in the afternoon. I have just woken up from another nap. I'm on the front porch with a small stack of newspapers piled in front of me, unread from the last few days. Annie left before I went back to sleep, saying that she had a ton of errands to run and was driving to Olean to pick up a free TV.

"How'd you find out about a free TV an hour away?"

"Just a friend of a friend. I don't have a TV and this one is only a few years old. It's not color but that's okay."

§

I made a decision the other day when sitting at the funeral. I cannot help Ashley. The punishment for inaction is regret.

Mike's obituary was in today's paper, the cause of death listed as an aneurism. But I knew that. The obituary listed his high school and other accomplishments: 3-letter sport star (football, wrestling, and baseball), Junior Achievement, Boy Scouts, and more. I did not know he was an Eagle Scout. He never told me. It even mentioned his heroism at Kinzua Dam but only said he tried saving a local teen. I clipped the obituary from the paper and placed it in my journal.

I tried reaching Dr. Laighles via international long-distance, but they were not at the number they gave me. I spoke briefly to Emily's sister. She said that Emily and Floyd drove to Stonehenge yesterday, then they are driving to Glasgow for a day before flying home.

I did not go to work today.

§

It is 10:00 p.m., and I have just returned from driving Karen home. Have I not learned to stop hurting people?

Karen and I took a shower together. She wrapped my arm in a garbage bag and washed me. It was wonderful. It was romantic, much more so than the other night when it was awkward and intimidating. We were both more relaxed tonight. I love touching her body with my hands, and she loves wrapping her arms around me. I like that, too.

I had taken another day off from work, and Karen came over after I had woken from my nap. She said we had talked about helping me clean the house, but I didn't remember that. It took us the afternoon to dust, vacuum, wash the kitchen floor (Annie didn't do that, which is okay), and wash clothes, and bathe the dogs, etcetera, etcetera, etcetera. I helped as I could, doing the easy jobs that required one arm, kind of like the man in *The Fugitive*. Karen did most of the heavy cleaning. When the wash was finished and we were folding bath towels and placing them in the upstairs closet, Karen turned around, and I kissed her. We began biting each other's lips and fell into the closet and onto all the towels and blankets. I screamed in pain when she rolled onto my shoulder.

After the shower and while Karen towel-dried her hair, I threw on my jeans and tip toed down the spiral staircase to the kitchen, where I thought I had heard something. I found nothing, but when I walked back upstairs, Annie was walking down the hall.

"Hey, there you are," she said to me.

"What are you doing here?" I asked. "I thought you were in Olean buying a TV."

"Yeah, I did. It was free. But it's only an hour away."

Annie stood no more than ten feet from the bathroom where Karen was drying her hair.

"I stopped by to see how you're feeling and to see if you want to watch TV tonight on my new TV set. We can get Chinese food or something."

"How'd you know I was here?"

"I called your office and Roy said you laid out. I called here but no one answered."

"I just woke up from a nap and wasn't expecting anyone."

"You look shaken up. Are you sure you're okay? How's your arm feel?"

"I'm fine."

"Why's your hair wet?" she asked.

"Let's go sit outside on the porch. I need some fresh air."

"Or, we can get a pizza," Annie said. "I haven't been to The Pub in a long time. They've got the best. We can order take-out."

"Not tonight. Maybe another time."

"I thought we might need to talk about Mike, raise a glass to him. But, also, there are some things I want to tell you about Mike and Steven, and Julie. She and I were girlfriends and I was her maid of honor when she married Walter."

"Emily and Floyd are coming home, and I need to stay around the house and straighten up."

"I'll help. We can play cards afterwards?"

"Normally, I'd say yes, but I have to wash clothes and I don't want to make you hang around while I do that."

I tried edging her downstairs to the porch, but she wouldn't budge. She stood in the upstairs hall and wanted to talk.

"I don't mind. I'll help you fold."

"Are you saying something to me?" Karen asked as she opened the bathroom door and walked out into the hall with a towel wrapped around her.

"Karen?" Annie questioned.

I slumped back against the hallway wall when Karen turned toward Annie, gasped, and ran back into the bathroom.

"Robert!" Annie yelled. "My God. What's going on?"

I closed my eyes.

"Karen!" Annie yelled, as if to make her come back.

"I'm sorry," I said. "I didn't mean for you to see this."

"How dare you!" She slapped me across the face. I absorbed the sting and didn't budge. "She's only sixteen."

"I'm only nineteen."

"How dare you?"

"It's not like I'm twenty-six," I said.

Annie slapped me again. This time, her hand did not bounce off my face, but stopped flat against my cheek. It hurt. I felt the sting all the way down into my arm.

"How could you? Everyone trusted you."

"What do you mean trusted me, Annie? This has nothing to do with trust. This isn't bad. This is healthy. This is nothing to be ashamed about."

"Is this the first time?"

"This is between Karen and me. And now between us and you."

"Don't worry, I'm not going to spread the news around town."

"I'm sorry," I told her.

"No, you're not. I thought we were—. You're not ready for this responsibility."

"You're not my mother."

"No, I'm not, but you're just a little boy."

Annie pounded down the stairs, almost tripping on the last couple of steps. When she opened the front door, she turned around and looked up at me, as I leaned on the staircase railing. I followed right behind her to the bottom of the stairs.

"I'm just a little boy? What about the other night?"

"That's different. I hope to hell you two are smart enough to be using birth control."

And Annie was gone.

I hesitated for a few seconds before running out the door after her, but she was already on her bicycle and near the end of the driveway when I reached the edge of the porch. I watched her pedal away down the street and under the streetlight.

§

Upstairs, Karen had dressed and was lying face-down on the bed, crying, when I entered the room. I noticed the thin white lines of her bra beneath the pale-yellow blouse. She and I lay on the bed for a while until our hearts stopped beating so hard.

"Do you need to go home?" I asked her. "I'll drive you."

"My parents think I'm at Susie's house and they'll want to know why I'm home early."

"You don't have to go until you need to."

We fell asleep on the bed for a while. When it was late, I drove her home. From there, I drove to Annie's apartment.

"Open the door, Annie. I want to talk."

"Go away," she said, muffled from behind the door.

"Come on. Open up. We need to talk."

"About what? You're going to do what you want regardless."

"You shouldn't be mad at me," I said.

"Don't you understand? I'm not angry, Robert, I'm hurt. Very hurt. Now, go away, before my neighbors start wondering what's going on."

She finally cracked open the door, but the chain was locked across the opening.

"I want to talk about what happened with us," I said.

"There's nothing to talk about. It was a mistake. It never happened. Go away before I call Buck Cline."

She closed the door and locked it. I leaned against the wall, believing Annie would open the door again, but she did not. I waited ten minutes, then left.

On the ride home, the truck crept through the sleepy little town where no other car was on the road and the only streetlight flashed yellow. In the driveway, I turned off the engine and sat in the truck, listening to the quiet and all the things wrong in my life.

Friday, September 7

Early this morning, I drove by Annie's apartment but did not stop as her car was not there. Even if her car was there, what was I going to do—wake her up at 5:45 a.m.? How much more angry can I make her? Instead, I had breakfast at The Big Tree. I read the newspaper and laughed at myself, because I was supposed to eat here throughout the summer but never made it back. Life interrupted my plans. I waited for the Trading Post Hardware store to open at seven. I bought a bottle of odorless wallpaper paste. Who knew such things as odorless paste existed?

I worked from home today, reading and finishing *Rubyfruit Jungle*.

At three o'clock this afternoon, when I walked outside for the mail, Dr. Laighles and Emily pulled up in the driveway. Dr. Laighles had shaved off his beard and mustache and looked ten years younger. He had even lost some weight. If not for Emily being with him, I would not have recognized him.

Dr. Laighles shook my hand and tapped his knuckle on my cast. Emily hugged me. From the open windows, the dogs howled and barked for their owners. They ran all over the house trying to get to Emily and Dr. Laighles. Harry peed on the hardwood floor.

"We're so sorry we couldn't get back sooner," Emily said as we stood in the driveway. The small gravel stones crunched under my bare feet, catching between my toes.

"My sister left a message at the Glasgow Airport for us, so we didn't find out about Mike until yesterday," Emily said.

I made several trips into the house carrying their luggage with my one good arm and told them about everything that had happened to both Mike and Caroline's band of marauders. Dr. Laighles kept rubbing his smooth face, a contour cut with steel, rugged and wrought with fire.

It's odd. I feel as if they are intruding into my space by being home. I am typing one page at a time but then hiding it, so they do not see or read what I have written. My freedom to leave things out has been disrupted. But, of course, this is their house.

Emily made a pot of coffee and sat on the front porch, talking for more than an hour. I explained how I broke my arm. Dr. Laighles said he did not recall having Caroline or her brother in his classes. Sitting around reminded me of when I was a little boy and my grandparents would visit, and for the first hour, the adults sat and talked about everyone in town and all the happenings.

After they took a nap and showered, Dr. Laighles asked me into his study.

"The house looks wonderful. You must have cleaned it every day from the way it looks. Did things proceed on the straight and narrow for you this summer?" he asked, sitting in his leather chair and smoking a cigar.

"Pretty much."

I watched the smoke dissolve above his head like a swirling fog.

"Good, good," he chuckled. "Just checking. It feels great to be home. I haven't smoked a cigar since we left. Can you believe it? I can't say that I really missed them. I started walking two miles a day, so you may have notice that I've trimmed down a little bit, huh?"

"Yes, sir. You look pretty good without a beard, too."

"Do you want these cigars? I've quit smoking. I don't even like the taste anymore."

He had about a dozen fat cigars in a wooden case.

"No, sir. I don't smoke."

"Me neither," he replied. "This one here is my last. I'm tossing them out unless you want them."

"Roy might want'em."

"Here. They're his. Is there anything you might want to tell me, something that may have slipped your mind?"

"No, sir. Nothing off hand," I replied.

"Let's see. About a year and a half ago, I pulled a step ladder down from the garage, and when I did, I scraped the left front fender of the Corvette. That was my son's car, Steven. Did you know that?"

"No, sir."

He blew smoke into the air.

"It's odd, but the scratch isn't there. I've read about such things occurring by osmosis, but I can't figure this one out. You wouldn't happen to have a theory?"

"Yes, sir. I drove the Corvette and I wrecked it, but it was just a small fender bender. I ran into a lamp post in the grocery store parking lot. When they made the repair, I paid to have the whole car painted."

"Steven bought that Corvette from a local man, Herm Walters. It had been driven into the lake and stayed submerged for two weeks before it was retrieved. It needed a complete restoration, so for two years during high school, that's what Steven and I did together in our garage."

He did not say so, but I could tell that Dr. Laighles was angry with me. I apologized several times.

"Well, I understand. A Corvette's like a piece of pussy, you cannot resist the temptation."

§

This summer, I read nineteen of the twenty-three books Roy gave me. When Emily and Dr. Laighles took a nap this afternoon, I took the books to The Book Cellar on North Main Street and sold the entire lot for fifteen bucks.

Emily and Floyd stayed in this evening because they are tired from traveling. Floyd placed a take-out order at The Beechwood Restaurant and he and I drove down the street to pick it up. When we returned, Emily had the kitchen table set. I felt strange having dinner with them because I figured I probably sat in the same chair Steven did when they ate as a family. I wonder if my being there made them think of their son. If so, I hope it brought joy and not pain.

Floyd's on sabbatical this fall semester, and now with his research, he's going to write a book. He and Emily spoke a lot about their trip, his research, and me starting school in a few days. He's going to stay at home and write his book.

I surprised them with some news of my own, "I'm not going to college this semester."

"Is it money?" Emily asked. If I had asked, I think she would have given me the money.

"No, ma'am. I'm leaving for Paris. I want to live there and study painting."

"That's out of the blue," Floyd said as he pulled a crescent roll apart and buttered it. "Have you thought this out?"

"I've been painting a lot this summer, right out there on the deck, overlooking the backyard. Sometimes, I've painted from the porch," I explained.

"Well, you might as well go while your young, because once you're tied up, you can kiss that shit good-bye," Floyd said.

"Floyd," Emily scolded him.

"Well, it's the truth. I'm not about to sugarcoat it."

"Put a dollar in the jar," she said to him. He pulled a dollar from his pocket and handed it to her. Emily placed it in a jar that was half-full of one-dollar bills.

"I'm going to find a job and paint until I enroll. I'm not even sure where I want to study, but I know I need to leave."

"Sweetie, have you told your parents?" Emily asked.

"Not yet. I was going to call them after dinner to say I'm leaving on Tuesday."

"Did something happen between you and Annie," she asked.

"I don't know. Why?" I asked.

"When I heard you to were dating, I thought you'd make a wonderful couple," Emily said.

"She's too old for him," Floyd told her.

"What do you know," Emily snipped back.

"I know she's too old for Robert," Floyd said.

"Well, we're just friends, I guess. I'm not sure you can say we're dating. Maybe we were. I'm not sure what you'd call it."

"Robbing the cradle," Floyd laughed.

"Floyd, stay out of his business," Emily told him.

"Where're you staying in Paris?" Floyd asked.

"I don't know yet. I haven't gotten that far in my planning."

Saturday, September 8

Emily made breakfast this morning: oatmeal, grapefruit, plain toast, cranberry juice, and black coffee. I told them I had a job, which was fine by them. They didn't think I would stay in the house all day long. Emily said that if I changed my mind about Paris, I could live in the house during the school year if I wanted. I could have the guest room. No charge.

"We've been invited to Dean Stanton's house for dinner tomorrow," Emily said. "You're welcome to come along."

I declined the invitation. I need to find Annie and talk to her!

Dr. Laighles was so happy to see Harry and Bess that he kept feeding them food from the table, even though Emily fussed at him for doing it. She made him another stack of toast, but he fed most of it to the dogs when she wasn't looking.

"Did Annie say anything about she and Steven?" Emily asked.

"No, ma'am. I never asked about him and she never said anything. Once in a while, Mike asked where Steven was," I said.

"I wouldn't imagine Annie would say anything. She keeps these things to herself, close to her chest. It's been five years and I know it was hard on her. She and Steven were sweethearts," Emily explained.

"Since the seventh grade," Floyd interjected.

"Steven had already planned on marrying Annie. They both had planned on it after college," Emily said. "They weren't engaged yet, but it was the next step. Steven talked to us about it many times."

§

In his office, I handed Roy the cigars, which he sniffed.

"These are top-tier. Cubans. Where did you get Cubans?"

"Dr. Laighles. He's stopped smoking them, so he gave them to me to give to you."

"I'll have to send him a bottle of scotch."

"He stopped drinking, too."

"No kidding. Well, maybe I'll buy he and Emily a few pounds of smoked white fish from Westfield."

"He might enjoy that. I don't think he's stopped eating fish." That made Roy laugh.

"Louise and the girls are in Warren visiting her mother and won't be back until late tonight. After work, meet me at The Triangle. I'll buy you dinner."

§

I finished writing several reports today on the last few books I've been reading. I liked *Rubyfruit Jungle*, but I never finished reading

Breakfast of Champions, even though I still wrote my report. I made up a bunch of stuff.

I listened to Casey's Top 40. My favorite song is "Live and Let Die" but also a new song I heard, "Ramblin' Man." It's by the All Man Brothers or the Almond Brothers—something like that. Casey doesn't spell out the band's name.

§

I met Roy at The Triangle at 6:30.

"Take a look around at this place," Roy said. "It's my favorite restaurant, but it won't be here much longer, a few years maybe."

"Why's that?"

"They want to widen the road, and this wonderful place is smack dab in the middle, and when you're in the middle of the road, everyone and everything runs you over. Too bad, really. It's my favorite restaurant. It's where I had my first date with Louise."

"Really?"

"Yeah, we sat right over there in the corner and talked for hours. It might not be for a few years or even ten, but it's on the way. This place is history, gone like it never existed."

"That brings up my situation, a dilemma really."

"It's a woman, isn't it? It always is."

"Pretty much."

"Let me guess. It's Annie?"

"How'd you know?"

"What the hell, Robert, who else would you be sleeping with? I got to tell you, I saw her this morning at Brad's Hardware and she was pissed off about something."

"What'd she say?"

"Nothing. She was getting every carboard box they had. I asked her what she was doing, and she said she was packing up."

"Like, to move?"

"I guess so. She didn't go into detail, but she was angry at the world."

"I got to go," I said as I stood up.

"Where?"

"To Annie's. I've got to talk to her."

"Look, sit back down. First off, it takes a few days to pack up all your shit. Have a drink, a steak, and go over later. She'll be home. Take her some flowers. There's nothing so bad that you've done that cannot be fixed with flowers. Louise and I've been married for nineteen years. In that time, I've screwed up so much. Believe me, flowers. It works every time. Just tell her you're sorry. Never forget that owning up and apologizing is the most important thing you can do."

Roy had a whiskey sour, and I had a Coke. Until the waitress brought our food, I did not say another word to Roy. I listened to him talking about a swimming pool he wanted to get next year. He had a steak. I had breaded fish, which overlapped my plate two inches on each side. I didn't want fries, so I ordered mashed potatoes and gravy. Fish is easier to eat with a fork while using my right hand—no heavy cutting with a knife—but I barely ate my food and asked the waitress to box it up.

"I have to go but let me leave the tip."

"You're that worried?"

I tossed five dollars on the table.

"Is that enough?"

"Leave seven."

So, I did.

"You'd better hurry because some other guy's going to step in and take care of business and then where will you be," he laughed.

"It's not like that," I told him.

"It's always like that."

§

It was 7:50 when I arrived at her apartment. I knocked so loud on the red front door that the man next door opened his door.

"She's not home," he said.

"Do you know where she went or when she's coming back?"

"By the looks of it, never."

"What do you mean?"

"She just left about twenty minutes ago. She gave me her apartment key to give to Mr. Lenna."

"Did she say where she's going?"

"No, not really. Just something about everything being a mistake and she's going to law school now."

"Where?"

"Hell if I know. I thought she was going to be a doctor or something."

"Did she give you any indication where she was going?"

"No. None whatsoever. Some guy drove up in a small U-Haul. He helped her pack up some, but she packed most of it herself. He hitched the car up to the trailer then she said good-bye. I was standing here because I asked if she wanted any help, but she said no. She gave that guy a hug then a kiss and then she drove off in the truck."

"Were they together, like a couple?"

"No, no. Nothing like that. She gave me the key and a letter. Are you Robert?"

"Yeah."

"Here, this is for you. She said you'd stop by."

The man handed me an envelope with my name written across it in blue ink. I sat in the truck and read her letter.

> Robert,
>
> I never want to see you again. EVER! I'm leaving so don't bother following me or looking. You will not find me. I guarantee that. Everything this summer was a mistake. You need to grow up.
>
> -A

I drove back to the office to call Lauren, to see if Annie was at their folks' house. She was not.

"I don't want you calling here anymore."

"What'd I do?"

"You hurt Annie."

"That's why I'm calling. I want to talk to her and fix things. I want to apologize."

"Well, you can't. She's not here and I don't know where she's headed. She wouldn't tell anyone. Even if I knew, I wouldn't tell you.

She simply hit the road and said she'll call in a few months. But most of all, she doesn't want you to know where she's going. So, don't try to follow her."

Annie did not tell Lauren what I did, which is honorable of her, kind of like how I haven't told anyone about driving Lauren to Canada. We all have secrets we are required to keep.

Bottom line, neither Lauren nor her parents know where Annie was heading. Lauren wouldn't even speculate.

"She left the suds in the bucket and vamoosed, which is not like Annie. What did you do to her?"

"I made a mistake."

"Yeah, a big-ass mistake. My parents are pissed off at you. Don't ever show up here or my dad will shoot you. I'm not kidding."

§

I called my parents late tonight and told them I was leaving for Paris, said I wanted to learn to paint. I'll be behind a semester, but I'll enroll next spring and change my major.

My mom was not happy with my decision to use my tuition money to fund my life in Paris, but I told her I would get a job. I didn't tell her about the Corvette and only having about a quarter of my tuition money left. I don't have a ton of money, but I'll find some way to make do. I heard of students being tutors. I read that the poet, W.S. Merwin was a tutor for a rich family, long before he was a poet. I could do something like that.

My mom kept saying, "Robert, I don't know if this is a good idea. Give Chautauqua one more year."

When she asked me about the house, I simply told her that it was something I had to do.

"I'll tell you all about it when I come home for Thanksgiving."

"Your father's going to be angry about the money."

"I'll pay you back."

"It's a girl, isn't it?" she asked. "Is it Annie? She's a nice girl. Don't let her get away."

"Mom."

"You do that, you know—a girl breaks your heart and you run away."

"No, mom. It's not like that. I broke her heart. I'm the one who's at fault this time."

"Win her back."

"It'll never happen. I was told she'd left for good, to start a new life without me in it. Plus, she wrote me a note and said she never wants to see me again."

"Oh, yeah. That sounds pretty definite. I'll tell your father. Remember, there are other fish in the ocean."

Sunday, September 9

Early this morning before he would leave for church, I stopped off at Roy's house to tell him I was leaving and quitting my job.

"Kind of short notice, isn't it?" he said.

"Sorry."

"Come on inside."

We sat in the kitchen and had a few cups of coffee. Roy said he would give me a recommendation.

"When you arrive, go to these two bookstores and apply for a job. You're well-read and a good writer, and they'll probably hire you. Librarie Galignani and Shakespeare and Company. Both are famous. You'll meet more woman there than you can handle. You'll forget about Annie before you know it."

That's what I was afraid of but didn't tell him.

If Annie is gone and wants me out of her life, as she said, "I never want to see you again . . ."—I can make that happen. If Lauren won't tell me where she's run off to, then I will disappear, too. She can be on one side of the Grecian Urn, while I'm on the other side.

Like Jim Croce sings in one of my favorite songs, "If that's the way that you want it, well that's the way I want it more."

I'll give her more invisibility than she ever expected. I'll be a mystery. I'll become a ghost.

§

Karen stopped me outside of her house before I left. She was upstairs eavesdropping on my conversation with her father.

"Are you really going to Paris?" she asked.

"Yeah, I'm leaving Tuesday morning. Heading to Buffalo on the bus and flying to Boston then to Paris."

"How come?"

"I don't want to end up like Ricky Weislogel," I told her.

"What's that mean?"

"He was a guy who was killed in Vietnam. I say that so I don't end up like him. I'm not really going to die in Vietnam because that's probably never going to happen, but what it really means is I need to live an adventure. Live life before I die."

"I get it. My grandfather used to tell me that he was never going to slow down. He used to say he was going to live life to the fullest until the bear tracked him down and ate him. He said he was never going to let the old man inside."

"Yes, exactly. That was his way of telling you to always keep living life to the fullest. Is he still around?"

"No. A few years ago he got eaten by a bear."

"No way!"

"No, really. He got attacked by a grizzly bear in Alaska when he was hunting. He shot the bear and then it turned on him and killed him. He shot it a few more times and killed it, but not before the bear killed him."

"That's wild. How old was he?"

"Eighty-two."

"That's what I'm talking about. You keep living hard until the bear kills you. Not literally, of course, except in regard to your grandfather, but you get the idea."

"What's going to happen with you and Annie?"

"I don't know. She's pretty angry at me."

"Me, too!"

"No, this is all me. She's run off. I'll probably have to hire a private investigator to find her. I mean, she's gone. No one knows where she ran off to."

"If I see her, I'll be nice and tell her how sorry you are. Maybe she can visit you in Paris."

"Yeah, maybe."

"Can I visit you in Paris?" Karen asked.

"Sure.

"I read where lovers go to the Eiffel Tower and have sex underneath it at night, right out in the open. Is that true?"

"I don't know but I can ask around."

"I still have that joint Jenny gave me. You wanna blaze that up?"

"Naw."

"I got nothing going on today. Can I come over to your house?"

"Not right now. Emily and Floyd are back. The house is not a good place. Plus, I'm busy until later this afternoon."

"I'll make a picnic basket and tell my parents were going to Long Point, but let's go to the creek where Mike and Annie drove us. I'll bring a blanket. I won't wear any underwear."

§

While Emily and Dr. Laighles are having dinner at Dean Stanton's, which is occurring at this exact moment (they left ten minutes ago and should be gone two or three hours), I will carry my summer's efforts to the secret room (as soon as I finish typing this) and give back all that I have taken. I will restore light to darkness.

I have carefully cut a 20x25-inch piece of wallpaper from the old roll and have matched it perfectly to the opening of the secret room. I'm going to seal it so no one realizes the room is there. It will take a super sleuth, and that's if they are looking for it. Metaphorically, I'm rolling a stone in front of a tomb. My journal will lay in darkness, isolated, its pages to be read by one who can discover the secret room, as I have done.

I cannot stop thinking about what lies ahead this afternoon with Karen.

One last time, I keep thinking.

§

I wanted to apologize to Annie and talk to her about many things, including Steven and what Floyd and Emily told me. I don't care about her and Steven and how she hasn't gotten over him. That's the past, a part of who Annie is. I want to help with that. In fact, I'm glad she was in love with Steven and has had a difficult time getting over him. It proves she loved him. Well, I love her as well, and I need her to know this.

I have typed a quick letter to Annie explaining how I feel. I apologized for my behavior. I have asked her for forgiveness, and perhaps by the time I see her again, she will have forgiven me. I did not mention Paris or anything about my future plans. I mailed my letter to her apartment and assume it will be forwarded to wherever she ends up.

§

The wallpaper and paste are ready.

My journey has taken eleven years and this glorious summer. I have come back to where I began, and now I feel I can move forward in spectacular clarity. I am, at this moment, a broken young man. I have made a disaster of my personal life with Annie. I do not deserve to be loved by a woman like her. If she does not speak to me for twenty-five years, she would be justified.

Here are the following items I'm placing in the secret room before I seal it:

* My journal
* Annie's naked picture (which I stole)
* Annie's vengeful letter
* Mike's obituary
* Ashley's letters
* Twenty-six watercolor and acrylic paintings I created this summer. They are small paintings and not that great, but it's a start, perhaps.

Above everything, I love Annie and wish she were traveling with me to Paris.

I miss Kimberly, now dead eleven years. And, still, I cannot stop thinking about what my life and the life of our family would have been like with her.

I miss my parents.

The house hears the clicks of the typewriter, and this house, my house, knows I will be back. From down the hall, the grandfather clock is chiming three o'clock, and across my path, the late afternoon sun shines through the window onto the hardwood floor and Oriental rug. Karen will be here in thirty minutes.

It's time to move on. The curtains are fluttering as a breeze glides across the lake. The house hears the echo of my thoughts, reverberating as I declare to the page, "I will return, and when I return, I will arrive as a better man. I promise."

Acknowledgements

I would like to thank the following people who have helped keep this book in focus over the past thirty-nine years—friends and family, my Uncle David, and those who read early versions and offered insight and support: Christopher Noel, John Williams, Beth Day, and most especially, Nikki Bowen, without whom this book would never have been resurrected from the bottom of a filing cabinet. She worked diligently as my early editor to see this novel to fruition. Thanks to Mark Roberts, Wayne Glowka, and Donna Little at Reinhardt University for their creative support, friendship, and fellowship. Special thanks to Philip Lee Williams, who's eleventh hour advice proved insightful and indispensable, and who for many years has been my benchmark of literary achievement. Thanks to my editor, Mallory Matthews, for her insightful comments. I am truly grateful for my friendship and artistic comradery with David Waehner, who for nearly forty years has listened to every plot, character nuance, storyline, and funny bit of dialogue I could think of, and he has been a good friend through all of it. Most importantly, to the people and the town of Lakewood, New York, where I grew up, moved away, but return to on a daily basis, if only in my imagination. I may be miles away, but each day Lakewood is in my heart.

About the Author

William Walsh is the author of seven other books, including the award-winning collection of poems, *Fly Fishing in Times Square* (Červená Barva Press). Widely published in some of the finest journals including *Five Points*, *The Georgia Review*, *The Kenyon Review*, and *Literary Matters*, he is also known for his literary interviews, which have included: Czeslaw Milosz, Joseph Brodsky, A.R. Ammons, Richard Blanco, Eavan Boland, Pat Conroy, Harry Crews, James Dickey, Rita Dove, Mary Hood, Ursula Le Guin, Andrew Lytle, and Lee Smith. Born in Jamestown, NY and raised in Lakewood until moving south in 1972, his historical family has resided in Chautauqua County since pre-Revolutionary War. A graduate of Georgia State University and Vermont College, he resides in Atlanta with his family. He is the director of the undergraduate and graduate creative writing programs at Reinhardt University, in Waleska, where he teaches literature and creative writing. He is the editor of the *James Dickey Review*. When not writing, he spends time with his family, enjoys competitive tennis and golf, as well as playing chess internationally.

CPSIA information can be obtained
at www.ICGtesting.com
Printed in the USA
BVHW072054150422
634018BV00003B/21

9 781956 851090